A

TASTE OF EVIL

Recent Titles by Patricia Matthews from Severn House

THE DEATH OF LOVE
MIST OF EVIL
NIGHT VISITOR
OASIS
SAPPHIRE
THE SCENT OF FEAR
THE UNQUIET
VISION OF DEATH

TASTE OF EVIL

Patricia Matthews

This first world edition published in Great Britain 1993 by
SEVERN HOUSE PUBLISHERS LTD of
9–15 High Street, Sutton, Surrey SM1 1DF.
Simultaneously published in the U.S.A. 1993 by
SEVERN HOUSE PUBLISHERS INC., of
475 Fifth Avenue, New York, NY 10017.

British Library Cataloguing in Publication Data
Matthews, Patricia
  Taste of Evil
  I. Title II. Matthews, Clayton
  813.54 [F]

  ISBN 0-7278-4505-5

This book is a novel. No resemblance to actual persons
living or dead is intended.

Typeset by Hewer Text Composition Services, Edinburgh.
Printed and bound in Great Britain by
Redwood Books Ltd, Trowbridge, Wiltshire.

ONE

Across the arena, the gate to the chute swung open, and a black mass of muscle and fury plunged out. Bellowing and bucking, in a savage frenzy, the bull attempted to rid himself of the man on his back.

Dust billowed up, drifting toward the stands where Casey Farrel and her son, Donnie, sat on the worn, wooden bleachers.

Donnie leaned forward, tense with excitement as the big Brahma bull, with an angry buck-and-twist, sent his rider into the air.

The man hit the ground, apparently stunned, and the angry animal spun towards him, head lowered. Casey felt her gut tighten, wondering if the clown would be in time. Then a large, colourfully painted barrel came rolling out in front of the angry bull, and a collective sigh came from the crowd.

'What's that?' asked Donnie.

Casey took his hand.

'That's Bobo, the rodeo clown. He's inside the barrel. It's his job to distract the bull so that the riders can get away.'

'Wow!' said Donnie, obviously impressed.

The bull had seen the barrel now, and drove towards it, his heavy head and horns sending it rolling, as the bull rider was helped to safety.

After another pass at the barrel, the bull, angry and frustrated, stood blowing, until two riders came out and drove him towards the corrals.

1

As they did so, Bobo climbed out the barrel and took a broad bow. A small man, he wore loose, short-legged trousers with a wide waist, held up by flaming red suspenders; a long-sleeved, old-fashioned men's undershirt, and a *very* small Stetson, held to his head by a band under the chin. A painted smile and red nose hid his real face and a wild, red wig protruded from under his hat. From the stands he looked comic and silly, but Casey had noticed earlier, when he had been entertaining the children in the stands, that he was wiry and well-muscled. Now he was loping easily around the edge of the arena, honking a horn he had taken from a pocket in his baggy pants.

Donnie let out a heavy sigh. 'That was neat!'

Casey smiled. They were attending the Prescott Rodeo, said to be the oldest in the country, and it was Donnie's first time. He was enjoying it with all of a ten year old's enthusiasm for action and violence.

The announcer's voice boomed from the speakers. 'That was Roy Burke, folks. Give him a big hand. The judges' rating is seventy-five!'

Casey glanced down at her programme. The next rider was listed as Buck Farrel. She felt a surge of recognition as she saw her own surname. She didn't often run into other Farrels; it didn't seem to be a very common name.

Donnie tugged at her sleeve. 'Can I have another hot dog, Casey?'

Casey lifted a hand and smoothed back his unruly blond hair. 'No, my little sees-all-eats-all. You've already had three, plus an ice cream bar and two colas. I don't want you getting sick all over our new car, and I expect you to eat a good, healthy dinner. Okay?'

'Okay,' he said reluctantly, and she sighed in mock exasperation.

'Besides, this is the last event. We'll leave before it's over, and avoid the crowd.'

He nodded, his attention again on the action in the arena, where the next bull and rider were about to be released.

Casey gazed at the boy with her affection clearly disclosed on her face. Once Donnie Patterson, he had become, as of five months ago, Donnie Farrel, her adopted son; filling a void in her life that she had not, until then, realized was there.

Donnie glanced up at her, his blue eyes bright with excitement. She resisted the impulse to give him a hug. In the year they had been living together, she had learned what not to do and say in public. In front of spectators, hugs were definitely out, but in private they were happily accepted.

He said, 'I'll bet Josh would love this, huh?'

In a teasing voice she said, 'I thought Josh only liked football and baseball.'

'Aw, Casey.'

She laughed. 'Yeah, kiddo, he would love it, I'm sure. Too bad he had to work today.'

Thinking of Josh gave Casey a pleasant glow. Sergeant Joshua Whitney, a homicide officer with the Phoenix Police Force, had come into Casey's life at the same time as had Donnie. Friend, lover, and sometimes antagonist, he kept her on her toes, and gave her support and love. The problem she occasionally had with the relationship was with the last part. Josh wanted to marry her, now! Donnie, who worshipped Josh, wanted it too. But an earlier relationship had left Casey scarred and she wasn't certain that the hurt was healed, although the adoption of Donnie had gone a long way to making her feel whole.

The announcer's voice interrupted her thoughts: 'And now, coming out of Chute Two, is Buck Farrel, folks. Give him a big hand!'

Donnie looked at her with round eyes. 'He said, "Farrel", Casey. Is that man related to you?'

Casey shook her head. 'Not that I know of, kiddo. Lots of people have the same last names, but they're not related. Look! Here he comes.'

The gate opened and the bull leaped out as if released by a spring. Instantly, Casey could see that something was wrong. The rider, a wide-shouldered man wearing a black hat and black chaps, already seemed to have lost his grip on the bull-rope.

Even as Casey thought this, the bull's feet hit the ground, the rider slumped, then went plummeting off the bull's rump, landing limply in the dust where he lay without moving.

The bull, still bucking and twisting, moved away. The crowd was silent. Two riders quickly herded the bull towards the arena gate and men came running to kneel beside the fallen man. It was then that Casey realized that something was missing from the picture. There had been no distracting barrel. Where was the rodeo clown?

Donnie said, 'Is the man hurt bad, Casey?'

She looked down at him. His face looked pale and his eyes looked too big, but she wouldn't lie to him. 'I don't know, kiddo; but it looks that way.'

'Will they get him a doctor?'

'Of course, see?' She pointed to where the limp figure of the bull rider was being carefully loaded on to a stretcher. Donnie tugged at her shirt. 'Let's go, Casey. I don't think I want to see any more, and I'm hungry.'

Casey nodded, but kept her eye on the figure on the stretcher that was now being carried out of the ring.

'In a minute, Donnie; but first I'd like to check on that bull rider. There's something not quite right here.'

Donnie looked up at her apprehensively. 'Aw, Casey, you're not working. This is supposed to be our vacation. Remember what Josh said? He told us to have fun, and he told you not to go poking in dark corners.'

He narrowed his blue eyes in an approximation of

4

Josh's interrogational stare: the effect was humorous, but she found it annoying. 'Look, kiddo, I didn't bring you up here to be a mouthpiece for Josh Whitney's homilies. I get enough of that at home.'

Donnie looked hurt, and she regretted her snappishness. 'All right. I'm sorry. But this will only take a few minutes. Can you give me that?'

He nodded reluctantly. 'Are you worried about that man 'cause he's got your same last name?'

She took his hand and started down the steps. 'No, that's not it. I'll explain it to you later. Okay?'

When they reached the entrance to the area behind the arena, they found their way blocked by a short, weathered-faced man with hard eyes.

Casey took a card from her purse and held it towards him. 'I'm Casey Farrel, with the Governor's Task Force on Crime. I need to talk to someone back here.'

The guard looked over the card, looked over Casey – taking considerable time about both – and finally shrugged his beefy shoulders. 'I guess it's okay. Go on through.'

Casey, controlling her urge to give him a kick where it would do the most good, smiled too sweetly and led Donnie through the gate. She had learned long ago that certain types of men reacted in certain ways, and it was usually better – if you could stand it – just to play along. Most of the time they were too stupid, or too arrogant, to know they were being condescended to.

A considerable crowd was gathered around the area where the bull rider lay. A fire department ambulance was backed up to the spot, and two paramedics were working over the man on the stretcher. A tall young officer wearing a uniform that Casey recognized as that of the Prescott Police Department, stood over them, writing in a notebook.

Casey led Donnie away from the group, to where she could keep an eye on him, but he couldn't directly see what was going on. 'Donnie, I want you to stay here,' she told him firmly. He began to open his mouth, and she raised a finger. 'No. No arguments. This is serious. I want you to wait right here until I come back. Okay?' Eyes big, he nodded.

She left him and hurried over to the group around the fallen rider. The two medics seemed to be conferring with one another, then one of them, the short blond one, looked up at the young officer. 'This man's dead.'

The young officer wiped his forehead. His face was very pale. 'What happened? Did the fall snap his neck?'

The medic shook his head. 'Nope. Nothing's broken.' He hesitated. 'We won't know for sure until there's an autopsy, but I think he may have been poisoned.'

The other medic nodded. 'It might have been cyanide. I've never worked on a cyanide case, but all of the classic symptoms are there; the odour, the colour of the skin . . . The only thing is, cyanide acts within seconds, and this guy was on a bull . . .'

The other medic shook his head. 'Maybe he committed suicide, took the stuff just before they released the bull.' He shrugged. 'Stranger things have happened.'

He looked up at the young cop. 'Well, so what do we do, take him in to the morgue, or wait here until you check the scene? We've never had anything like this before.'

The young officer flushed. It seemed clear that he hadn't had anything like this before either. He cleared his throat.

'I'll call the station.'

He moved a few feet away from the tableau on the ground and spoke into a hand radio.

The medics placed a sheet over the body of the bull rider. The onlookers looked away, not meeting one another's eyes. Casey glanced over to where Donnie stood, saw that he was all right, then stood quietly, deep in thought.

The young officer returned. 'They're sending out the homicide sergeant. He'll be here in a few minutes.'

He turned to the onlookers. 'I think that anyone who isn't involved should be on their way.'

Casey touched his sleeve. 'Officer?'

He looked at her without seeming to see her. He seemed shaken. 'Yes, Ma'am?'

She held out one of her cards. He took it, read it, read it again, then looked into her face. 'The Governor's Task Force on Crime. Yes, I've heard about it. What do you want?'

Casey took pity on him. 'I was in the stands. It didn't look like a natural fall. I thought I'd see if I could help.'

He stared at her, still puzzled. 'I don't see how.' He scanned the area as if looking for someone to advise him.

She touched his arm again. 'I think there's something you should check. Where was the clown?'

He looked at her blankly. 'What clown?'

'Bobo, the rodeo clown. He was supposed to come out in his barrel as soon as the rider fell. He didn't.'

The young cop still looked puzzled. 'It could be important,' Casey said, gently. 'Maybe he saw something. Or maybe someone wanted him out of the way.'

The young cop's face brightened. 'Oh. Yeah.'

He turned to a tall, greying man who seemed to be in some position of authority. 'Jeff, send somebody to look for the clown. And anybody that was working the chute, or that was standing nearby when Farrel went into the chute. Tell them to get over here.'

He looked back at Casey, who nodded approvingly. 'I'll get out of your way now.'

She gave a last look towards the sheeted figure of the man with the same surname as hers, and a great sadness filled her. He had been a young man, in the prime of

7

his life. The sadness was followed by a sharp surge of anger at whoever had snatched that life away from him. She knew that this was one of the reasons she was in law enforcement, this feeling that no human being had the right to arbitrarily take the life of another; that, and the anger at those who did.

Donnie was uncharacteristically quiet when she went to retrieve him. Neither of them spoke as they left the area of the arena and made their way through the crowd towards the parking lots. So much for missing the crowd, she thought, then focused on the task of keeping Donnie and herself from being crushed in the press of humanity, or from tripping over the uneven cement. The fairgrounds were old and in poor repair.

The parking areas were not paved, and clouds of dust filled the air, making breathing a hazard. She spotted her new Cherokee Laredo, white and sparkling in the late afternoon sun, and despite herself, she felt cheered. She really couldn't afford it, but she had needed better transportation, and a four-wheel drive was a big plus, especially for travelling in snow and ice in the winter and for off-roading and camping, both of which Donnie loved. Despite his tender age, his knowledge of cars and trucks was amazing.

When they reached the vehicle, she smiled as Donnie performed his customary inspection; marching around it, then proudly announcing. 'No dents or scratches, Casey.'

She reached for her keys, and pronounced the ritual reply: 'Well, that's good. If anybody scratched us, I'd run 'em in!'

It wasn't until they were slowly making their tortuous way toward the main part of town, that Donnie finally asked what she had known he would: 'Is that man dead, Casey?'

She nodded slowly. 'Yes, kiddo. I'm afraid he is.'

She could hear his deep sigh, and sneaked a look at him. Death was a large concept for a small boy, but it was one that he had faced before with the death of his parents, and then with his dog, Spot I, who had been one of the victims of the Dumpster Killer. He said no more, and she didn't push it. She had learned to let the boy get things out when he wanted to, to be there if he wanted to talk, but not to push him. Truthfully, she was relieved that her simple answer seemed to satisfy him. Sometimes question led to question until she thought her nerves would frazzle.

But now they should think of happier things. They were on vacation, and were going to enjoy themselves.

Because of Frontier Days, the down-town area was crowded and parking was difficult to find. Luckily, Casey and Donnie were staying at the Hassayampa Inn, and they were able to park in the Inn's reserved parking lot, which was only a block away from the courthouse plaza, where the action was.

Casey had always loved down-town Prescott. The Prescott Chamber of Commerce called it 'Everybody's Home Town', and that's just how it looked: the classic, old stone courthouse surrounded by the grassy plaza; the white bandstand; the tall trees; the wide streets surrounding the square lined with shops and stores in turn-of-the-century buildings.

Now, the plaza and the roped-off streets around it were covered with booths selling food, drinks, hand-crafted items, art works, and other specialty items. There were huge crowds in the plaza, a happy mixture of tourists and town-folk, all enjoying the entertainment and the beautiful day.

South of the plaza, on Montezuma Street, was Whiskey Row, scaled down now from the days of its prime when a dozen or more saloons and brothels used to offer entertainment to visiting miners, ranchers and cowboys, but still where the action was on Friday and Saturday nights, and a great tourist attraction.

North of the plaza were the antique shops, another great tourist draw. Casey remembered one in particular that had a beautiful mahogany bar brought in years ago from the nearby mining town of Jerome, but now it served ice cream instead of booze.

All in all, the town looked like it had been taken, complete, out of a Norman Rockwell painting, and set down in the lovely mountain valley full of ponderosa and pinon pines, and guarded by the sentinel of Thumb Butte. Its charm and beauty were advantages it owed to the fact that, instead of just growing, unplanned, as so many old mining towns had, it had once been the Territorial Capitol of Arizona, and had been laid out like the towns the builders had come from, back in the East and Midwest.

Casey and Donnie headed down the hill towards the plaza. Casey wanted to buy a small gift for Josh and something for Donnie as a memento of the trip.

They walked around for a half-hour or so, looking at the booths, and Casey bought Donnie a boy-sized stetson. As soon as he put it on, he began to walk with the rolling gait of a cowboy. She also bought Josh, and herself, beautiful hiking staffs fashioned from the hardened ribs of a dead saguaro cactus. They were light and strong and ornamented with leather wrist straps bearing Indian fetishes.

As the seller prepared her receipt, Casey looked at her watch, then turned to Donnie. 'It's getting late, kiddo, and I'm getting tired. We have dinner reservations for six-thirty, and we have to have time to shower and dress.'

Donnie nodded cheerfully, and tipped back his new hat in a gesture learned from watching countless Western movies. 'Yeah. I'm starving.'

She smiled and shook her head, wondering where all the food went in that small frame.

After the noise and bustle of the plaza, the Hassayampa was refreshingly quiet and soothing. The beautifully restored interior mingled history, comfort, and grace in equal parts. It was, Casey thought, a classy place, and she loved staying there.

After a relaxing shower and fresh clothes, Casey felt that she might make it through the evening.

Donnie, his face shining and his hair combed back in a semblance of order, wanted to wear his new hat, but was finally convinced that gentlemen did not wear hats to dinner.

Taking his hand, Casey let him escort her down stairs to the Peacock Room, where Donnie handled matters with the Maître d', telling him proudly that they had a reservation.

Casey felt herself smiling, thinking how far he had come. It had taken a while for Donnie to become civilized enough to be taken to a good restaurant. Life with his blowzy aunt and her live-in lover had not given him much preparation for dealing with situations that required good manners; but he was very bright, and naturally considerate of others, and now, after only a year, he was – or at least could be when necessary – a model of deportment. She was very proud of him.

After dinner – a steak for Donnie and an excellent piece of swordfish for Casey – Casey lingered over her coffee while Donnie demolished a slice of chocolate ice cream pie.

Casey was just finishing the coffee when she glanced up and saw a tall, lean man in his sixties, wearing jeans and cowboy boots, coming towards her. To her surprise, he stopped before their booth. She looked up at him uneasily. His strong, craggy face looked drawn with pain, and his pale blue eyes were swollen and rimmed with red, as if he had been crying.

11

He held a roll-edged, sweat-stained Stetson in his big hands, and stared down at her for a long moment.

At last he spoke, in a raw, hoarse voice. 'Casey Farrel?'

Cautiously, Casey said, 'Yes?'

The man swallowed painfully. 'Well, I'm Dan Farrel, your uncle.'

Casey looked at him unbelievingly. 'But I don't have an uncle named Farrel!'

He swallowed again. 'I'm afraid you do. Your father, Roger Farrel, was my brother.'

TWO

Casey was, quite literally, stunned. Her mind groped dazedly for understanding. 'That isn't possible!'

'It's true. What reason would I have to lie?'

'But my father never mentioned a brother.'

'It's a long story, Casey, and not a very pretty one, I'm afraid.' He gestured. 'May I sit down?'

For a moment she considered telling him to get lost. Her life was relatively in order now – a place for everything, and everything in its place – and this complication she did not need. But she was moved by the obvious pain on the man's face, and her curiosity had been aroused.

'Yes, sit down,' she said, moving to make room for him. 'But if this is some kind of scam . . .'

'It's no scam,' he said. 'I almost wish it was.'

He bent down and slid heavily into the booth, as if his body were unwilling to obey his mind's commands. Donnie was staring at the man open-mouthed. She felt very much like doing the same. She found herself searching the man's tired face for resemblances to her father, who had died so young, but this man was so much older, it was difficult to find similarities.

She motioned to her waiter and turned to the man. 'Would you like a cup of coffee?'

He nodded. 'I would.'

She gave the order to the waiter and asked for a refill for herself, then turned to the man. 'All right, Mr . . . Farrel. What's all this about?'

13

He sighed and leaned back. 'I'll try to explain. Roger, your father, and I were never close. It wasn't your father's fault; I was twelve years older, and we were very different in nature, didn't have much in common.

'By the time Roger was big enough for me to take an interest in, I was already out of the house, working the rodeo circuit. Our father and I didn't get along too well, and I was, well, sort of wild. Thought I knew it all.

'Dad, your grandfather, died of cancer soon after I left home, and your grandmother went back to Texas, where she died of the same thing.'

He shook his head. 'If I believed in such things, I'd swear that there's some kind of curse on our family; most of us seem to die young.

'At any rate, I didn't see much of your dad after I left home, and we drifted even further apart. Then, Roger married your mother.'

He looked at Casey and his eyes seemed to plead for understanding. 'Now, I'm not proud of this part of it, but when he married your mother, I was pretty angry with him. I've learned better since, but in those days I thought that the only true men and women that God made were white, that anybody with a brown, yellow, red, or black skin was inferior, and should stick to their own.

'The last time I saw your dad, we had a terrible argument, and I beat him badly. When it was over, I told him that if he married that . . . excuse me, that . . . squaw, he was no brother of mine, and that I never wanted to see him again.

'Later, I wanted to take it back, but the separation had gone too deep; he had taken me at my word; he wouldn't see me or talk to me. Then I spent a couple of years in prison because of a drunken brawl. That pretty much put the cap on things. I certainly don't blame him for not wanting to mention me. Then he died, so young, and I never had a chance to apologize.'

He looked at her then, straight in the eyes, and she was sure he was telling the truth. The knowledge filled her with a great sadness, for her father, and for him.

'How did you know that my father had a daughter?' she asked.

'A friend of mine sent me a Flagstaff paper with your birth announcement in it. After that, I tried to keep track of you. Last year, I saw the article about your being appointed to the Governor's Task Force on Crime, and the one about your solving the Dumpster Killer case, and the illegal alien thing. Your dad would have been proud of you.'

'But how did you find me? How did you know I was in town?'

'After the . . . After Buck was killed, and I was talking to the police, a young officer mentioned your name – he was struck by the fact that we had the same last name – and he said that you had been there, and had given him your card. As for finding out where you were staying, well, Prescott's not a real big town, and I've got lots of connections. You see, I'm respectable now, a regular pillar of the community. I've got a good-sized ranch outside of town where I raise good saddle horses and a few bulls.'

'But why have you come forward now, after all this time?'

'Because now there's a reason. You might be able to help me, and I hurt too much not to take advantage of that.'

Suddenly, Casey put two and two together. 'The man at the fairground, the bull rider . . .?'

He nodded again, slowly. 'That was my boy, my Buck. Robert William Farrel.'

Casey felt herself slump, thinking of that still form on the stretcher, feeling something of what the man beside her must be feeling.

'Oh, God. I'm so sorry.'

15

Slowly the sorrow left Farrel's face to be replaced by a cold anger. 'It's a terrible thing to lose a child, Casey; but even more so to lose one to a senseless killing. I want that killer found!'

Casey drew in a deep breath, and looked at Donnie, who was taking this all in. She wished that she had sent him away before this conversation started, but he had heard the worst part already, so he might as well stay for the rest.

'Have the police declared it a homicide?'

He nodded. 'I just talked to the homicide sergeant before I came over here. He and I are old friends; we go way back. He told me that they had finished the preliminary autopsy, and that Buck had been poisoned. They found whisky in his stomach, not much, and it was laced with cyanide. Buck liked to take a drink, just one shot, before the bull was released; it was sort of a good-luck thing. They figure that this time somebody handed him a lethal shot.'

Casey fingered her chin. 'Did they say anything about the rodeo clown? He should have come out when Buck fell off the bull, but he didn't appear.'

'Yes. He mentioned the clown. The clown was seen near the chute just before the gate opened; but nobody saw him give Buck anything to drink. And the thing is, it wasn't even the original clown. That guy, Bobo, was found stripped to his underwear and bound and gagged, in one of the horse barns.'

'Did he see who did it?'

Farrel shook his head. 'He was struck from behind, knocked cold, didn't see a thing.'

'Well, the police seem to be on top of it.'

'Maybe, but they aren't real experienced with this kind of thing around here. This isn't like Los Angeles, or even Phoenix. Here, we have so little crime that our local paper can list them; and usually the worst thing that occurs is a

16

robbery, a breaking and entry, or some drunk gets in a brawl down on Whiskey Row. Now, you've handled this kind of thing before, and I'm certain that the police would work with you – in fact, I have their word on it.'

Casey shook her head, a little annoyed by the fact that he had talked to the police about her working with them, before asking her if she would.

'I'm terribly sorry about what happened, but there is nothing that I can do. This isn't in my jurisdiction. As you must know, this isn't the kind of thing the Task Force does. Also, I'm only here for a week, then I have to go back to Phoenix, to my job. I wish I could help you, but it's just not possible.'

He leaned toward her, a determined gleam in his grey eyes.

'But you can. I've taken care of everything. The Governor and I are old friends, and I called and spoke to him before I came here. He says that things are quiet for the moment, and that he would be happy to assign you to this case. He said he would explain things to your immediate boss.'

Casey felt heat wash up her neck and into her face. This man had just been through a horrible experience, and allowances should be made; but she hated being manipulated.

'That was pretty presumptuous of you, Mr Farrel,' she said in irritation. 'You might as well know that I don't take well to being pushed.'

He managed a thin smile. 'That just shows that you're a real Farrel, Casey. I know, I'm coming on pretty strong; but if I've learned one thing in my long, hard life, it's that when you've decided on what you know is the right course, you have to charge ahead. It's the only way to get what you want, and right now I want to see my son's killer taken off the streets. Is that too much to ask?'

Casey felt her anger leak away. He was right, in his way;

and Buck Farrel, although she had never known him, was her cousin, her flesh and blood. As the anger left, she felt excitement take its place. Still, she didn't want to appear to give in too easily.

She took a sip of her coffee, and set down her cup. 'You're a hard man to say no to, Dan.'

'Then you'll do it?'

She shrugged. 'I'm thinking about it. But if I do work on the case, don't expect miracles. You make it sound as if all that is needed is for me to investigate, and *voilà* the case is solved. It doesn't work that way.'

'I have faith in you, Casey. You're a Farrel, after all, and we're made of tough material.'

Donnie was fairly bouncing in his seat, his eyes bright. 'Then we're going to stay here in Prescott, Casey? Are we?'

Casey let out a sigh. 'I guess so, kiddo; at least I am. I think that maybe you'll have to go home, and stay with Josh.'

Donnie stopped his fidgeting for a moment, his face creased in thought. He loved Josh dearly, but Josh would be working, and this was summer vacation. Also, Phoenix was miserably hot in summer, while here in the mountains it was far more comfortable, and there were lakes for fishing, and hills for climbing.

Finally, he said, 'Aw, Casey. I don't want to go back to Phoenix. You said that we were on vacation, that we were going to have fun!'

Casey felt a twinge of guilt as she heard her words thrown back at her.

'I know, kiddo; and I meant what I said; but this is what you call an emergency. Mr Farrel needs my help.'

Farrel broke in. 'I have a suggestion. As I said earlier, I have a ranch outside of town. You and the boy can stay with my wife and me. There's plenty of room –

only Alice, my wife, and me living there now . . .' He broke off, looking away.

'Alice and I can look after the boy while you're working.'

His glance went to Donnie, and he smiled slightly. 'I'll bet that you'd like to stay on a real ranch. Do you like to ride?'

Donnie's eyes lit up, and Casey knew that her last objection had been taken care of. And she was intrigued. It would be a little different from her usual type of case, and then, of course, there was the fact that the dead man had been her relation.

Instantly, one of what she thought of as 'Josh's Homilies' popped into her mind: 'Never get drawn into an investigation involving friends or relatives. Too much emotional involvement prevents a clear mind.'

Well, be that as it may, she had already been drawn into this, and her participation seemed inevitable and ordained.

She looked up at her father's brother. 'All right,' she said. 'Now tell me about your son. What was he like?'

Dan Farrel looked down at his hands, and then up at her face 'I'm not going to lie to you. Buck wasn't any angel. He was just a man, with all of a man's weaknesses and faults; but there was no real meanness in him. He almost always means . . . meant well, and he had a lot of what the New-Agers around here would call "positive" energy.

'In some ways he was a lot like me. He loved rodeoing, and anything that had a bit of danger to it. He was a great rider – better than I ever was. And he was willing to work. When he wasn't on the circuit, he really kept the ranch in shape. He liked living out here. His brother now, Clint, never did care for ranch life. He was a real estate office here in Prescott. You'll meet him later.'

So, there was another relative that she hadn't known

19

about, Casey thought. 'Did they get along well, Buck and Clint?'

Dan looked away. 'Not all that well, I must admit; but I figured that when Buck finally settled down, they'd have more in common.'

'How old was Buck?'

'He was going to be thirty-four in two months. Clint is three years older.'

'Was Buck married?'

'Not now, but he was. He and this little girl ran off to Vegas. It only lasted a couple of years. They weren't much more than children.'

'Does his ex-wife still live around here?'

'Yeah. I heard that she married again, and they live in Prescott Valley.'

'Do you happen to know her address?'

'No, but I suppose I can get it. Why? What can she tell you? I happen to know that she and Buck haven't seen each other in years.'

Casey shrugged. 'Maybe so, but I'd still like to talk to her. It's routine in a case like this.'

'All right, if you say so. I'll find her address.'

'Now, what about enemies? Do you know if there was anyone who hated Buck enough to kill him?'

'Wild and scrappy as Buck was, he made a few enemies, sure. What one of us hasn't? But I can't see any of them hating him enough to kill him.'

'How about a current girl friend, or friends?'

A slight smile, edged with melancholy pride, touched his lips. 'Sure. Buck was popular with the ladies; had a real way with them.'

'Can you give me a list of his friends, acquaintances, and women he dated?'

He nodded. 'Yes, although I didn't know everyone he knew. He met a lot of people when he was on the circuit.'

'And what about you? Is it possible that someone wanted to get back at you by killing your son?'

His face sagged. The thought seemed new to him. He said slowly: 'My God, I hope not. I'm not sure I could handle that.'

Casey knew that this was hurting him, but it had to be done.

'We have to look at the possibility,' she said gently. 'Can you think of anyone?'

He lifted a work-roughened hand, then let it fall limply. 'I've made my own share of enemies, but most of them were in the past and in other places.'

'No one in this area?'

'Well, maybe one. Darrel Dyce. The Dyces own the spread next to mine, and last year we had some trouble over the water rights. There's a good-sized creek runs through both of our properties, and he built a dam, stopping the flow of water into my property. I had to take him to court over it. I won, and it left him pretty pissed.'

'And?'

'And what?'

'Did he make any threats?'

'Well, yeah, he made some threats,' Farrel admitted grudgingly. 'Told some people he felt like killing me; but it was all talk. Dyce is too much of a coward to do anything directly.'

'Well, I want you to think about it; see if you can remember anyone else who might carry a grudge towards you or Buck. And I'll need the real name of that clown. I'll want to talk to him right away. I also need the name of the homicide cop who will be handling the case.'

'The clown Hank Wilder. He's a good man.'

'I'll contact him first thing in the morning. I guess that's about it for now.'

He shifted his large frame, reached into his pocket, and

handed her a card. 'Here's my address and phone number. Give me a call when you're ready to go in the morning, and I'll give you directions.'

'Are you sure you want us to stay with you?'

He managed a thin smile. 'I'm sure. It will be nice to have a child around again. Alice will be thrilled.'

He reached over and ruffled Donnie's hair. 'Besides, he looks like a pretty strong fella to me. Might be able to make a good hand out of him.'

Donnie grinned, his eyes asking Casey 'please'.

She put the card into her purse. 'Okay then.'

Dan Farrel leaned forward. 'Casey, I can't tell you how much this means to me. And afterward, when this is all over, maybe we can get acquainted, be a real family. Even if you find me hard to take, you'll like your aunt Alice, and Clint, your cousin, is bright and sharp.'

'Maybe,' she said. 'We'll see what happens.'

It was only eight o'clock when Casey and Donnie returned to their room. Casey sent Donnie into the bathroom to brush his teeth and get ready for bed, then she sat down on the edge of the bed and stared at the phone. After a few moments' thought, she picked up the receiver and punched out the number of her mother's brother, Claude Pentiwa, on Second Mesa. He didn't have a telephone in his home, but he did have one in his shop, and he often worked late, particularly during the tourist season.

The phone was picked up on the third ring, and Claude Pentiwa's deep voice growled, 'The store isn't open now. Call back tomorrow if you have anything important to say.'

Casey said quickly, 'Hello, Uncle.'

There was a moment's silence, then, in a different, lighter voice he said, 'Hello, *Nesseehongneum*.' Her Hopi name, he never called her anything else. It was amazing, she thought, how he could go from what she thought of as

22

'Indian Primitive' to 'Sophisticated Contemporary' in the blink of an eye, to suit his purpose. In his youth, Claude had spent some time as an actor, both in Hollywood and in Europe, but had come back to his Hopi roots an Indian activist.

With a smile in her voice she said, 'How are you, Uncle?'

'I'm fine. But if you visited me more often, you'd know that.'

Casey felt the familiar mixture of affection and aggravation that she often felt when dealing with her uncle. He was not an easy man to get along with. There had been a long period when she, and her parents, had not been welcome in his house. He had felt about Casey's white father the same way that Dan Farrel had felt about his brother's Indian wife.

'We were up over the Christmas holidays,' she reminded him. 'And my job keeps me very busy.'

'Yes, your very important job. How is the boy?'

'He's fine. Do you want to talk to him?'

'Of course.'

Donnie had just come out of the bathroom, and she held the receiver towards him. 'It's Uncle Claude, Donnie.'

The boy's face lit up, and he snatched the receiver. She sat back, smiling fondly as Donnie talked excitedly to Claude Pentiwa. After that near-fatal encounter with the Dumpster Killer on Second Mesa, Donnie and Claude had become fast friends. Whenever she and Donnie visited her uncle, he and the boy roamed the Mesa while her uncle taught him the beliefs and the old skills of his Hopi ancestors, and Donnie ate it up. For a ten year old, there was nothing greater than to have an Indian for a great uncle.

Donnie held the receiver out to her. 'He wants to talk to you.'

Casey said into the receiver, 'Uncle?'

'I think we've already established that,' he said mockingly. 'The boy tells me that you're in Prescott, on vacation. You couldn't have spent the time here?'

Casey held back a sigh. 'I brought Donnie to Prescott to see the rodeo and the Frontier Days celebration. Besides, you know that at this time of year it's almost as hot on the Mesa as it is in Phoenix. I wanted to get out of the heat.'

The disparaging sound that he made indicated his opinion of such a weak excuse. Before he could say anything else, she broke in. 'Uncle, do you know if my father had a brother, a Dan Farrel?'

There was a long silence before Simon spoke. 'Your mother spoke of him only once. She said that your father had severed relations with him because he would not accept her, an Indian, as his brother's wife. She was, I believe, trying to make a point! I take it that they never mentioned him to you?'

'That's right. I got a big surprise tonight when he came over to our table while Donnie and I were having dinner. It happens that he has a ranch here, just out of town.'

'And how did he find you, and why?'

'His son was killed today, at the rodeo. He was a bull rider. The father knew I was in town, because I talked to the police just after the son's death.'

'That's a terrible thing. But why come to you?'

'Because he knows who I am, what I do. He's been following my career. He wants me to find his son's killer.'

'His killer?'

'Yes. The preliminary autopsy indicates cyanide.'

'And are you going to take the case?'

'Yes, I am. He sort of boxed me in; he's already talked to the Governor – a buddy of his – and my boss. I have their blessings.'

He sighed heavily. '*Nesseehongneum*, how long are you going to continue to hunt down the killers of the white

24

man? The more whites that are killed, the better for the Indians.'

This was an ongoing argument between them. She said lightly, 'If you will remember, Uncle, my last case concerned the killing of three Mexicans and two Mexican Americans, and all of them probably had a good share of Indian blood in them.'

He said abruptly, 'Good-bye, *Nesseehongneum*.'

Her 'Good-bye, Uncle,' barely preceded the click of his receiver. She hung up slowly, shaking her head. Claude could really be aggravating. Whenever he found himself at a perceived disadvantage, or when conversation turned to any of the many things he did not wish to discuss, he abruptly cut out.

Donnie interrupted her thoughts. 'Casey, are you going to call Josh?'

'Sure, kiddo. Hold your horses.'

Josh was working the day shift this month, so he should be home now. She punched out his number.

He answered on the first ring. 'Hello?'

'Hi, Detective.'

'Hi, babe.' His deep voice was warm with pleasure. 'How goes it with the bucking horses?'

'It's been great. Donnie loves it. I think he wants to be a rodeo rider.'

'No way! He and I have agreed that he's going to be a NFL wide receiver for the Cardinals. Maybe by the time he's ready to play they'll have a decent team.'

'Yeah, right. Wait, I'll put him on.'

Feeling rather guilty, she handed the receiver to Donnie. She knew very well that Donnie would tell Josh that they were going to stay in Prescott, and that she was going to be working on a case there. She also knew that this would be easier than breaking the news herself. All that would be left for her to do was to explain why.

Knowing the conversation would take a while, she went

into the bathroom to remove her make-up and put on her nightgown and robe, hoping that when it was her turn to talk to Josh, she could make him understand. He wasn't going to like it.

Her turn came sooner than she had thought as Donnie yelled, 'Hey, Casey, come talk to Josh!'

Reluctantly she walked over to Donnie and took the receiver from his outstretched hand.

'What's this about your staying in Prescott to work on a case? I thought this was supposed to be a vacation?'

'It is. It was. I didn't plan for this to happen, Josh.'

'Donnie said something about a bull rider being killed at the fairgrounds? Why are you involved?'

'It's a long story, Josh.'

'Well, condense it. What's going on?'

Quickly she repeated to Josh the same information she had just given to her uncle Claude.

There was a pause, and Casey could almost see Josh shaking his head. 'Jesus! Trouble certainly finds you, doesn't it? And you said you'd take the case?'

'There wasn't much I could do, he sort of boxed me in. He had already talked to the Governor – they're good buddies – and the Governor said he'd clear it with Wilson. Also, I must admit that I'm intrigued. Although I didn't know that Buck existed, now I do, and he *was* my cousin.'

'Shit, Casey. Have you forgotten what I told you about working on cases involving family or friends?'

She sighed. 'No, Josh, I haven't forgotten; but like I told you, I didn't really feel I could say no. So how about giving me some support, and your best wishes?'

It was his turn to sigh. 'Okay, babe. But you're sure this guy, this "Uncle Dan" isn't lying to you?'

'Pretty sure. I called Uncle Claude and asked him if he knew anything about my dad having a brother, and he corroborated Dan's story.'

26

'Just what you need, another eccentric uncle.'

'Well, this one doesn't seem to be eccentric, just tough. From what he says he was pretty wild when he was young; but now he seems to be well off, and well connected to boot.'

'Well, I guess you're set on doing this. But I'll miss you, and Donnie.'

'We'll miss you too. We'll call often. And Josh, there is something you can do for me if you will?'

'Yeah. All right, what is it?'

'Run a check on Dan Farrel. He said that he's done some time, so there should be a sheet on him.'

Josh groaned. 'A con, yet. Just what kind of a family do you come from, girl?'

'Just your ordinary, every-day type of family. Don't you watch the soaps? Will you run the check?'

'Depend on it. I'll get back to you tomorrow evening.'

'Call me at this number.' She reached for her purse, pulled out her uncle's card, and read off the phone number.

'We'll be staying at the Farrel ranch. Mrs Farrel is going to look after Donnie while I'm working the case.'

'You think that's wise?'

'Under the circumstances, yes. After all, the Governor of the state and the local police trust this man, why shouldn't I?'

'Okay. You'll do what you want to anyway; you always do. I'll call you tomorrow night. Remember, I'm always here for you.'

She said softly, 'I'll remember, Josh.'

THREE

The next morning, while Casey and Donnie were packing, the phone rang.

Wondering if it could be Josh calling back with some information, Casey grabbed up the receiver. 'Hello?'

'Good morning, Casey. This is Dan Farrel. I'm downstairs in the lobby.'

Taken by surprise, Casey was silent.

'I didn't wake you, did I?'

'Oh, no. We were just packing. It's just that I didn't expect you here. You said you were going to call with directions to get to the ranch.'

'Well, I got to thinking last night about that rodeo clown, Hank Wilder?'

'What about him?'

'Well, I'm concerned that he might take off before you get to talk to him. I know him slightly – he's been working the Prescott Rodeo off and on for years – so I called him. He said that if you'd come up to the Sheraton at ten sharp, he'd be happy to talk to you. He can give you some time before he has to leave for the fairgrounds.'

Casey felt a surge of irritation. She wanted to handle things in her own way, at her own pace.

'I really should talk to the officer in charge first. If I get off on the wrong foot here, it could hamper the investigation.'

'I don't think you need to worry about that. Like I told you, I know most of them, and they're not like

28

those big city cops. They're friendly, easy to work with; and I've told the chief that you're going to be working with them.'

Casey gave a soft, disbelieving grunt. It had been her experience that most cops, big city and small town alike, weren't too crazy about someone from out of town butting in on their cases; and she really couldn't blame them.

'What about Donnie?'

'That's simple. I'll take him along out to the ranch. It'll give me a chance to show him around. You can come out later, after you've talked with Wilder and the sergeant. Okay?'

Covering the mouthpiece, she turned to Donnie, who was watching her expectantly. "You want to go on out to the ranch with Mr Farrel?'

He nodded eagerly.

"Okay,' she said to Farrel grudgingly. "We'll be down in a few minutes.'

The Sheraton Hotel stood on a large hill off Highway 69, near the edge of town, on Yavapai Indian land. The exterior was probably meant to be derivative of Indian architecture; but somehow it came off looking institutional. Most people, seeing it for the first time, assumed that it was a hospital or a prison.

However, the interior more than made up for the stark façade, being attractive, gracious, and offering a marvellous view of the city of Prescott from the large, glass-walled restaurant. The lobby and wide hallways boasted a continuous art gallery that exhibited the best work of Arizona artists.

Casey was a little early, so she spent a few minutes walking about the lobby, studying the exhibits. As she did so, she passed a pair of closed doors guarded by two large men in dark suits. The door opened and closed behind a middle-aged Indian couple. The rattle and clink of slot

29

machines, and the buzz of voices could be heard from inside. Casey paused. She had read about the opening of the casino at the Sheraton. It had caused considerable controversy. In fact, her last case, dubbed the Organ Pipe Murders by the media, had as its basis the thorny issue of legalized gambling in the state of Arizona.

She moved on, attempting to think of something else. There was still some pain associated with that case.

As she neared the lobby desk, a slender, muscular man dressed in khaki and worn cowboy boots approached her. He wasn't tall, only about her own height, and had a weathered but handsome face, with shrewd, pale blue eyes. It was difficult to judge his age; he could have been forty or sixty.

'Are you Miss Farrel?'

She nodded. 'Yes. You must be Henry Wilder?'

'That's right.'

He looked her over appraisingly, but there was nothing offensive in the look. It was the same look you sometimes got from cops, just taking measure.

'So you're Dan Farrel's niece?'

'So I just discovered.'

He raised sandy eyebrows. 'A long-lost uncle, eh? I thought those only existed in books.'

She found herself smiling; there was something likable about him, despite his obvious guardedness. 'So did I, but life is full of surprises.'

'You can say that again. It's pretty coincidental, you being a policewoman, and being here in town when this happened.'

She raised a hand. 'I'm not a policewoman, Mr Wilder, at least not *per se*. I'm part of a task force on crime set up by the Governor.'

He shrugged. 'Same thing. At least Dan says that you've been assigned to the case. Look, would you like some coffee while we talk? I haven't eaten yet.'

'I could use some coffee, sure.'

He led the way into the restaurant, where they were shown to a table by the window.

As the waitress took their orders, Casey studied Wilder. He had an easy manner, but he was obviously a careful man who guarded his boundaries. She had an impression of strength and caution. An interesting combination.

When the waitress had left, Wilder pulled out a small metal case from his pocket, and removed a toothpick. He looked over at Casey. 'I'm trying to stop smoking. This helps a little.'

He stuck the toothpick between his teeth. 'Now, what was it you wanted to ask me?'

He had, Casey noticed, a nice mouth. Speaking around the toothpick gave him an added air of toughness.

'Tell me what happened in the horse barn, Mr Wilder.'

'Hank, please.' He shifted in his chair. 'I'm afraid that I have nothing to tell you that will be of much help.'

'Just tell me what you remember.'

'Well, it was just before the bull riders were due to go on. I had to go to the john, so I told the handlers where I was going, and took the short-cut through the barn. It was pretty dark in there and about halfway through, I heard someone step out of one of the stalls I had just passed, and footsteps behind me. I started to turn and something hit me.'

He reached to touch a spot on the back of his head. 'I went out like a smashed light bulb. When I came to, I was in the stall, face down in the hay, a gag in my mouth, my hands and feet tied behind me.'

'You didn't get a look at your assailant?'

He shook his head. 'No. I feel stupid saying this – somebody always says it in every cop show I've ever seen – but it happened so quickly. I just heard steps, started to turn, then wham . . .'

31

'Could you tell if it was a man or woman?'

'I told you. Nothing. It could have been a kid, for all I know.'

'So whoever struck you, then took your place. He would have had to be already in costume, and made up to look like you.'

'Yeah, that's the way I figure it. I can't think of any other way it could have happened. *Somebody* came out and did my turn, and it sure wasn't me.'

'So it would have to be somebody who knew your routine, somebody who knew how to work the bulls?'

'Yeah, and somebody who knew my habits. You see, I've got weak kidneys – too much bull riding in my younger days – and I don't like to work with a full bladder, so I always relieve myself just before the event.'

'So your assailant waited in the barn, knowing that you would be coming through?'

'That's what I figure. It's the only thing that makes sense.'

Casey thought for a moment before she spoke. 'And why do you suppose your assailant did this, took you out?'

Wilder frowned. 'It seems obvious that he wanted me out of the way. I can only suppose that it had something to do with Buck's death.'

'Yes, that does seem the reasonable conclusion. Tell me, how well did you know Buck Farrel?'

'Oh, I'd seen him around. Knew him to say hello to and all. Used to see him on the circuit now and then.'

'What did you think of him?'

He shrugged. 'Like I said, I didn't know him all that well. He seemed to be about par for the course, for his type.'

Casey tilted her head. 'And what type was that?'

'Well, he was something of a hot-shot, always going for the glory. There's a lot of them like that, devils with the ladies, keen on drinking and partying; I think they go into rodeoing just for the excitement and the women. Only a very few top performers earn the big money, and even they usually end up crippled before they're middle-aged.'

'But you're still at it.'

'True,' he grinned crookedly. 'It gets in the blood. But rodeo clowning isn't glamorous like riding broncs or bulls. It's part hard work, and part laughs for the kiddies. I tried bronc and bull riding for a while, but one day I drew a real mean old bull, a seventeen hundred pound black devil that tossed me within two seconds, then tried to stomp me to death. If it hadn't been for the clown, I'd have been killed or crippled. It was then that I switched to clowning. Been doing it ever since, except for the time I spend at my ranch. I have a little spread outside of Elko, Nevada. It's pretty country.'

'Is that where you're from originally?'

'Yep. Elko's my home town.'

'So back to Buck. You say he was a womanizer?'

'From what I could see. He always had a different girl on his arm.'

'And a brawler?'

'That too, when he'd had too much to drink.'

'Was he a good rider?'

Wilder chewed on the toothpick thoughtfully. 'He wasn't bad. Took a purse now and then, and the crowd liked him; particularly here, in his home town. He'd never have been one of the great ones though, didn't take it seriously enough.'

'Do you know if he had any enemies, someone who hated him enough to kill him?'

Wilder shrugged. 'Some irate husbands and boyfriends, maybe; and some women that he loved and left behind; the usual.'

Casey raised her eyebrows. 'The usual?'

He nodded. 'Passions run pretty hot among rodeo people. A lot of them tend to be real basic: you take my woman, I punch your lights out. But usually it doesn't come to much. A lot of sound and fury.'

'Signifying nothing.'

He smiled. 'That's right. You're surprised I know that, aren't you? Didn't expect a rodeo clown to quote old William S.'

Casey smiled back. 'Not at all. Now, just a few more questions. Who found you tied up in the barn?'

'One of the local cops. Somebody realized that the clown hadn't shown up when Buck fell, so they went looking for me.'

He grimaced, and rubbed the back of his head. 'I had managed to work the gag out of my mouth, and was doin' some hollering.'

'Have the police asked you to stick around for a while?'

'Yeah, but I was going to anyway. I have a couple of weeks before my next rodeo, and I was going to spend it here.'

Casey stood. 'Good, I may have some further questions. Thanks for talking to me.'

He stood also. 'Any time. Glad to help any way I can. I'd like to see Buck's killer caught.' He shook his head. 'It sure must be hard on Dan.' He paused, and looked down at his hands. 'I know what it's like to lose a child. It's a hard thing to deal with.'

He looked up, and held out his hand. Casey shook it briefly. His grip was firm and his hand rough and warm.

'Maybe, if luck is with us, we'll nail the killer before you leave.'

Privately, she wondered why she had said that. This was going to be a hard one, she could feel it in her bones. The killer had planned well, which usually meant that he, or she, was the careful type, which meant that

34

he, or she, would probably have left little or no evidence at the scene.

After leaving Wilder, Casey went in search of a telephone. When her call was answered at the Prescott Police Station, she was informed that Sergeant Steve Randall was presently out at the fairgrounds.

Although it was still three hours before the afternoon rodeo, the fairground was bustling. The most activity seemed to be centred around the barns lining the back two sides of the arena.

Casey found Sergeant Steve Randall in the barn where Hank Wilder had been attacked. Randall was standing before a stall roped off with yellow crime-scene tape. He was a tall, thin forty-ish man, with thinning blond hair, a narrow face, and tired-looking brown eyes.

When Casey introduced herself, he nodded. 'Yeah, Dan Farrel said you'd be dropping by today.'

He gave a slight smile. 'Nice to meet you. I read about your work on the Organ Pipe case.' He shook his head. 'I don't suppose I should say this, it's probably not "politically correct" but I expected someone more . . . well . . . older, and more . . . formidable.'

'If you are trying to say in a nice way that I don't look like a woman wrestler, you need to overhaul your stereotypes; but no offence taken.'

He shrugged ruefully, and she smiled. 'Did Dan tell you that he has asked me to work on the case with you?'

Randall nodded. 'Yeah, he said the Governor had given his approval.'

'Do you have any problem with that?'

'None at all. I figure that I can use all the professional help I can get. We don't get this type of case around here very often – in fact never, in my experience. Now and then a body is found in the desert, and some of them have involved pretty gruesome murders; but here

35

in town, well, there hasn't been a murder committed since I've been here. I'll be happy to pick your brains.'

'Great. So fill me in on what you've found so far.'

He sighed. 'Nothing. That's the problem. That spot over there,' he pointed to a long indentation in the hay in the stall next to them, 'was where Henry Wilder was found bound and gagged. His attacker left nothing in the stall, at least nothing we can find.'

'The killer evidently came to the fairgrounds already dressed and in make-up,' Casey said, chewing on her lower lip. 'You'd think that somebody working around the barns would have noticed him.'

'Some people probably did – at least they saw a clown – but they don't know if it was Wilder or the killer. There's nothing we can go on.'

'I gather that it's been definitely established that the victim was poisoned, and that it was cyanide?'

'Yeah. The autopsy has been completed.'

'And how does the coroner figure the poison was administered?'

'In a jolt of whisky. The clown . . . a clown . . . was seen giving Buck a shot just before he and the bull left the chute. We found the bottle on the ground beside the chute. There were a few drops of whisky left. It was loaded with cyanide.'

Casey shook her head. 'Sounds foolish to me, taking a drink when you're sitting on fifteen hundred pounds of sudden death. I should think Buck would have wanted a clear head.'

Randall shrugged. 'Yeah, I know, but some of the riders do it. Maybe when the alcohol hits it helps deaden the pain. I don't know.'

'No fingerprints, I suppose.'

Randall shook his head. 'Wiped clean.'

'And what was the last time that the fake clown was seen?'

36

'As far as we can tell, there at the chute. Of course we haven't gotten around to talking to everybody yet. There were dozens of people in the area, so there's still a chance that someone saw him. We're going to run an announcement on the news tonight, as well as in this afternoon's edition of the *Courier*, asking anyone who might have seen anything to get in touch with us. People here in town are pretty community oriented, and we hope somebody will come forward with something.'

'Did you know Buck Farrel?'

'Never met the man. Seen him ride a few times, but never met him personally.'

'I understand that he's been in a few brawls down on Whiskey Row. I thought you might have seen him at the station.'

'Nope, never did, but I found a file on him.'

'Do you have any suspects yet?'

He shook his head. 'It's too early for that.'

Casey held out her hand. 'Well, thanks for your cooperation. I appreciate it.'

'It's no big deal; as I said, I'm glad to have the help. But there is one thing: you find out anything, anything at all, I want to know about it right away. Okay?'

'Okay. But that cuts both ways.'

He smiled. 'Of course. Share and share alike.'

FOUR

Leaving the fairgrounds, Casey took Miller Valley Road out towards the airport, then turned left on Highway 89 heading toward Chino Valley and points north.

She followed Dan Farrel's instructions, driving through the small town of Chino and taking a left on a gravel road about three miles beyond the city limits. The so-called monsoon season had started early this year, and the grass on each side of the road was green. Cattle grazed placidly in the fenced fields. Here and there a windmill turned lazily in a light wind.

About two miles down the gravel road she came to another gate with a square wooden arch above it. The top of the arch had the words 'Double D Ranch' burned into it. She turned on to this road, clattering over the cattle guard, and proceeded for about another half mile, until she saw the approach to the ranch house. The drive was framed by tall flagstone pillars, and surmounted by a handsome wrought-iron arch bearing the name Farrel.

The entrance was on a rise, and from it Casey could see the main ranch house and its outbuildings. The house was long, low, and Spanish, with a wide, shady veranda across the front. Its walls gleamed white in the afternoon sun. Shade trees softened its outlines, and a large circular cement turnaround offered parking for several vehicles. Behind the house, and to the left and right, she could see outbuildings and well-kept barns and corrals.

When she got to the turnaround, she saw two dusty

Ford pickups and a late model Cadillac. Parking behind the Caddy, she got out of the Cherokee and took a deep breath. The air smelled of country. She smiled. Donnie was going to love it here.

As she thought this, she noticed two figures seated on the top rail of the large corral to the left of the house. It was quite a distance away, but she was sure that the smaller figure was Donnie.

She started toward the corral. Halfway there, the smaller figure turned around, saw her, and jumped down from the corral railing. With a delighted yelp, Donnie raced toward her.

'Casey! This is great! There are real bulls and horses and real cowboys!'

Forgetting that he had said he was too big now for mushy stuff in public, he threw his arms around her and hugged her.

She bent to hug him back. 'Well now, how about that, kiddo?'

She ran her fingers through his hair, her gaze going to Dan Farrel, who had climbed down from the fence and was waiting for her. She took Donnie's hand in hers and walked with him to the corral.

Farrel, weathered face wreathed in a smile, said, 'The boy is having a fine time, Casey.'

Donnie looked up at her with shining eyes. 'Uncle Dan is going to teach me to ride, and everything!'

Casey ruffled his hair. 'That's great, kiddo.'

She looked up at her uncle. 'He's never ridden before.'

'Not to worry, Casey,' Farrel said reassuringly. 'We have some horses around that have pretty much been put out to pasture. They haven't got enough energy left to be dangerous. I'll look out for the boy.'

Casey was touched by the look of affection he gave Donnie. It was clear that the two were getting along famously.

Donnie said, 'I'll bet that Josh would really like it here.'

Casey smiled, thinking of Josh in Western wear. 'I'm not so sure about that, kiddo. Josh is pretty much a city guy.'

Farrel said, 'Who is this Josh, Casey? The boy seems to mention him with every other breath.'

Casey felt her face grow warm. 'Josh is a friend. Donnie and I met him when he was in charge of the Dumpster Killer case. He's a homicide officer with the Phoenix police.'

Farrel's glance was shrewd. 'Boyfriend?'

'Something like that, yes,' she said a little stiffly. 'I talked to the rodeo clown, and to the Prescott homicide sergeant.'

'Did you learn anything?'

She shook her head. 'It's hard to tell. At this point, I'm just gathering information; I won't know until later if it's useful or not. By the way, I need the name and address of Buck's former wife. I thought I'd drive out there and talk to her.'

Farrel nodded. 'Come on up to the house. My wife can give you the address. I'm no longer in touch with the woman, but Alice still sends and receives a card at Christmas.' At his gesture, they started towards the house.

'And I also want to talk to your neighbour, Darrel Dyce.'

Farrel grunted. 'Lots of luck. He probably won't even talk to you.'

'This is a murder investigation. He'll have to talk to me, if he likes it or not.'

Farrel's lips twisted in a sour smile. 'That shows just how much you know about the ornery bastard.'

As they approached the house, the front door opened, and two people came out on to the veranda. One was a

40

plump, greying, sweet-faced woman, about Dan Farrel's age. The second was a man, probably in his late thirties, of medium height, with thick brown hair and cold grey eyes. The eyes regarded Casey appraisingly. The man looked out of place in this setting, with his tailored grey suit, polished shoes, and styled hair.

Dan Farrel said, 'Casey, this is my wife, Alice. Alice this is Casey, my long-lost niece.'

Alice Farrel, smiling warmly, stepped forward to take Casey's hand in both of hers. 'Casey, I'm so happy to meet you. It's a shame that we haven't met before.' Despite her pleasant manner, there was a deep sadness in her brown eyes, which were red and slightly swollen.

Casey liked her immediately. 'I'm sorry about your son, Mrs Farrel. I know that this is a bad time to intrude, but Mr Farrel insisted that it would be all right.'

'Oh, it is. We're happy to have you here. You're family, and family should be together. And to have a bright youngster like Donnie here, well . . .' she swallowed, 'It helps.'

'Now, Mother,' the man beside her said stiffly, 'you should be resting, not looking after somebody else's kid.' He gave Casey an accusing glance, and she could feel her hackles rise.

Dan Farrel sighed heavily. 'Casey, this is our other son, Clint.'

Casey looked the man straight in the eyes. This one, she didn't think she was going to like. Mr Uptight, with an attitude. She nodded coolly. Getting his cooperation would not be easy. The elder Farrel appeared to be embarrassed by his son's behaviour.

'Clint, this is Casey Farrel, my brother's girl. Casey is a member of the Governor's Task Force on Crime. I've asked her to look into Buck's death.'

Clint frowned disapprovingly. 'I should think you would

41

leave that up to the local police. Why do you want to bring an outsider into it?'

His father's face reddened, and Casey surmised that this son and his father didn't see eye to eye on many things. 'Casey isn't an outsider, she's my niece,' Dan said. 'Also, she is one of the best investigators in the state, and I feel very lucky that she happened to be here at this time. She's doing us a favour, taking on this job, and I'll thank you not to insult her. Do you understand?'

Clint's face grew white, and his lips thinned. 'Oh, I understand, all right,' he said. Then, bending to kiss his mother's cheek, he strode down the veranda steps, and got into the Caddy, before Casey could speak to him.

Casey turned to Dan. 'Maybe we should call this off. I don't want to cause trouble between you and your son . . .'

Farrel waved a large, weathered hand and shook his head. 'It's not you. Clint has a policy of not agreeing with anything I say or do.'

Casey looked at Alice Farrel, who nodded wearily. 'It's like that sometimes, you know. Just being born into the same family doesn't mean people will get along.' She tried to smile. 'Maybe it's in the genes; after all, we don't all get the same package, do we?'

Casey, not usually demonstrative with strangers, put her arm around Alice's shoulders, and Alice reached for and took Casey's free hand with hers. Casey felt a swell of affection, and a pang of longing for her own mother, dead now for many years.

Dan said, 'I apologize for my son's rudeness, Casey. I suppose I could say that he's grieving over Buck's death; but I'm not sure that would be true. The two boys never did get along after they were grown.'

'Well, that's enough of that,' said Alice, removing her hand from Casey's and straightening her back. 'Let's all go into the house and have something cool to drink.'

'Oh, I'm sorry,' Casey said, 'but I have to get going.'

'Yes,' Dan said. 'She wants Pam's address, honey.'

Alice looked surprised. 'Pam? Whatever for?'

'I need to talk to her about Buck,' Casey said.

Alice looked at her questioningly. 'Surely you don't think that she had anything to do with Buck's death?'

'It's only procedure.'

'Oh.' The older woman appeared relieved. She added briskly, 'Well, come on into the house, dear, and I'll get Pam's address, and show you where you'll be sleeping.'

Casey wasn't familiar with Prescott Valley, having only seen it as she passed through on the way to Prescott. Located seven miles from Prescott, at a lower altitude, the valley was very different physically. Here, treeless, flat prairie stretched for miles, broken by the distant blue peaks of the mountains to the east. The town proper had the raw, new look of recent development. Along 69 small shopping centres and tidy industrial buildings sat hopefully, set off by the slender whips of young trees. Back from the highway were rows of new homes, the homes growing sparser the further one proceeded from the highway.

It was hotter here than in Prescott, and Casey turned up the air conditioning in the car.

The residence of Pamela Morgan was situated about a mile from the highway. A low, stucco structure, it was painted a light tan, and looked to be about two or three years old. Inside the chain-link fence, the yard was covered with tan gravel, punctuated with islands of drought-resistant plants. The backyard could be seen from the street, and there Casey could see a swing and slide set, and a plastic playhouse. Three small children, all tow-heads, ranging from about three to nine, were running through the yard, shrieking delightedly. A blonde woman, apparently in her early thirties, sat reading in a lawn chair in the shade of an awning attached to the back of the house.

There was a gate on the side of the house where Casey had parked, and she went up to it. 'Mrs Morgan?'

The woman glanced up, putting down her book. She looked at Casey uncertainly. 'Yes?'

'Can I speak to you for a moment?'

As the woman struggled to her feet, it became apparent that she was pregnant.

As she came closer Casey could see that her face was quite pretty, or had once been, for it bore the signs of lack of care, and too much sun. Her expression, and the downward curve of her rather weak mouth, made her appear the classic victim. Looking at her, Casey felt a familiar mixture of pity and annoyance. She saw women like this every day. They had abusive husbands or boyfriends; unmanageable children; health problems; thankless, low-paying jobs; any or all of these in various combinations. They were born to get the fuzzy end of the lollipop, or at least perceived themselves that way. When she was around women like this, Casey always felt the urge to shake them and tell them to shape up and handle things, be a mensch!

But that was not the way to get the information she wanted, so she smiled non-threateningly, and held one of her cards out through the mesh of the fence.

Mrs Morgan took it hesitantly. When she looked up from it, her faded blue eyes were apprehensive. 'Task Force on Crime? What on earth do you want with me?'

Casey smiled again. 'I'm investigating the death of Buck Farrel. May I come in?'

The woman looked down at the card again. 'It says that your name is Casey Farrel?' She looked up, a question in her eyes.

Casey clamped down on her annoyance. It had been a busy morning, she was hot and thirsty, and she didn't want

44

to waste time having to explain herself, but diplomacy was the key here.

'Yes. I am related to the Farrels. If you let me come in, I'll explain.'

The woman hesitated again, and then finally, reluctantly, unlocked the gate and held it open.

'I guess we can sit out here in the shade.'

She walked awkwardly toward the chaise in which she had been sitting, and motioned to another beside it.

Carefully – it didn't look too sturdy – Casey lowered herself on to the chaise as Mrs Morgan, with some effort, did the same with the other. The children were on the swing set now, still shrieking. The two eldest, girls, seemed to be having a contest as to who could swing the highest. The little boy was laboriously climbing the steps of the slide.

'So you're related to Buck?'

Casey nodded, and told the woman briefly about her relationship to Dan Farrel, omitting the fact that until yesterday she had not known he existed.

This seemed to satisfy the woman, and she relaxed a bit.

'Well, what do you want to ask me?'

'Just a few questions about Buck.'

The woman shrugged. 'I don't see why. I haven't even seen him in over ten years.'

'I know that, but I need to flesh out a picture of Buck Farrel, to find out what he was like, who he knew, and what he was involved in. In doing this, I hope to come across something, a thread, and connection, that will lead me to whoever killed him. Do you understand?'

Pam nodded doubtfully, and Casey sighed. 'At any rate, I would appreciate your telling me what you know about Buck. How did you meet, for example?'

Pam's eyes looked inward. 'It seems like a hundred years ago. We were both in high school, here in Prescott.

45

We were both freshmen, and had some of the same classes. I got a crush on him right away, but he didn't have time for me then. I wasn't you know, real developed yet, and he was already popular, and ran with kind of a wild bunch of kids. He liked to date older girls, the fast girls, you know. But all the girls were crazy about him.'

A piercing scream came from the play yard. Pam leaned forward. Casey looked up to see the little boy and the younger girl engaged in a tug-of-war over a plastic bucket. The girl was much larger, but the boy hung on tenaciously, proclaiming his claim to the bucket with bellows of outrage.

'Mary Sue, you stop that this minute,' Pam shouted in a surprisingly loud voice. 'Now don't you hit him. I've told you not to hit him. He's just a baby. If you don't stop it this minute, I'm going to put you in your room!'

Giving her mother a baleful glance, the girl reluctantly released her side of the bucket. The toddler gave a grunt of victory, and threw the bucket aside.

Pam Morgan sighed heavily. 'Kids. Sometimes I think I'm going to give out before I get them raised up. They always seem to know when you're feeling bad; and do their worst. Now what were we talking about?'

'You and Buck. So when did you finally get together?'

'It was later, when we were seniors. Buck was captain of the football team that year, and I had sort of blossomed, like they say, and was on the cheerleading squad. One day he noticed me, and the next thing I knew he had asked me out.'

'And so you dated?'

'Yeah. We dated.'

'And then you got married?'

Pam nodded. 'Yeah, we got married not long after we graduated. I was happier than I've ever been before or since. I was real young, you know, and I thought that

46

being married to Buck was the best and greatest thing that could ever happen to me.'

'So what led to the breakup?'

Pam frowned. 'Whisky and other women. Buck couldn't keep his pecker in his pants, and he always drank hard. On the rodeo circuit there's always women, groupies, you know. When he was home, he'd be good for a while; then he would start getting restless. Pretty soon hc'd be slipping off down to Whiskey Row. He'd get loaded, then pick up some woman. Each time I caught him at it he would swear that it wouldn't happen again, but it always did.'

Casey nodded. Pam's was a sad and familiar story. 'Well, it was probably lucky that you didn't have any children by him.'

Pam looked up. 'Well, that's a whole other story. I didn't know it at the time, but Buck had had one of those operations, you know a vasectomy.'

'Did his parents know about this?'

Pam shook her head. 'I don't think he wanted them to know. We were living with them at the time, and he told me not to mention it; he said it might upset his mother.'

'How did you get along with his parents?'

Pam smiled, and the expression brought up a quick glimpse of the pretty girl she must have been when Buck married her. 'Oh, I get along fine with Alice. She's a good woman, and she liked me. She was always kind. But Dan . . . Dan never did care much for me. I think he believed that marrying young hurt Buck's rodeo career.'

Her smile faded. 'He wanted that for Buck, you know; wanted him to be a big rodeo star.'

'How about Buck's brother, Clint?'

Pam frowned. 'Me and Clint never did get along; but then neither did he and Buck. Clint thinks that he's so much better than everybody else that his . . . well, let's just say that he's sure got a good opinion of himself. He couldn't get along with anybody in the family except Alice,

47

and she's a saint. He and Buck fought about everything. Clint thought that rodeo was for hicks, and Buck thought that Clint was what he called a "Prescott Yuppie".'

'Do you think it's possible that Clint disliked or hated Buck enough to kill him?'

Pam looked shocked. 'Kill his own brother?'

When Casey didn't answer, Pam said slowly. 'I don't know about that. Lots of brother and sisters fight, but sometimes they still love each other, deep down. I don't think they see . . . saw much of each other. They stayed out of each other's way. So what would be the reason?'

'It's just a question I had to ask. By the way, have the Prescott Police talked to you yet?'

An expression of alarm crossed the other woman's face. 'Will they do that?'

'I believe so.'

'But I don't *know* anything! You just found that out, didn't you?'

'Oh the contrary, I learned quite a bit.'

Pam shook her head. 'Ted – that's my husband – I don't know how he's going to take this, me talking to all of these cops. He doesn't like to be reminded about Buck. He says he doesn't like to think of me ever being married to someone else.'

Casey leaned forward, 'He won't hurt you, will he? He isn't abusive?'

Pam's face closed tight. 'Of course not. Why would you ask a thing like that?' Something flickered behind her pale eyes, and Casey wondered if she was telling the truth.

A sudden bellow from the play yard interrupted their talk, and brought Pam to her feet. The second girl crouched on the ground, small arms above her head. Standing over her was the oldest child, with a plastic shovel in her hand.

Pam struggled out of her chair with amazing speed, and,

walking heavily, arrived in time to intercept the second blow. Casey got to her feet. Over the squalls and shouts of the children, she shouted, 'I think I have all I need. Thanks for your cooperation.'

Pam turned her head, nodded, and turned back to her children. Casey returned to her car thinking of Donnie with relief and pleasure.

After leaving Pam Morgan's house, Casey stopped at a coffee shop where she got an iced tea, and used the pay phone to call Steve Randall at the Prescott Police station. She caught him at his desk.

'Sergeant Randall, this is Casey Farrel.'

'You just caught me on my way out. What can I do for you?'

'Just wanted to ask you something. Did the autopsy report on Buck Farrel mention anything about his having had a vasectomy?'

There was a pause at the other end of the line, then, finally, 'A vasectomy? I don't really know, the Medical Examiner didn't mention that when I talked to him, and I have yet to see the written report. Why do you want to know?'

Casey hesitated. 'I'm not sure, but Buck's ex-wife said that he had had one just after they married, and it struck me as strange. I mean, a man that young doesn't usually do that, does he?'

Randall chuckled. 'You're asking me? I don't even like to have my toenails cut. But you're right, it would be unusual. Usually a man has already had a few kids when he decides he doesn't want any more. Of course if there was something wrong with him, a reason why he shouldn't have children . . . Anyway, I can't see why it would be pertinent to this case.'

'It probably isn't, but I'd like to know anyway. Could you find out for me?'

'Sure. I'll be back in the office late this afternoon, about four-thirty. Can you drop by then?'

She nodded, thinking that would give her time to grab a bite of lunch, and, hopefully, talk with Clint Farrel about his relationship with his brother.

FIVE

Clint Farrel's real estate office was located in a new brick building on East Gurley. Casey found a place to park in the small lot that framed the building.

A sign over the front door spelled out: 'Farrel & Associates: Real Estate Sales and Development.' Displayed in the window were a number of colour photos of properties for sale. Casey got out of the Cherokee and approached the window. Most of the pictures seemed to be of homes in a development called Shady View Estates.

Inside, there was a reception desk; several chairs; a small couch, framed by potted palms; and a low table brightened by colourful magazines. Hanging on the wall over the couch was a handsome painting of Thumb Butte, the local landmark.

Behind the reception desk was a hall, and number of doors. Some of the doors were open, and Casey could see that behind them were small offices.

The plump, blonde receptionist was just putting down the receiver of the telephone, and she smiled at Casey brightly.

Her 'May I help you?' was cheery and chirpy as a bird's trill.

Casey returned the woman's smile. 'Yes, please. I'd like to see Mr Clint Farrel.'

'May I give him your name?'

'Of course. Tell him it's Casey Farrel.'

51

The woman raised well-plucked eyebrows. 'Just let me see if he's free.'

Turning slightly away, she picked up the telephone again, punched a button, spoke into it softly, then turned back to Casey.

'May I ask you what this is about, please?'

Casey sighed. 'You may tell Mr Farrel that this concerns the death of his brother, and that I am here in my official capacity.'

The woman's large, blue eyes widened further, but she relayed the information into the telephone, then put it down.

'He says to go on back. His office is the last one on your left.'

Before Casey reached the last office on the left, the door opened and Clint Farrel stood in the doorway. He moved aside to let her pass, then closed the door firmly behind her.

Not waiting until she took a seat, he said, 'What do you want, Miss Farrel? I'm a busy man, and I don't appreciate being interrogated at my place of business.'

Casey, uninvited, took one of the two comfortable chairs before the large desk, and looked up at him calmly.

This seemed to throw him off-stride, and he hesitated, as if not knowing if he should stand or seat himself behind his desk. He opted for the latter, and Casey turned to face him.

'This isn't an interrogation, Mr Farrel. I just have a few questions. And truthfully, I find your attitude curious. I'm attempting to find out who killed your brother – something I should think you'd be in favour of – but for some reason I detect animosity, even downright hostility towards me. May I ask why?'

'I'm perfectly willing to cooperate with the local police,' he said stiffly.

'But not me? Look, I'm not here because I want to intrude, or because of some hidden agenda. Until yesterday, I was happily on vacation. I didn't even know you, or your family, existed. Your father asked me, begged me, to look into your brother's death; and due to his influence with the Governor, I'm now assigned to the case. I didn't ask for it, but since it is now a fact, I intend to do my job; a job that you're not making any easier. Now, as a favour to your father, and the Governor, stop jacking me around and answer my questions.'

Her cousin's face paled and his eyes widened for an instant. Casey suppressed a smile. It was obvious that Clint Farrel was not used to being spoken to in this way.

Maybe it would do him some good.

He was silent for a moment, and then he visibly relaxed. 'All right,' he said. 'Let's get on with it. What do you want to know?'

Casey looked at him levelly. 'First, I'd like to know why you are so hostile to me. We've hardly known one another long enough for you to develop a dislike of me personally.'

His mouth thinned. 'To be honest, Miss Farrel, I find this long-lost cousin bit a little hard to accept. It seems very strange to me that my father has never mentioned the fact that he has a niece!'

'But surely you must have known that he had a brother?'

Clint waved his hand dismissively. 'It was mentioned, but just in passing reference to old pictures in the family album. He never talked about him, and there was no contact. I assumed that he was dead.'

Casey nodded. 'He is, but it wasn't that long ago, and from what your father says, they were estranged long before that, in fact from the time my father married my mother.'

53

'Well, that's neither here nor there. As I told you, I'm a busy man. Ask your questions, and let me get on with my work.'

'Fair enough. First, where were you during the time your brother was killed?'

'Here in my office. My staff can verify that. Weekends are our busiest days.'

'How did you and your brother get along?'

'Not all that well.'

'Would you care to explain?'

He gave her a cold look. 'Not really, but I suppose you might as well hear it from me as from someone else. Buck and I did not have a great deal in common. I have a family; a stable business; and a standing in the community. Buck was pretty much a bum. He was supposed to be helping Dad work the ranch: but he spent most of his time rodeoing; drinking down on Whiskey Row; or chasing women.' His lip curled. 'I didn't approve of the way he lived his life, and he knew that. We didn't see one another often.'

She looked at him appraisingly. 'So there was no love lost between you?'

He returned her look coldly. 'Yes, you could say that; but if you're fishing around for a motive, no, I had no reason to kill him. There is no benefit for me in his death.'

Casey nodded. 'Do you know of anyone who had a grudge against Buck, someone who might have hated him enough to kill him?'

Clint grunted. 'There were probably dozens, jealous husbands, jilted women; Buck cut a pretty wide swath, and he ran with some pretty rough people. However, I can't give you names; as I told you, we didn't see much of one another, and I didn't want to know his business.'

Casey made a note on her pad. Clint was the second person to mention jealous husbands or lovers. 'Can you

54

give me the name of someone who was close to Buck, who might be able to give me the names of some of his friends?'

Clint thought for a moment, then shook his head. 'I told you, I pretty much stayed away from Buck, so I don't know who he was hanging out with. Maybe Dad can tell you.'

Casey closed her notebook, and got to her feet. 'I guess that's it, Mr Farrel,' she said. 'For now.'

He stood also, his face a study in mixed feelings. 'I suppose that means that I'll be seeing you again?'

Casey smiled sweetly, and, borrowing Josh's favourite phrase, said, 'Depend on it.'

After leaving the real estate office, Casey drove the few blocks to the centre of town, and parked near the police station, a low, modern building. Inside, Casey was surprised to find the place empty except for two women behind the counter. She found it amazing. In Phoenix, or Los Angeles, almost any station was bustling with activity, or, in rougher precincts, downright chaos. Smiling, she approached one of the women and asked for Sergeant Randall, and was directed to his office.

Randall was on the phone. He raised an eyebrow and motioned her to take one of the chairs in front of his desk.

Hanging up the receiver, he gave her a wide grin. 'Your timing couldn't be better,' he said, nodding toward the telephone. 'That was the medical examiner's office. The autopsy is completed, and it's pretty much like they said at first, cyanide, and he died within a few minutes of ingesting it. Nothing else pertinent, except that, just as you said, he had had a vasectomy.' He paused, grinning.

Casey searched his face. 'Now, why do I have this feeling that there's more?'

55

'I guess because you're a good investigator. Yes, there's more. The vasectomy had been repaired – recently, it would seem.'

She made a sound of surprise. 'Well, I'll be damned!'

'Gives you something to ponder, doesn't it?'

She nodded. 'The question is, does this have anything to do with his murder?'

'That's a good question. Probably not. Still, I learned long ago that often, what seem like irrelevant details, turn out to be crucial. This early in the game, it's hard to tell. At any rate, it's an interesting fact.'

'Yeah. Anything else I should know?'

'That's it. You?'

She shook her head. 'I talked to Hank Wilder, the rodeo clown, this morning and checked out his story. He claims that he didn't know Buck well, so I didn't get a lot; but I found out that Wilder didn't have a great opinion of Buck. And this afternoon I talked to Buck's brother, Clint. Evidently Clint and Buck didn't get along very well, too different. Clint admits that he disliked his brother; but as far as I can see now, he certainly had no reason to kill him. He was at his office all afternoon, and the staff verifies that.'

'So he's pretty much out of it too?'

'It would seem so. One interesting thing, though. When I asked him if he knew of any enemies Buck might have had, he mentioned possible jealous husbands and jilted women. This morning, Wilder told me almost the same thing. Evidently Buck was quite a womanizer, and not very politically correct about it.'

Randall smiled. 'Womanizers seldom are. But it's something we should look into. So what's your next step?'

Casey sighed. 'Just plough ahead with the footwork. Have you checked out the man who found the clown?'

Randall nodded. 'Yep. It all checks out. He found Wilder about fifteen minutes after Buck's death, bound hand and foot. He swears that it was impossible that Wilder could have done it himself, so it all computes. He's in the clear.'

Casey shifted in her chair. 'We need to get a list of Buck's friends. His father should know at least some of them. And then there's Darrel Dyce, Dan's neighbour. Do you know about him? It seems that there is bad blood between the two families, something about water rights and a lawsuit. Maybe things got out of hand there.'

'Possibility.'

'By the way, I'll be staying at the Farrel ranch, if you should need to get in touch. I'm going to head out there now. It's been a long day.'

The phone on Randall's desk rang. He scooped up the receiver, listened intently, and then hung up, his face grave. 'I'm afraid you won't be going home just yet, Casey. They've just found the body of a man at Granite Dells. He's been shot between the eyes.'

Casey leaned forward. 'You think there's a connection between this and Buck Farrel?'

'Looks very much like it. The dead man is Red Pollock. He worked as a stable hand at the rodeo. We just don't get murders here in Prescott, and it has to be more than coincidence that we now have two murders in two days, both tied up with the rodeo. Coming with me, Casey?'

Casey stood. 'You couldn't keep me away!'

SIX

The area called Granite Dells was a strange and beautiful place. Huge granite boulders, carved by thousands of years of wind, water and weather, stood in towering piles and clusters amid low oak trees and brush. Above the stream bed stood the old, white frame bath house with its ruined pool, and the deserted dance hall, both closed since the early sixties. Casey tried to imagine what they had been like in their heyday, when local families had come here during the day to swim and sun, and at night the dance hall had spilled out its light and music into the darkness.

She turned back to the scene in the stream bed. The slender body of a man lay on its stomach at the edge of the stream bed, one foot touching the narrow rivulet of water that was all that remained of the stream at this time of year. At the base of the skull was a strangely neat, dark hole. From it, a trickle of dried blood crawled like an obscene worm. The red hair that had given the man his name moved slightly in the gusty wind.

It was a sad scene, and Casey turned away from the sight.

Two men in the uniform stood nearby. One was the young officer whom Casey had seen at the fairgrounds. The other was a stocky man in the uniform of the Country Sheriff's Department. The Deputy was holding back a scattering of spectators who had appeared, as they always did, seemingly out of nowhere. Casey felt a slight shiver. She always found this sudden gathering of spectators eerie.

Steve was talking to the Prescott officer. 'You took the call, Ray?'

The young officer nodded, and managed a weak smile. 'Yeah, I was patrolling Willow Creek Road. Bill . . .' he pointed to the Sheriff's Deputy, 'got here just after I did. Technically, I guess it's their jurisdiction.'

'Who found the body?'

'A couple of kids. They live nearby. They ran home, and their mother called 911.' He turned and pointed to where a young woman and two small boys, about eight and ten, huddled beside a large boulder. 'They're over there with their mother, if you want to talk to them.'

Steve nodded. 'Later. Any identification on him?'

'No, but I knew who it was right away. Red's been hanging out at the fairgrounds for as long as I've been here, picking up odd jobs, making enough to buy a little food and keep himself in liquor.'

'Yeah, he was a boozer. Poor old bastard.'

Ray shook his head. 'There wasn't any harm in him, though. I figure he got paid yesterday and somebody offed him for what he had in his pockets. Maybe some wino or tramp. Sometimes they camp out around here.'

'You figure that, do you?'

Ray nodded earnestly. 'Yes, sir. Clearly, robbery was the motive. As you can see . . .' The officer pointed a finger. 'His pockets are turned inside out.'

Steve smiled. 'But have you asked yourself the key question, what was Red doing out here in the first place, and how did he get here? We haven't found his old truck, or any other vehicle. And, why would someone bent on robbery be hanging around here? This isn't what you might call a happy hunting ground for muggers.'

The young officer looked sheepish. 'It could have

59

been some wino, camped out here, and Red just ran across him.'

'I suppose it's possible, but if it was a wino, and he had gotten his hands on a gun, he would probably have hocked it to buy booze.'

The young officer's face reddened. 'Maybe that's true, but maybe it wasn't a wino, maybe it was one of those nuts, you know, the ones in the camouflage suits. Some of them are real touchy.'

Steve nodded. 'That's a possibility; but we're still left with the question of why Red would come out here in the middle of the night. When we know the answer to that, we'll have the first piece of the puzzle.'

'Yes, Sir,' Ray nodded. 'I guess we will.'

Steve clapped him on the shoulder. 'Don't worry about it, Ray. That's what they pay me for.'

Steve turned away, and walked over to the body. Casey followed him. 'Are there many street people around Prescott? I haven't seen any.'

Steve nodded. 'A few, during the summer months. Since there isn't much competition, they find pan-handling fairly easy. In the winter, most of them make their way down to Phoenix.'

Steve glanced at her with a grin. 'You thinking along the same lines as Ray?'

'Not exactly. But it appears that someone wants us to think that way.' She pointed to the turned-out pockets.

Steve nodded. 'Of course, like Ray said, winos aren't the only loose nuts we have around here. There are the squatters, although they mostly camp out in the deep woods. A lot of them are Vietnam vets, or survivalists, and, like Ray said, some of the them are, to put it mildly, "real touchy". But you usually don't find them this close to civilization. There are quite a few houses around here.' He stared down at the body. 'The thing is, if it wasn't robbery, what was it? Why would somebody

60

want to blow away a harmless old wino? And why was he shot in the back of the head, execution style? I still think there's a connection with Buck Farrel's death.'

Casey glanced down at the body, then away. 'You think he knew something, or saw something?'

Steve shrugged. 'Or somebody thought he did. The first thing to do is find out if he was working at the fairgrounds at the time of Buck's death. If he was, we'll go on from there.'

He glanced towards the two uniforms. A third man, stocky and grey-haired in a brown suit, was coming toward them. He was carrying a medical bag.

The man in the brown suit trotted up, somewhat out of breath. His expression was unhappy. 'Hello, Steve,' he said briskly, as he neared them.

'Hi, Doc,' Steve said. 'This is Casey Farrel, with the Governor's Task Force on Crime. Casey, meet Dr Peter Flood, our medical examiner.'

Casey nodded. 'We've talked on the phone. I'm Casey Farrel.'

Dr Flood nodded curtly. 'Miss Farrel.'

He turned back to Steve. 'So, what do we have here?'

'Another killing, Doc, if you can believe it.'

The doctor shook his head. 'I've never seen anything like this.' He looked down at the body. 'My God, it's Red Pollock! For God's sake. Who would want to kill that poor harmless man?'

He squatted down beside the body, pulling on a pair of plastic gloves. 'Shot in the back of the head with a small calibre gun.'

He reached forward, touched the dead man's hand, then lifted it. 'Probably killed sometime in the middle of the night; rigor mortis is almost gone. I'll give you a better estimate after the autopsy.'

He raised his head. 'You know, I think this is the same place that they found that girl's body. Poor little thing.'

61

'What girl was that?' Steve asked.

'Oh, you wouldn't remember it, it was years ago; but a young girl was found here, in this same spot. I remember because she was my first autopsy after I came to Prescott. Poor little thing, shot herself in the head. We do get a suicide, once in a while, but two murders inside of a week . . .'

Steve put a square brown hand on the older man's shoulder. 'I know. This just doesn't happen here in Prescott; but somebody doesn't seem to know that. Doc, I'd like you to do me a favour. Granite Dells is county, so the Sheriff will have jurisdiction; but I think this ties in with Buck Farrel's death. Perform the autopsy as soon as you can, will you? And get back to me. Okay?'

The doctor nodded, and pulled out a small tape recorder which he clicked on as he turned his attention back to the body.

Steve turned to Casey. 'Do you want to help me look around, see what we can find before the Sheriff's squad gets out here? It's probably too much to hope for, but maybe we can find the shell casing . . .'

The doctor broke in. 'How about the bullet itself?'

Steve looked down at him. 'What?'

The doctor gave him a grim smile. 'It's still in his head. No exit wound.'

Steve scrubbed his hand over his face. 'Well, thank heaven for small favours. Let me know as soon as you get it out.'

He turned back to Casey. 'Well, at least that's one break.'

Two Sheriff's Department vehicles pulled up in the area in front of the old bath house and ballroom.

'We might as well get out of here,' Steve said. 'They'll take care of the details.'

Casey looked up at him. 'So what's next?'

'Well, I think that I'd like to have a look at Red's

62

trailer, before anybody else gets a whack at it. He lived in a trailer park just up the road.'

Casey nodded. 'Sounds reasonable. Let's go.'

The trailer park was one of those sad little parks, dusty and barren, which looked like a trailer graveyard to which old trailers came to die. The trailer in which Red Pollock had lived was one of those bulky, old, aluminium jobs, showing signs of wear, but surprisingly well kept up. Steve had obtained the key from the man who ran the park, but as he reached out to use it, the door swung open under the pressure of his hand.

Casey and Steve exchanged looks. The detective motioned Casey back, and slid his service revolver from the holster beneath his jacket. Easing the door open with his foot, he entered the trailer in a crouch, holding the revolver in both hands.

Holding her breath, Casey listened anxiously, hearing only the sounds of Steve's footsteps, then a muttered curse: 'Goddamnit, we're a little late!'

Casey came through the door and found Steve standing in the middle of the living area, his gun dangling at his side. The room had been thoroughly, and roughly, tossed. Cabinet doors and drawers hung open. Books, tapes, magazines, personal articles lay scattered over the floor. Bits of rubber foam and cotton from ripped pillows and upholstery were spread over the mess like a foul, yellow-white frosting.

Steve holstered his gun, disgustedly. 'It's the same in the bedroom and the bathroom. Whoever tossed it, did a thorough job.'

Casey shook her head. 'A burglar? Or our perp?'

'My guess would be the last. Anything else would be too much of a coincidence.'

'I wonder what he could have been looking for? What could Red have had that would be that important?'

Steve shrugged. 'Who knows; but whatever it was, it's gone now, or was never here.' He ran his hand through his hair, leaving it tousled. 'Well, I guess we might as call it a night. There's not much we can do till we get the autopsy report, and the Sheriff's Department will be on it. I'll check with them in the morning.' He holstered his gun, then reached out and clapped her on the shoulder. 'So go home, Casey. I'll take you to your car. Get a hot meal and a good night's sleep. I'll see you in the morning.'

It was growing dark by the time Casey picked up her car from the police parking lot. She settled herself in the Cherokee feeling tired and a little depressed.

Heading toward Chino Valley, she felt the need to forget the case for at least a little while. She needed to touch base with what she thought of as the real world.

Every cop Casey knew had his or her own way of coping with the horrendous and depressing burden that they all carried. There was, Casey thought, a terrible chasm between the people and things that the average law enforcement officer saw and experienced every day on the job, and the life of the average citizen. You often spent your day, or night, in the company of the dregs of society. You saw things that made your soul tremble: abused children; tortured wives; battered old people. Then, when your shift was over, you were expected to return to your family and friends: to cross over into their world; to take care of your kid's problem at school; commiserate with your spouse over the broken washing machine; worry about paying the bills; all of the normal, ordinary details of everyday life in a world where people read about the terrible things that happened in the world, but didn't, ordinarily, experience them.

For some, it was a difficult adjustment to make. For others, impossible. Casey had seen more than a few good officers burn out and go down in flames, and she was determined not to do the same.

Now, she slipped a Carlos Nakai tape into the car's cassette player, and punched the play button. Nakai might be a Navaho, but she could forgive him that because his music was so beautiful.

As the liquid notes of the flute filled the car, she took a deep breath, held it, then exhaled. By the time she had done this two more times, she could feel her tension and depression leaching away with the setting of the sun.

She turned her thoughts to Donnie, then to Josh. She must call Josh tonight. He would be worrying about her, as usual. She smiled. Nakai's flute floated peace into the corners of her mind. She passed the turn-off to the Dyce ranch without a second glance and only a passing thought; she would take care of that tomorrow.

It was almost dark when she drove up before the Farrel ranch house. As she parked, Donnie came barrelling out of the house, running up to hug her as she got out of the Cherokee.

'Casey! This is a real neat place!' He looked up at her with shining eyes. 'I got to see cowboys herd the cows, and work the bulls, and I got to ride a horse!'

Casey smiled and hugged him back. He smelled of soap, and his enthusiasm rubbed off on her like some marvellous elixir. She laughed. 'Well, a horse. Did you like it?'

He nodded enthusiastically. 'Boy, yes. It was great! Uncle Dan showed me how to get on – you gotta get on a special way, you know, or the horse will throw you off. And he showed me how to sit, and everything.'

'Everything?'

'Well, maybe not everything, but a lot. He's going to show me more tomorrow. He says in a week or so I'll be riding like a real cowboy. He says I'm a natural!'

'So, it's Uncle Dan, is it?' she said dryly, feeling a guilty twinge of jealousy.

Donnie seemed not to notice. 'Yeah. Sure. He said I could call him that. He's real neat, Casey. He let me call Josh.'

Casey lifted his chin with her hand. 'Call Josh? Why?'

Donnie's small face assumed an expression of anxiety. 'To see if Josh could bring Spot Two out here. Spot would like it here, there's rabbits to chase and everything.'

Casey, imagining the little dog chasing other things, like the stock, frowned. 'Are you sure Dan said that it would be all right. Spot isn't used to cattle. He might be a bother.'

Donnie shook his head, and grasped her hand. 'Uncle Dan said it was fine. He said he'd like to have a dog around. Please, Casey. I really miss Spot.'

Casey looked down into the boy's pleading face, trying to remember how it was to feel that strongly about such a simple thing. She smiled. 'Well, it's "Uncle Dan's" ranch. If he says it's all right, well, I guess it's all right. Now let's go in the house. I feel a pressing need for a hot bath.'

As Casey and Donnie walked across the veranda, Dan Farrel swung open the door. He wore a wide smile. 'Casey! Alice and I were worried that you wouldn't make it back for supper. It'll be ready in about half an hour. Would you like a drink?'

'I need a shower and a change of clothes, then a drink would be good.'

'Fine,' he said heartily. He placed a hand on Donnie's shoulder. 'You know where your room is. Donnie and I were watching a rodeo show when you drove in. This boy of yours sure loves rodeos and horses.'

'So he was telling me. It looks like baseball and football will have to take a back seat for a while.' She glanced down at Donnie with a smile. 'Shows you just how fickle he is.'

Donnie looked up artlessly. 'What's "fickle" Casey?'

She reached out and ruffled his hair. 'Don't try to con me, kiddo. You know what fickle means.'

A wide grin lit up his face, causing her to laugh.

'We'll be parked in front of the TV in the family room,' Dan Farrel said.

Casey nodded, and started down the hallway to the bedroom in the rear of the house. As she passed the kitchen, the savoury odour of pot roast made her pause. Inside, Alice Farrel was working over a large, butcher-block table. She smiled as she saw Casey, and waved. Casey returned the gesture, and continued on to the guest bedroom. Donnie had been given the room that had belonged to Clint, just across the hall.

Her room was cheerful with a comfortably old-fashioned decor. The bed, dresser, chifforobe and rocking chair were fashioned of warm, golden oak, and the bed was covered with a bright, handmade quilt. White curtains filtered the outside light, hiding pull-down blinds with tasselled pulls. A large ceiling fan moved lazily overhead. Casey had never had a room furnished like this; but it almost seemed as if she had. She smiled at her own fancy.

After a relaxing bath in the old fashioned claw tub in the bathroom across the hall, Casey felt her energy returning.

She put on a pair of soft, tan trousers, a loose, beige blouse, and a pair of tan moccasins. The materials felt smooth and comfortable against her clean skin.

The TV in the study was muted, and Dan Farrel was alone in the room, at the oak bar that took up most of one wall. He faced about as Casey came in, holding a heavy glass of dark liquor in one hand.

His face lighted. 'Casey. What would you like to drink?'

'A martini would be fine. Very dry.'

'Gin or vodka?'

'Gin.'

'Coming right up.' He lifted the bar flap and went behind the bar. 'Not too many people drink martinis these days.'

Casey smiled. 'A friend of mine, I mentioned him, the Phoenix homicide cop, got me hooked on them.'

'In case you're wondering, Donnie is helping Alice in the kitchen. I think he's getting hungry and wanted to hurry things along.'

Casey watched as he rinsed the interior of a silver shaker with vermouth, then carefully added the gin. Looking up, he said, 'Did you make any progress today?'

Casey watched him shake the drink. 'Not much. Of course it's hard to know, at this stage, just what is and is not going to be useful.'

She paused, and he poured the martini into a glass, handed it to her, and watched as she took her first sip, his expression questioning.

She nodded. 'You make a good martini, Dan. Thanks.' She took another sip. The fluid was icy, and faintly bitter, much like the information she was about to give him.

She sighed. 'Dan, there was another murder today, a man called Red Pollock. Do you know him?'

Dan had been reaching for the bar towel. He stopped and his face paled. Then he shook himself, like a big dog, shaking off water. 'Red Pollock? Sure I know Red. Hell, I went to school with him. He wasn't what you might call an upstanding citizen, but he never did anybody any harm. But why? How?'

Casey spoke softly. 'We found him out at the Dells. He had been shot. Probably happened sometime during the night. We don't know why, but both Sergeant Randall and I think that there must be some connection with Buck's death. We think that Pollock may have seen something and that the killer wanted him out of the way.'

Dan shook his head, and came out from behind the

bar, taking the stool next to Casey's. 'This is all getting to be too much,' he said. 'First Buck, now old Red. What the hell is this town coming to. Is there anything else?'

'Well, I talked to your ex daughter-in-law . . .'

Dan grunted. A bit of colour was coming back into his face. 'Don't pay too much attention to what she says. The woman's got about as much sense as a goose, and the parting between her and Buck was bitter.'

'That's pretty much what Clint said, too.'

Dan looked surprised. 'You talked to Clint, too? Did you get anything out of him?'

Casey shrugged. 'He wasn't exactly friendly, but after I explained to him that I was only doing my job, he did talk to me.' She paused a moment, wondering how to put what she wanted to say. 'It's pretty clear that he feels a lot of hostility toward me. Would you have any idea why that should be?'

'Oh, Clint's all right,' Dan said with a shrug. 'He's always been a bit nervy, you might say; and a little close minded, but he'll settle down eventually. Right now he's blaming Buck's death on Buck's wild ways. He says that Buck brought it on himself.' His voice rose in annoyance. 'I think he sees this investigation as a plan to embarrass him, personally. He always was a bit selfish; but he's a good enough boy. He'll come around. Did you learn anything useful from him, or from Pam?'

Casey took another sip of her drink. 'I'm not sure. There was one thing I found curious, and I'm not sure why it sticks in my mind, but it does. Pam told me that just after she and Buck got married, that Buck had a vasectomy. Did you know about that?'

Dan's face blanched, then reddened. 'Why that's got to be a goddamned lie! Buck would never have done anything like that! He was hardly more than a boy! He'd never of let some doctor cut on him like that! And his mother! He knew how much his mother and I wanted

69

grandbabies. I told you that woman was crazy. She'd say anything to bad-mouth Buck.'

Casey, startled by her uncle's anger, spoke even more gently.

'Lots of men have vasectomies, Dan. It's nothing to be ashamed of. You don't need to feel angry. Buck probably had a good reason.'

He shot her a dark look. 'Well, I know my boy, and he would never have done something like that, and not told me.'

Casey sighed, feeling the pain and pressure of the afternoon again closing in. 'I'm sorry, Dan, it's true. The autopsy confirmed it. It also confirmed that he had the operation reversed, fairly recently.'

He glared at her. 'Even saying that it's true, what in the damn-hell does this have to do with Buck's death? Why are you asking questions about this kind of thing instead of trying to find out who killed my boy?'

Casey reached out to touch his arm, but he pulled away. 'Dan, I'm trying to do just that. The fact of Buck's vasectomy may have nothing to do with his death; but I've learned, from experience, to check out all leads, no matter how strange.'

He got off the stool stiffly. 'You call this a lead?'

'It may be. I don't know yet.' How could she explain this to him? 'Dan, most people who are murdered are killed by someone they know; often by someone close to them. One of the ways to find out who the killer is, is to study the victim's life. Do you under-stand?'

He pushed away from the bar. 'I understand that you're poking into private matters that don't concern you, and that don't have a thing to do with my boy's death!'

Turning away from her, he strode out of the room.

A few seconds later, Casey heard the front door slam violently, and Alice call out, 'Dan? Is that you? Where are you going? I'm just putting dinner on the table.'

SEVEN

When Casey joined Alice and Donnie for breakfast the next morning, Dan Farrel was nowhere in sight. Casey, feeling a little guilty, asked after him.

Alice smiled at her understandingly. 'Don't fret, girl. Dan gets these spells sometimes. He'll be back later, acting as if it never happened, whatever it was.'

Casey winced. 'It was something I said. I don't suppose he told you?'

Alice shook her head. 'Not a word. You saw; he stormed out right after talking to you in the study. Haven't seen hide nor hair of him since. Probably slept in the bunkhouse. He does that sometimes.'

Donnie, all eyes and ears, fidgeted in his chair. 'What are you talking about, Casey? Where's Uncle Dan?'

Alice leaned over and plopped three steaming, fat pancakes on to his plate. 'He'll be back in a little while, Donnie.'

She gave Casey a knowing smile. 'He's out doing man things.'

Donnie stared down at the fragrant hotcakes, and then at the door. 'But he said I could help him today. He said . . .'

Alice set down a blue, ceramic pitcher filled with warm maple syrup, and a plate holding two cubes of golden butter. 'Oh, he won't forget that. Dan never breaks his word. Now you'd better dig into those hotcakes so that you'll have the energy to keep up with him.'

72

Donnie, with no further urging, reached for the syrup and the butter. Alice motioned to Casey with her head. 'Donnie, I want Casey to help me with something. We'll be back in a minute.'

Casey followed the older woman out of the room. 'Little pitchers . . .' said Alice, closing the kitchen door behind her. They were in a so-called Arizona room, surrounded by green and healthy plants. Alice motioned Casey to one of the comfortable looking wicker chairs. 'Now we can talk.'

Casey settled back into the chair. 'I didn't mean to upset Dan. I had no idea he'd react like he did . . .'

Alice waved her hand. 'Dan's a wonderful man; but like most men, he has a few odd notions, a few blind spots.' She smiled. 'I think it's all that testosterone. Men are always talking about women and their hormonal moods; but they never talk about how *their* hormones affect them.'

Casey found herself grinning. She had often thought the same thing. Still, she hesitated, worried that bringing up the subject of Buck's vasectomy would have the same effect on Alice as it had on Dan. Alice sensed her discomfort.

'Casey, you don't have to tell me what it was that set Dan off; but if you'd like to; or if you think it's pertinent to the case . . .'

Relief allowed Casey to relax. This was really an exceptional woman. She wondered if Dan knew how lucky he was. She leaned forward. 'Thanks, Alice. I don't know yet whether or not this means anything, but, did you know that Buck had had a vasectomy just after he married Pam?'

Alice nodded. 'Yes. I knew about it.'

Casey let her surprise show. 'It seemed to come as a shock to Dan. He got pretty upset. He refused to believe it.'

Alice sighed. 'I told you he had some strange ideas. To

73

Dan, having that kind of operation would make a man less than a man. And, he wanted grandchildren from Buck. I knew that if he found out about the vasectomy it would have hurt him terribly.' She shook her head again. 'He worshipped the ground that boy walked on, and he let his feelings blind him. Buck was my son too, and I loved him; but he had his flaws and his problems. I never talked to him about the vasectomy – it wasn't the kind of thing that Buck and I could have discussed – but I suspect it had something to do with his drinking, and his . . . fooling around.' She looked directly into Casey's eyes. 'Yes, I knew about that. Buck could never resist the women, and they couldn't resist him. When he was in high school I used to worry that some angry father with a shotgun would come pounding at our door; but he got through school, then married Pam. But there were still other women. People talk, you know, and I love my boys, but I'm not blind to their faults. And I suppose it showed a certain kind of responsibility, not wanting to get some other girl pregnant.' She looked down at her hands, folded in her lap. Casey followed her gaze. They were good hands, strong and capable, but right now they looked helpless and vulnerable.

Casey cleared her throat. 'Do you have grandchildren by Clint?'

Alice looked up. 'Yes, but somehow, for Dan, it's not enough. He's always favoured Buck, ever since the boys were small. I never understood why, or maybe I did. Buck was more like Dan, they had more in common. I tried to explain to Dan that his favouritism showed, that it hurt Clint, but . . .' She shrugged. 'At any rate, that's why I never let Dan know about Buck's operation.'

Casey leaned forward. 'How did you find out about it, if Buck didn't tell you?'

'Pam told me.' She looked thoughtful, and her face

paled. 'I suppose they, the police and all, found out about it when they . . .' She hesitated, and Casey didn't have to be told that she was thinking about the autopsy. It often hit people like this, the thought of their loved ones' bodies being, as they saw it, violated.

'Yes,' she said gently. 'But there was something else. The operation had been repaired. Did you know that?'

Alive blinked away her previous thoughts, and surprise rose in her eyes. 'Repaired. You mean the operation was undone?'

Casey nodded. 'The medical examiner said that the second operation had been performed recently.'

Alice shook her head. 'No. I didn't know that. I wonder why?'

'Could you give me the name of Buck's doctor? Maybe we can find out.'

Alice's lips thinned, and Casey reached out and touched her hand. 'It's not just curiosity, Alice. I'm not just being nosy. It's possible that this all has something to do with why Buck was killed.'

Alice nodded. 'Yes. I suppose so. Buck went to Dr Wheaton, here in Prescott. Of course he wasn't a surgeon, but I guess he would have referred Buck to someone who was.'

Casey took her notebook from her pocket, and jotted down the name. 'I assume he's in the phone book.'

Alice nodded. 'We'd better get back in the kitchen before Donnie thinks we've left home. He should be about ready for some more hotcakes.'

Forty-five minutes later, after her own breakfast, and after she had said good-bye to Donnie, Casey got into the Cherokee, and started the engine. Before she could put the car in gear, Dan Farrel drove up behind her, and got out of his truck.

As he walked toward the Cherokee, Casey steeled herself for a confrontation; but as he leaned to look in her open driver's window, she could see that he was smiling ruefully.

'Casey? I hope you can forgive an old blowhard for making a fool of himself.' He paused, and she realized that it was taking an effort for him to make what was obviously intended as an apology.

'About last night, well, my remarks were uncalled for. What you told me came as a real surprise; but I had no call to jump on you for it. I know that you're just doing your job, and I appreciate that you're doing it.' He stuck a weathered hand into the car. 'Am I forgiven?'

Relieved, Casey took his hand without hesitation. It felt strong and rough. 'It's forgotten. I'm sorry if I upset you.'

He shrugged. 'I have a quick temper sometimes; just can't seem to help it. Alice say's I'm a knee-jerk reactionary, act first, think later. I guess she's right. But you do whatever you have to do to find Buck's killer. If I start carrying on again, just ignore me. I'll get over it.'

She couldn't help smiling. 'Well, I hope you remember that if I bring up something sensitive again. I'm going to hold you to it.'

He returned her smile, seemingly relieved. 'You do that, girl. Now, you get on with your job while I go in and get me some breakfast and apologize to Alice for missing dinner last night.'

He stepped back from the window, and Casey put the Cherokee in gear. As she drove away, she glanced in the rear view mirror. He was still standing there, looking after her, and he seemed shrunken, a melancholy, lonely figure.

She shook her head briskly, and drove on, thinking of one of Josh's preachments: 'Never get involved with anyone in an investigation; it clouds your judgment.'

Turning off the side road to the Dyce Ranch, she turned her mind to the business at hand.

The Dyce ranch house, which came into view after a rise and a dip in the road, came as something of a surprise. It was a real period piece. Casey judged it to have been built in the late eighteen hundreds. Bright flowers bloomed in beds bordering the front of the house, and a TV satellite dish faced skyward off to the left. It was all very cheerful and homey.

As she parked the Cherokee and got out, three people came out of the house and arranged themselves in a line on the wide, cement entry, almost as if they had been waiting for her. It was a little off-putting. She studied them for a moment before approaching. All wore western attire: faded jeans, western shirts, and cowboy boots. Two men: one middle-aged; one young; both wiry and of medium height; and a young woman, as tall as the men, but more gracefully built, with long, ash-brown hair. Darrel Dyce and his son and daughter, no doubt.

She moved toward them, and at closer range, she could see that the older man's narrow face bore an expression of anger. He had small features, and close-set, pale, blue eyes. The younger man looked much like his father, except that his face was unlined, and the pale, blue eyes could best be described as blank. The girl's expression was unreadable. She was attractive, with nicely rounded hips, and surprisingly full breasts, which strained against the fabric of her shirt.

The older man took a step forward, turned his head aside, and spat a brown stream of tobacco juice into the flower bed. The gesture held a world of contempt. It took an effort, but Casey smiled pleasantly. 'Mr Dyce?'

The man hooked his thumbs in his belt and stared at her challengingly. 'Yep. Who wants to know?'

'I'm from the Governor's Task Force on Crime, and I'm working with the local police on the death of Buck Farrel. I'd like to ask you a few questions.'

Dyce spat again, taking his time about it. 'Got some identification?'

Damn it, Casey thought, knowing that as soon as he saw her name he would become even ruder, if that was possible. She pulled the folder out of her purse, and held it out to him. He took it and looked at it carefully, his face growing tighter as he did so.

He handed it back to her with a sneer. 'Farrel! Just a coincidence, or are you related to that side-winder Dan Farrel?'

'Yes,' Casey said coolly. 'I do happen to be related to the Farrels, but that does not alter the fact that I am assigned to this case, and that I would like to ask you some questions. Now, will you cooperate, or do I have to call Prescott and get a police officer out here to take you in to the station?'

Dyce let loose another brown stream into the flower bed. The girl's glance followed the brown cascade with a displeased look, but she did not protest. Casey figured that she was the one who was responsible for them, but it was clear that she was reluctant to protest to her father. Casey had to wonder how the poor plants survived.

Dyce shrugged. 'Come on in, if you have to; but I'm doing this under protest.' He looked at his son and daughter as if to assure himself that they were impressed. Neither of them said a word; but they followed him as he turned and went into the house. Casey trailed along behind.

It was cool inside the house, the hiss of air-conditioning like a lulling whisper. Dyce took a few steps along the hallway, then turned left into what appeared to be an office-study. From the glimpse Casey had caught of the living room, off the hall to the right, the interior of the house was as old-fashioned as the outside. This room was a typical man's room: with an old roll-top desk and swivel chair; faded green filing cabinets; a small, leather-covered couch; and an easy chair shaped by many years of human bottoms.

Dyce took the easy chair, and looked up at her coldly. The man had a nasty sneering way that triggered Casey's anger; but she made sure he didn't know it.

Keeping her expression pleasant, she seated herself on the couch. The young woman took the desk chair, and her brother remained standing, arms folded across his chest.

Removing her pad and pen from her purse, Casey looked at Dyce expectantly, until he began to squirm. 'All right,' he finally said. 'Let's get on with this nonsense. I don't know what I can tell you. I don't know damn-all about Buck's death.'

Casey leaned forward. 'Well, for starters, I understand that there was, and is, ill feeling between you and the Farrel family.'

Dyce grunted. 'That's putting it mildly. We hate one another's guts, Dan Farrel and me; and there's good reason, at least on my part. That pig-headed bastard took me to court just because I built a dam on my *own* property!'

'And won, I understand.'

'I had a fool for a lawyer. And people around here were all on Farrel's side. They don't cotton to me much, around here. I tend to my own business, and don't mess with theirs, and I'm not much of a one for socializing.'

'You don't think it might have had something to do with the fact that you were blocking water that, by law, belongs to other ranches as well as yours?'

He shot her a hard look. 'You sound just like the pious bastards. What I did was on my own property, and as far as I'm concerned, it was my business.'

'So you hate Dan Farrel.'

'That's what I just said, isn't it?'

'Enough to want to even things up with him?'

He gave her another cold stare. 'What are you getting

at, girlie? If you're asking me if I killed Buck Farrel, you're way out of line. There are a lot of things I might do, but killing someone isn't one of them. And even if it ever came to that, I'd do it man to man, not the sneaky way Buck Farrel was killed. The paper said it was poison. That's a woman's weapon, isn't it?'

He stared at Casey challengingly. She gave him a slight smile, said, 'Not necessarily,' then turned her attention to her notebook.

When she looked up again, Dyce was staring at his daughter. The girl's expression was sullen.

Before Casey could say anything, Dyce said: 'Lissa, there's no need for you to be here. Why don't you get on with your chores?'

With another sullen glance at her father, Melissa got up from the chair, and moved to the door. Casey thought of stopping her, but she could talk to her later. Better get what she could from the father, first.

She turned back to Dyce. 'So, you had no problem with Buck, it was just his father?'

Dyce lowered his head. 'I didn't say that. I got no love for Buck, or for anybody else in that family.'

The young man, Barney, shifted his arms and leaned forward, speaking for the first time. His voice was rather high, and raspy. 'Buck was messing around with Lissa . . .'

'You shut your yap!' his father barked. Casey felt a surge of excitement. She looked up expectantly, but nothing else seemed to be forthcoming. 'Mr Dyce, is it true that Buck Farrel was . . . seeing your daughter?'

Dyce snorted, shifting in his chair so that he might look out the window. When he spoke his tone changed. Some of the hostility was gone, replaced by something that might have been sadness. 'I suppose you'll find out one way or another, and think I'm hiding something. Yeah, he damned well was, if seeing is the word for it. Even if there wasn't bad feeling between

80

his father and me, I wouldn't have approved. Buck was a womanizer, a good- for-nothing. He said he wanted to marry Lissa, but he'd said that to lots of other girls to get what he wanted from them. Melissa's a good girl, but she knows nothing about men. I didn't want her to get hurt. I cornered him one day and told him to leave her alone. I told him that I'd blow his gonads off with buckshot if I caught him sniffing around her again.'

'And did he stop?'

Dyce snorted. 'Sure as hell did. He knew I meant what I said.'

'Just when was this?'

Dyce looked up at the ceiling. 'Oh, about six weeks, two months ago. That about right, Barney?'

''Bout right, Pa.'

'Did anyone else hear you threaten him?'

'Barney, and a couple of other guys. It was at the fairgrounds.'

Casey nodded thoughtfully. Dyce glared at her. 'Now, listen here, girlie. I may have threatened to blow off his balls, but I didn't threaten to kill him. I told you before that I wouldn't have done that; and that if I had, I wouldn't have used poison!'

Casey raised her hand protestingly. 'I haven't accused you of anything, Mr Dyce. It's my job to ask questions, and get answers, and I have to examine all possibilities before I can eliminate any of the suspects.'

He leaned forward in his chair. 'Are you saying that I'm a suspect?'

She looked at him levelly. 'I can't eliminate you at this time. You admit to hating the Farrels, and Buck was playing around with your daughter, against your wishes. These have to be considered fairly good motives.'

He sat back with a grunt, his face closed. 'Well, are you finished? I have work to do.'

'Just one more question. Were you at the fairgrounds on the day of Buck's death?'

He grunted again. 'Yes, I was at the fairgrounds that day. Lissa was riding in the arena parade, and Barney was entered in the calf roping. Won second place.'

'And were any of you around the chute area?'

Dyce glanced at his son, who stared back noncommittally. 'Yes, we were, along with several hundred other people.'

'Were you near the chute on or near the time that Buck got on his bull?'

Dyce shook his head. 'Nope. I was looking on from the side.'

Casey looked over at Barney, who uncrossed his arms and stuck one hand in his pocket. 'Not me. I was over at the end of the arena, talking to one of the girls.'

'And Lissa?'

'She'd gone on home,' said Dyce. 'She'd brought her own car, and left early.'

'Did you happen to see the rodeo clown anywhere along about that same time? Maybe near the chutes?'

This time both men shook their heads. Dyce said, 'Saw him in the ring during the previous rider's ride. Last I saw of him.'

Barney looked rather embarrassed. 'I told you, I was talking with a girl. Didn't see much else.'

'You know that Hank Wilder, the regular rodeo clown, was tied up in one of the barns, and that someone took his place?'

Dyce shrugged. 'There was something about it in the papers.'

'And you don't know anything about that?'

Dyce's eyes narrowed. 'Why would I? No, of course not.'

'Can anybody vouch for your location during that time period?'

Dyce shook his head. 'Don't know. Don't expect so, in all that mob. I didn't talk to anybody.'

Casey looked at Barney. 'The girl,' he said, 'Heidi Marshall. She's the one I was talking with.'

'And where can I find Miss Marshall?'

Barney's pale eyes grew even more expressionless. 'I don't know her address, but her Pa owns that big feed and grain store in Chino Valley, Marshalls.'

'There was another murder last night, a man named Red Pollock. Did you know him?'

'Sure, everybody knows old Red.'

'Did either of you see him around the fairgrounds yesterday?'

'I don't remember seeing him.'

Barney said, 'Me neither.'

'Do you know if he had any enemies?'

Dyce snorted. 'Hell no! Red was a worthless old coot, but for some reason people liked him.' He shook his head. 'Can't figure out why.'

Casey wrote her last note, closed her book and rose to her feet. 'Thank you for your cooperation.'

Dyce rose with her. 'Can't say that I did it willingly,' he said. 'I hope that this is the last of it.'

'I can't promise that, Mr Dyce,' said Casey, stowing her pen and pad in her purse. 'But I won't bother you unless it's necessary.'

Dyce scowled. 'Well, I surely hope that it won't be. I have better things to do with my time. Can you find your way out?'

'I think so,' Casey said coolly, and turned to the study door. She could feel the men's eyes on her back. Her mind was busy with what she had learned. Dyce was a difficult, disagreeable man; but she had the feeling that he was right when he said that he wasn't a killer. Despite his bravado, she figured him for a bit of a coward when it came to actual physical confrontation. Still, she could be wrong.

Both Dyce, and his son, were about Hank Wilder's height, and could easily have fitted into Wilder's clown suit. For that matter the same criteria applied to Melissa. She was going to have to talk to her, too; preferably without the presence of her father.

As the rise in the road blocked the ranch house from view, Casey saw a horse and rider galloping toward her at an angle. She slowed to a stop when she recognized the rider as Melissa Dyce.

As Casey thumbed down the driver's side window, Melissa dismounted and approached the Cherokee, leading the horse by the reins.

Casey looked at the girl expectantly, 'Melissa?'

The girl swallowed. Her expression was nervous and apprehensive. 'Miss Farrel, I wanted to have a few minutes alone with you.' She looked back, in the direction of the house. 'I wanted to tell you that I will do anything I can to help you find Buck's killer.' She looked back in the direction of the house again. 'Did Daddy tell you that I was dating Buck?'

'Yes, he did. He also said that he put a stop to it about six weeks ago.'

Melissa took in a long breath. 'He thinks he did; but Buck and me still saw each other as often as we could. We'd meet in the afternoons. We'd both ride out and meet each other at the old adobe; it's about half way between the ranches.' Her voice broke. 'The last time I saw him was the afternoon before the rodeo started.'

'And your father didn't know?'

'I'm sure he didn't. He'd have made a fuss otherwise.'

Casey looked at the girl seriously. 'If your father had found out, do you think he would have killed Buck?'

The girl shook her head. 'No way. Daddy makes a lot of noise; he likes to come on macho; but he usually doesn't really *do* anything about it.'

'So that's why you kept on seeing Buck?'

The girl hesitated. 'Well, yes. And . . . I might as well tell you, I can't keep it a secret much longer; Buck and I were going to get married. I'm going to have his baby.' Tears welled in her eyes.

Casey patted the slender hand that rested on the edge of the car window. 'I'm sorry, Melissa. Does your father know?'

She nodded, fighting back the tears. 'I went to our family doctor to find out for sure. Daddy saw the check, and kept after me until I told him why I'd seen the doctor. He wants me to have an abortion, but I won't. This baby is all that I'll ever have of Buck, and I'm going to keep it!'

'Melissa, I have to ask you this. Your father said that you left the rodeo early on the day Buck died. Is that true?'

Melissa nodded. 'Yes, I did. I could never stand to watch Buck ride the bulls. I was always afraid he would be hurt . . .' The tears welled up, and Casey fought back the sympathy that threatened to influence her.

'Did anyone see you leave?'

The girl shrugged. 'I don't know. I wasn't paying attention. I just wanted to get home.'

She looked up, frowning. 'You don't think I killed Buck? You can't, I love him!'

Casey shook her head. 'I just need to be able to eliminate you. It would help if someone saw you leave the grounds.'

Melissa shook her head. 'I suppose someone did. I just don't know who.'

'Is there someone in charge of the parking lots?'

Relief flooded the girl's features. 'Of course. Maybe they saw me.'

She glanced nervously over her shoulder. 'I'd better get back now, before Daddy misses me. You won't tell him that I talked to you?'

'I see no reason for him to know; but I can't promise.'

Melissa nodded, seeming to accept that, and pulled back from the window. As she mounted her horse, Casey watched her with a mixture of feelings. Melissa's story had dredged up memories of her own past, painful thoughts of the child she had chosen not to have. Of course their situations were not the same.

Casey had no idea of what Buck's real feelings had been; but Melissa was certain in her own mind that he had loved her, and she wanted his child. If all was as they said, if none of the Dyces was involved in Buck's death, then Dyce would probably, grudgingly, take care of Melissa and her baby; and probably grow to love the child. Maybe Melissa would marry, and have a home of her own. It could all work out.

In Casey's case, the man had betrayed her, and the thought of raising a child on her own, at that time, had seemed impossible. She had made the practical, sensible, decision; but at times it still bothered her.

But, she wasn't here to think about herself or her past. She was here to solve a murder, and that's what she would do. On the face of it, Dyce was certainly a suspect. Barney was less likely, unless his story about talking with a young woman didn't check out. More than one man had been killed for 'messing around' with someone's sister. And Melissa? The girl seemed sincere; but maybe she was just a good actress. Given Buck's M.O. with women, it was entirely possible that Melissa had found Buck with someone else, and had taken her revenge. As her father had pointed out, poison was often a woman's weapon.

EIGHT

Casey arrived at Dr Enos Wheaton's office a few minutes before the noon hour, hoping to catch him before he went to lunch.

The doctor's office was located in a medical complex off Miller Valley Road, across the street from the Yavapai Regional Medical Centre.

The young receptionist frowned when Casey asked to see the doctor. 'Do you have an appointment?'

'No. I'm not a patient.' Casey offered the young woman her card. 'I only want to ask the doctor a few questions. It won't take more than a minute. Why don't you give him my card, and see what he says?'

Still frowning doubtfully, the receptionist took the card gingerly in two fingers, and started toward the rear of the office, her voice trailing behind her: 'Doctor is awfully busy. I don't think . . .'

Casey sat down on one of the couches and began leafing through a medical magazine. She was alone in the outer office.

She had just finished the first page of an article on the necessity for detecting breast cancer in its early stages, when the young receptionist returned and directed her to an inner office.

Dr Wheaton was a tall man in his early sixties, with well- barbered grey hair and a ruddy complexion. He stood in front of a very large wooden desk, holding Casey's card in one hand. 'Miss Farrel?'

'Yes, Doctor. Thank you for seeing me.'

His warm, brown eyes crinkled at the corners. 'I gather that it's not a medical problem?'

She smiled back. 'You gather correctly. I'm investigating the death of Buck Farrel.'

'A tragic affair, that. It's upset the whole town.' He looked at her card again. 'Are you related?'

She nodded. 'Yes. I'm Dan Farrel's niece.'

He raised well-trimmed eyebrows. 'I didn't know that Dan had a niece.'

'Neither did I, until two nights ago.'

He put her card down on the desk. 'Well, how can I help you?'

Casey paused a moment before she spoke. 'I need some medical information about Buck Farrel.'

She raised a hand before he could protest. 'Of course I know that a patient's medical files are confidential; but in this case the patient is dead, and the contents of that file may have some bearing on the case. I can get a court order demanding access, but that would take time. I'm hoping that it won't be necessary.'

The doctor looked at her thoughtfully. 'You get right to the point, don't you? All right. I'll answer your questions, within limits. What do you want to know?'

'There is just the one thing. The medical examiner's examination showed that some fifteen years ago Buck had a vasectomy. Did you handle that for him?'

The doctor thought for a moment, then nodded. 'Yes, I remember the incident because he was so young, just out of high school. He consulted me about the operation, and I advised him against it. However, he insisted, so I referred him to a urologist in Phoenix.'

'May I have the doctor's name?'

'I suppose so. The urologist's name is Westin Phillips.'

Casey jotted down the name.

'Doctor, did Buck give you any reason for wanting the operation?'

'Yes. When I advised against it, he said that he – well, to put it bluntly – he said he wanted to play the field, and didn't want to get some girl pregnant. I told him that there were such things as prophylactics, but he said that – if you'll excuse my frankness – having sex with a condom was like taking a bath with your clothes on. Not a very original statement, I'm afraid.'

Casey smiled. 'No, not very. Did it strike you that this was his real reason?'

The doctor looked at her curiously. 'Strange that you should ask that. When he gave me his reasons, I remember thinking that he did so almost as a brag, very pious; but it didn't ring true. There was a certain smugness about his attitude that seemed out of place.'

'The medical examiner also said that another operation was recently done to repair the first. Did Buck come to you about that?'

The doctor shook his head. 'No. In fact, I haven't seen Buck in some time. He's not . . . wasn't one of those who come in for regular checkups. He only came in, or called, when he was sick. But I'm not surprised that he had the operation reversed. This often happens, particularly if the original operation was performed when the man was very young.'

Casey nodded. 'Well, thank you for talking with me, Doctor.'

'I just hope that I've been of some help. I'd like to see whoever did this thing caught and put away. It was such a cold- blooded crime. No man deserves to die that way. Buck may have been a bit of a rascal, yet he had a way about him. You couldn't help but like him if you knew him.'

'I never did, Doctor, but I'm beginning to think you may be right. Be assured that I'll do everything in my power to find his killer.'

*　　*　　*

89

Before Casey returned to the Cherokee, she walked over to the pay telephones just inside the building's main lobby, and called Josh at the station in Phoenix.

Someone else answered, but after a minute or so, Josh's familiar voice came on the line: 'Josh Whitney.'

'Hello, Josh.'

'Casey. It's good to hear your voice, babe. How's the case coming?'

'I'm not sure. There are a number of people who had reason to dislike Buck, and one or two who look like good suspects, but no real evidence. I'm going to have to do a lot of digging.'

'Well, that's how it usually is, babe. Like I've told you, most homicides are solved by leg work.' He chuckled. 'Besides, if it was easy, you'd be bored.'

'You're probably right.'

'Depend on it. How's Donnie?'

'Oh, Donnie's having the time of his life; riding horses, herding cattle. He's turned into a regular little cowboy.'

'Gone native, has he?'

'You could say that.'

'Well, I guess I'll just have to perform one of those intervention things on him when you get home; get him back to the sports-loving city kid he was when you left.'

'Yeah. Say, I hear he called you about bringing Spot up to the ranch. When are you coming up?'

'Not for a while. I've got a case of my own here, and it's going to keep me tied up for at least a few days. Explain to Donnie, will you? How is it working out, you staying at your uncle's place?'

'Pretty good. I'll tell you all about it when I see you. Josh, I know you're busy, but do you suppose you could do something for me?'

'Maybe. Tell me what it is.'

'Well, there's a urologist in Phoenix that Buck Farrel went to. Got a pencil and a piece of paper handy?'

90

She read off the name and address Dr Wheaton had given her.

'Got it,' Josh said. 'And exactly what am I supposed to find out from this guy?'

'Buck had a vasectomy fifteen years ago, and this Dr Phillips evidently performed the surgery. Buck was very young at the time, and I want to know if Buck told this doctor anything about his reasons for wanting the operation.'

'You think this may have something to do with Buck's death?'

Casey sighed. 'No, I'm just pruriently curious about my dead cousin's sex life.'

'Now don't get smart. It's a reasonable question, under the circumstances. All right, I'll check it out, but it may take a few days; I meant it when I said I was busy.'

Casey felt a surge of affection; she did miss the big bum. 'That's fine. I appreciate it. You know that.'

'Yeah, well you'd better.'

'Let me know if you find you're able to get away. Okay?'

'Okay. I miss you, both of you.'

'We miss you too, Josh.'

'Be careful, babe.'

'I will, Josh,' she said softly. 'Bye.'

Hanging up the phone, she stood bemused for a moment. She hoped that he would be able to get away and drive up for a day or two. Although she didn't often admit it, she had become used to the passion and comfort offered by his big, muscular body, and the stability of his presence. In addition, he was a good cop, and she appreciated the help and insight she received from his feedback.

One of these days, she thought, I'm going to have to make up my mind about Josh. Although an understanding man, his patience was not inexhaustible.

91

She gave her head a brisk shake. Back to the business at hand. She dropped another coin in the telephone, and called the Prescott station. She was told that Sergeant Randall was out at the fairgrounds.

Yesterday had been the last day of the Rodeo, but there were still quite a few people at the fairgrounds, loading livestock and working on clean-up.

Casey found Sergeant Randall just outside the building in which Hank Wilder had been found bound and gagged. Randall was talking to a man holding a shovel, who walked away as she approached.

Randall nodded as she walked up. 'Casey. What's up?'

'I just thought I'd see if you've turned up anything. I called the station, and they said you were out here.'

Randall shrugged. 'Nothing new. I've talked to at least a dozen people who were in this area at the time of Buck's death, but no one saw anything that could help us. How about you?'

'Well, I talked to the Dyce family.' Briefly, she filled him in. His eyes brightened. 'It seems to me that any one of them had a motive. Were any of them in the area when Buck died?'

She nodded. 'All of them. The father says he was watching from the sidelines, but doesn't know if anyone saw him. The daughter was supposed to be on the way to her car in the parking lot, but again, doesn't know if anyone saw her. The son, Barney, says he was talking to a young woman, named Marshall – her father owns a feed and grain store.'

Randall nodded. 'Marshall's Feed and Grain, in Chino Valley. Well, we can check that out easily enough. From what you've said, it looks to me as if both Dyce and his son had a motive. It could even have been the girl. Maybe Buck was going to leave her. What do you think?'

92

'I agree. I think it's more likely that it was one of the men, but I can't rule out the girl.'

Steve scrubbed at his chin. 'I was going to send a man out to question them this afternoon; but I think I'll do it myself.'

'That's a good idea. Maybe you can get more out of them than I could.' She smiled mockingly. 'They didn't really take well to being questioned by a woman.'

Steve answered her smile. 'Good ol' boys, huh?'

'You might say that.'

'Well, being local, I can come down harder on them than you can, in your position. I'll see what I can come up with.'

Casey raised a cautionary hand. 'I should warn you; Darrel Dyce is pretty tightly wound, and it doesn't take much to set him off.'

Randall lifted his eyebrows. 'Sounds more and more like he might be our man. And you say that you have a Phoenix detective checking out the doctor that performed Buck's vasectomy?'

'Yes, since I have a . . . connection. I hope you don't mind?'

'Hell no. Save me sending a man down there.' He looked down at her. 'So you have a friend on the Phoenix force.'

Casey felt herself flush. 'Yes. He's very good – as an investigator, I mean.'

Randall's eyes twinkled. 'Of course. What else?' He paused. 'Do you mind a personal question, Casey?'

Casey's face still felt hot. 'I guess not.'

'I know you have a son, but are you still married?'

Casey shook her head. 'I've never been married. Donnie is adopted. I'll tell you the story some time. How about you? You married?'

He smiled ruefully. 'Nope. Is that a proposal?' His eyes

93

twinkled, and she laughed; although she felt awkward with the turn the conversation had taken. 'Afraid not.'

To her relief, she saw Hank Wilder, the rodeo clown, approaching. As he neared, he doffed his Stetson. 'Afternoon, Casey.'

Casey nodded. 'Hank.'

Wilder's gaze moved to Steve. 'And if I recall correctly, you're Sergeant Randall.'

'That's right.'

Wilder's sombre gaze moved from one to the other. 'How goes the investigation?'

Casey let Steve answer. 'It's proceeding, Mr Wilder. Slowly, but moving along.'

Wilder shook his head. 'I was hoping that you'd get the bastard while I was still here.'

Randall's eyes sharpened. 'You planning to leave soon?'

'I have another few days, but then I have to get along.'

'Be sure to leave us your forwarding address before you go. We may need to talk with you again.'

'Of course. I'll do anything I can to help.'

Casey said, 'Have you heard about Red Pollock?'

An expression of sorrow crossed Wilder's lean face. 'Yes, and it came as quite a shock. Poor old Red. Not a mite of harm in him. Can't imagine why anyone would want to kill him like that.'

He frowned. 'You don't think that the two crimes are connected in some way?'

Randall shrugged. 'Well, it does seem odd, two murders within such a short time, and both victims associated with the rodeo. Of course it may simply be a coincidence; but then again . . .'

Wilder looked thoughtful. 'I see what you mean. Well, I hope you catch him.' He rubbed his head. 'I have a personal interest in this, you know. The bastard slugged me and tied me up like a trussed turkey. That does something to a man's pride. I'll keep in touch.'

As Wilder started away, Casey noticed that Randall was staring over her shoulder. She turned and saw a red pickup with a horse trailer attached, parked near one of the buildings. Darrel Dyce and his son, Barney, were leading a horse up the ramp into the trailer.

Randall looked at Casey questioningly. She shook her head slightly, and he turned and began walking towards the two men.

Casey watched as he approached them, knowing that her presence would only antagonize Dyce further. As it was, she could see the colour rise in Dyce's weathered face, and he aimed a murderous look in her direction.

After a few minutes of heated conversation, Barney Dyce broke away from the group, and stomped toward Casey.

Reaching her, he placed his hands in the back pockets of his jeans, and glared at her darkly.

Casey was somewhat surprised. So, Barney was capable of emotion! When she had talked with the family at the Dyce Ranch, the young man had shown no feeling at all. For all his apparent anger, Casey thought that she preferred him this way. At least he seemed alive.

Without any greeting, he said in a grating voice: 'Why'd you stick that cop on my daddy?'

'Hello, Mr Dyce,' Casey said equably.

'You got my daddy all riled, and when he's riled he takes it out on Melissa and me.'

Casey felt a surge of unbidden sympathy; he looked so like a small boy, angry at unjust punishment. Why do they put up with it, she wondered, all these women and men who chafed at the people who controlled their lives? Why did they never realize that they could leave? What held them in thrall to parents, husbands, wives, lovers, those who dominated and abused them either mentally or physically? Why in hell didn't they just get out and make a life of their own? Casey knew the psychological theories, but had never been satisfied with the answers.

Now, she looked Barney Dyce in the eye. 'I'm sorry for that, Mr Dyce, but this is a murder investigation, and since it's well known that there is bad blood between the Dyces and the Farrels, you have to expect to be questioned.'

His small eyes narrowed. 'You're going to be sorry you butted in. Don't think that because you're a woman you can get away with messing around with other people's lives.'

Casey gave him a cool smile that did not reach her eyes. 'I'm sure you don't mean that, Mr Dyce. It might be construed as a threat, and I'm sure you wouldn't want to threaten a law enforcement officer.'

A flash of panic scurried, rat-like, behind the boy's eyes, to be replaced by dumb meanness. He glared at her for a moment longer, then turned toward the pickup and horse trailer, shoulders hunched, his hands still rammed into the back pockets of his jeans, a menacing but awkward figure.

She watched as Barney returned to his father and Randall. The sergeant turned to the boy, and asked a few questions. Barney answered, but his body language expressed his sullen reluctance. Head down, he scratched the dust with the toe of his boot like an angry bull.

Then Darrel Dyce stepped between his son and Randall, his face pushed up to the taller man. He was shouting so loudly that Casey could hear his voice, but the words were unintelligible. Steve put his hand on Dyce's chest and moved him back, then turned on his heel and came back to Casey.

Casey looked at him questioningly. 'I told you they were an excitable family.'

Randall smiled meagrely. 'Well, you were right. What was the kid talking to you about?'

'Oh, just a little threat. He warned me to stay out of their business or I would be "sorry".'

Randall raised his brows. 'I'll put that in the file, in case he should follow through. I wouldn't have thought he had the sand.'

Casey shrugged. 'I'll admit I was surprised. When I talked to them at the ranch, he didn't say more than a few words. Did you find out anything?'

'Pretty much the same thing as they told you. But I agree with your assessment. They both had motive and opportunity, and after talking with them, I'd say they're both capable, despite all that shit of the old man's about how if he did it, it would have been face to face. The old guy's something of a weasel.'

Casey nodded. 'I agree. Are you going back to the station?'

'Yeah. Got some paperwork to finish.'

'Mind if I come with you? You said that there's a rap sheet on Buck. I'd like to look it over.'

'Sure.' He paused. 'Casey, I don't want you to think I'm being over-protective, but I want you to be careful. The Dyces are unpredictable, and we don't know what else we're getting into here. Okay?'

Casey smiled. 'Gee, this reminds me of home. You sound just like Josh.'

Randall gave a wry smile. 'He the Phoenix detective?'

She nodded.

'Well, he sounds like a smart man. Listen to him.'

NINE

Leaving the Fairgrounds, Casey followed Steve's car to the station. Inside the station, Steve escorted her to a small private room, gave her the file on Buck Farrel, and left her alone.

Reading the file didn't take long: several arrests for drunk and disorderly, and an arrest for drunk driving. He had spent a few nights in jail, paid a number of hefty fines, and had had his licence suspended once for six months.

But there was one entry that caught Casey's eye. Dated three months ago, the charge was assault and battery. The charge had been dismissed when the other party, one Eugene Taggert, had refused to press charges.

Casey put down the file thoughtfully. The picture of Buck Farrel that was emerging was not exactly that of an ideal citizen. He had a long-standing pattern of heavy drinking and minor violence. Yet, most of the people she had talked to, with the exception of Darrel Dyce, claimed that the dead man was likable and good natured, when he wasn't drinking. The question was, had Buck, while drunk, done something offensive enough to make someone want to kill him?

She returned the papers to the file, and went down the hall to Randall's office. He was on the phone when she entered. He waved her to a seat, and talked for a few minutes longer, face turned away from her.

He hung up the phone, and faced forward again. 'That

was the medical examiner's office. The final results on Red Pollock are in.'

Casey leaned forward. 'And?'

'Pretty much what we expected. The slug was a .22 calibre; which rattled around in the skull before spending its force. Pollock's blood alcohol level was high, well past the state of being legally intoxicated. The time of death has been narrowed down to the hours between eleven p.m. and one a.m. That's pretty much it. Find anything interesting in Buck's file?'

'Nothing you didn't already know, I'm sure. He did get into a lot of trouble, didn't he?'

Randall smiled. 'He got into his share of it.'

'That last charge, three months ago, assault and battery; why did this Eugene Taggert drop the charges?'

Randall threw back his head and laughed heartily. 'That's because Myrtle told him to.'

'Myrtle?'

Randall nodded. 'Myrtle is Taggert's girl friend, and when she says "jump" Taggert just asks "how far?".'

'Have you questioned Taggert about Buck's death?'

'Of course. Myrtle alibis him. She claims that Taggert was with her all afternoon and evening, up to the time she went to work. She's a bartender down on Whiskey Row.'

Casey frowned. 'Not much of an alibi, is it? She could be lying.'

'It's possible, but you can't arrest a man on the strength of a weak alibi.'

'I think I'd like to talk with them.'

He smiled. 'Couldn't do any harm, but I should warn you . . .'

She looked at him sharply. 'Warn me about what?'

His smile widened. 'Do you remember a few years back when Bruce Springsteen blew into Prescott with his motorcycle entourage?'

Casey frowned. 'There was something in the papers. He came to see someone, Bubbles the Biker Barmaid, wasn't it, at Matt's Saloon? He did a few sets with the band. What's that got to do with Myrtle and Taggert?'

Randall chuckled. 'Nothing, really; it's just that if it had been Myrtle he had come to see, the Boss might not have ridden out again. At least not right away.'

Casey stared at him, puzzled. He stared back, shaking his head. 'Tell you what, I don't think I'll warn you after all. I'll let you see for yourself. You're in for an interesting experience, Casey.'

Myrtle Carter resided in a small bungalow on a side street off Miller Valley Road. The house was old, but its white paint had been recently renewed, and the yard, though overgrown, was fairly neat. Sitting off to one side of the walkway was a nearly new Harley-Davidson. It was a state-of-the-art bike, equipped with just about every gadget on the market, and polished to a high shine. Off to one side was a much older machine, dusty and tired looking.

Casey walked up the cracked sidewalk to the front door – which had been painted a bright red – and rang the bell. There was no response, and she could hear no sound inside; evidently the doorbell was not working. Balling her hand into a fist, she pounded firmly on the door, and was rewarded by a shout from inside: 'All right, hold your water, I'm coming!'

The door was thrown open with considerable force, and a large form filled the doorway. Although Steve Randall had not given Casey a physical description of Myrtle Carter, Casey was pretty sure this must be her. Tall, muscular, broad-shouldered, with breasts that could have competed with Dolly Parton's, this was a formidable figure. She looked to be in her early thirties, with a tumble of thick, blonde hair, bright blue eyes, and strong, but not unattractive features. The blue eyes looked down at Casey, coldly. 'Yes? What the hell do you want?'

Casey stood as tall as she was able, and smiled pleasantly. 'I'm here to talk to you about Buck Farrel.' She held out her card.

The big woman took it, saying: 'You're not one of his women are you? If you are, there's no use in your coming to me . . .'

She looked at the card, read it carefully, then smiled. 'The Governor's Task Force on Crime? Gee, I didn't realize that I'd become *that* notorious!'

Casey laughed. There was something attractive about this Amazon, a fresh no-nonsense attitude that Casey liked.

She shook her head. 'No, nothing like that. It's about Buck Farrel's death. I have a few questions, that's all.'

Myrtle shrugged her impressive shoulders. 'Look, lady, I work nights; that means I sleep days – or try to, when people aren't banging on my door.'

Casey remained silent. Myrtle, she noticed was fully dressed in tight jeans, a sleeveless denim shirt, and low-heeled boots. Surely she hadn't been sleeping like that. She waited patiently, studying the woman's face, until Myrtle began to fidget and stepped away from the door.

'Oh, hell. Since I'm already awake, come on in; but I don't know what I can tell you that you don't already know.'

Casey smiled and followed the big woman into the interior of the little house. An old air conditioner rattled noisily in one window, but it didn't seem to help much, for the house was hot and uncomfortable. The small living room was cluttered with paperback books, pillows, magazines, and paper plates bearing the remains of food. The furniture was nondescript, and the worn couch was covered by a brightly coloured southwestern throw. The room smelled of cat-box and stale food.

101

As Casey surreptitiously looked around, she felt something touch her ankles, and looked down to see a large, grey tabby winding around her ankles.

Myrtle stomped her foot. 'Buck! Get away from the lady!'

The cat moved away insolently, rear end waving, its tail a statement of displeasure.

Casey raised her eyebrows. 'Buck?'

Myrtle appeared embarrassed. It was an odd expression on a woman of her size and apparent strength. 'Well, yeah. Buck gave me the critter, but that was back awhile, when he and I had a thing going. It seemed to me they had a lot in common.' She laughed, and Casey found herself smiling at the comparison, which, she had to admit, seemed to be apt.

'Look, let's go out to the Arizona room; it's not so hot in there.'

Casey followed her down a short hall, past two closed doors, which she assumed were those of a bedroom and bathroom, and into a glass-enclosed room. The windows stood wide, and a brisk breeze freshened and cooled the air. This room was relatively clear of clutter. An old, but comfortably cushioned rattan couch and chair were set so as to take advantage of the breeze, and shelves and plant stands bore a number of potted plants that looked healthy and well cared for.

Casey seated herself on the couch. On the rattan coffee table in front of it, stood two cups and saucers, a coffee carafe, and a copy of the *Arizona Republic*.

Myrtle saw the direction of Casey's glance, and grinned. 'So, I was stretching it a little. I'm usually slept out by this time. But I *was* asleep when the other cop came. So, do you want some coffee? I think there's some left.'

Casey nodded. 'I could use a little pick-me-up about now.'

'Yeah, I know the feeling, but I get it about two in the morning.'

Casey took a sip of the coffee, it was hot and fragrant. 'This is good,' she said.

'Yeah, I grind it fresh, it's a mixture of Colombian and French Roast. So what do you want to know? I've already spilled my guts to Randall.'

Casey set down her cup, and took out her notebook. 'First, what do you know about Buck Farrel's murder?'

'Nothing more than I read in the paper, hear on TV and the radio.' She had taken Casey's card out of her pocket, and was looking at it again. 'Look, I have to ask. You and Buck have the same last name, is that a coincidence, or . . .?'

Casey had wondered when the question would come. She was getting used to it. 'It's a little of both – I am a relative, but it was a coincidence that brought me here to town at this time. Buck's father asked me to work on the case, and the local police and my boss agreed.'

Myrtle nodded, her expression had softened. 'Buck was a good ol'-boy, you know. We had some fine times together there for a while. I think he liked riding my Harley almost as much as he liked riding horses, and that's saying something.'

'So, you and Buck were close?'

Myrtle gave a sniff, and put the card back into her pocket. 'Well, we *used* to be.'

She looked up. Her blue eyes looked a little misty. 'It was a sort of a on-again-off-again thing with us. We'd go together for a while, then one of us would get antsy, and take up with someone else, then later we would get back together. It wasn't love, or anything like that. Part of it was sex, but we were good buddies too. I'll sure miss that ol' boy.'

'So, you parted amicably?'

103

'There were no hard feelings, if that's what you mean. I took up with Tag, and he's kept me pretty busy.'

'You mean Eugene Taggert?'

Myrtle grinned. 'Yep! That's the one.'

'How did Eugene feel about Buck?'

'Oh, he was a little jealous. He's a mite possessive, you might say. But I keep him in line.'

I'll bet you do, Casey thought, trying not to stare at Myrtle's well-defined biceps.

'So the fight between Eugene and Buck was over you?'

Myrtle looked pleased. 'Yeah, I guess you could say that.'

'Did Buck often get into fights?'

Myrtle shook her head. 'Naw, I wouldn't say *often*. He was a little rowdy by nature, but so are a lot of the boys. They get into bragging matches, and sometimes things get a bit out of hand, but I can't say that Buck was any worse than the rest of them.'

'Are you saying that you never saw Buck get into the kind of argument, or fight, that was serious enough to make someone want to kill him?'

Myrtle hesitated, a brief flicker of something in her blue eyes. 'Naw. Never did.'

'And the fight with Eugene wasn't serious?'

Myrtle laughed aloud. 'No way. They were both drunk and acting stupid, that's all.'

'But both men were arrested. And Eugene was hospitalized.'

Myrtle sighed and rolled her eyes. 'It wasn't serious, just a broken nose and a few cracked ribs.'

Casey raised her eyebrows. 'And that's not serious?'

Myrtle shook her head. 'Not on the Row. Happens all the time.'

'And Eugene had no hard feelings? You know, you haven't told me how the fight started.'

Myrtle shrugged. 'I told you, it was stupid. I broke up with Buck before I started seeing Gene, and Gene knew that I wasn't seeing anyone but him; but the thing was, when Buck was liquored up, he'd still come on to me, and that got Gene pissed.

'On that particular night, Buck came in already sloshed to the brim, and started in on me; and Gene, who'd knocked back his own share, didn't take it kindly. I was in the john when it started, or I'd have put a stop to it!'

She noted Casey's expression, and grinned. Flexing her right bicep, she said: 'Ain't run into a man yet that I can't handle.'

Casey had to grin back. 'So, Eugene had no hard feelings?' she asked again.

Myrtle threw back her head and shouted in a voice trained to be overheard over bar fights, 'Tag! Get your sorry ass out here!'

She leaned towards Casey. 'But you'd better stop calling him Eugene. He don't like it much. Call him Tag, or Gene.'

Casey was surprised. Somehow it had not occurred to her that Taggert would be on the premises. But this was fine. Now she could talk to them both.

She heard a door open and close, and the shuffle of footsteps. In a moment, a thin, wiry little man stepped through the doorway, and stood exposed in the clear afternoon light.

He was clad in pyjama bottoms and thongs, and was rumpled from sleep. Thinning brown hair stood up from his scalp in tufts, and a patchy beard gave his face a scruffy look. His bare chest was narrow, concave, and hairless. It didn't seem possible that such a specimen could have won the affection of the big, attractive woman sitting opposite her; but Myrtle was gazing at the scrawny little man with every evidence of approval and affection.

'Tag, whyn't you go put on some more clothes,'

Myrtle said, then chuckled. 'You trying to turn the lady on?'

Fat chance of that! Casey thought, struggling not to smile. It was difficult to believe that this little man had challenged Buck Farrel to a fight. Yet, there was one thing. Taggert was small enough to have fitted into Hank Wilder's clown suit.

Taggert, sleepy-eyed, circled around Casey and stopped next to Myrtle, who put an arm around his waist. 'This here is Casey Farrel, sugar. She's investigating Buck's murder. Miss Farrel, this is Gene Taggert.'

'Mr Taggert.' Casey said.

Taggert said nothing, but seemed to draw himself inward, defensively.

Myrtle chuckled. 'Does Tag look like a killer to you?'

Casey smiled. 'What does a killer look like?' She turned her gaze on Taggert, who, this time, returned her gaze.

In a surprisingly deep voice he said: 'No, I didn't kill Buck, although I don't know what I might have done if he'd come rootin' around Myrtle again.'

Myrtle squeezed his bony waist, beaming proudly. 'Ain't he somethin' now?'

Taggert kept his gaze steady on Casey. 'One thing I got to say, Buck's death ain't no big loss, and there's probably plenty who'll be glad that he's gone.'

Myrtle gave the little man a shake. 'Now don't you go saying things like that, Tag. Buck had his faults, but he wasn't all bad.'

She turned to Casey. 'It's just the jealousy talkin'. Don't pay him no mind.'

Taggert set his thin-lipped mouth, and gave Casey a challenging stare. Casey turned her glance to her notebook. She wasn't about to get into it with a feisty little man intent on proving his macho.

When she looked up again, it was at Myrtle. 'Do you know of anyone else who might have had it in for Buck, the Dyces, for instance? I heard that there was some bad feeling between the Dyces and the Farrels.'

Taggert snorted, 'Old man Dyce and the Barn? Sure, they had some kind of a feud going with old man Farrel; but then they had some kind of argument going with almost everybody.'

This time, Casey directed her question to Taggert: 'Why do you call Barney Dyce, the Barn?'

The little man returned her gaze defiantly, but it was Myrtle who answered.

'The kid's got about as much in his head as an empty barn, and when he does get an idea, he moves in on you like a barn swept away in a flood. And since his given name is Barney . . .' She shrugged and smiled. 'It just seemed natural to call him that.'

'Has he ever come on to you, Myrtle?' Casey asked.

She nodded. 'Sure, he and the old man both; and I'll tell you, dumb as the kid is, he's not as disgusting as his old man. Darrel Dyce is an ol' horny toad, and just about as appetizing.'

She squeezed Taggert's waist. 'Not that I'd be interested, anyway. Tag here's my man.' She broke off, frowning. 'Come to think of it, I recollect Darrel and Barn talking at my bar . . . oh, about a month back. They were both slopping over with beer, and they were bragging to each other what they'd like to do to Buck, especially Darrel. He said that he'd like to dance on Buck's grave, and if Buck didn't behave, that's just what he'd do. And Barn, he agreed. Of course he'll do anything that his old man tells him to do.'

Casey finished writing, and put her notebook back into her purse. 'I want to thank both of you for cooperating.'

Myrtle looked at her intently. 'So, you satisfied now that Tag didn't do it? He's got an alibi, you know. He and I was in bed, going at it, all afternoon, the day

107

of Buck's death; and I'll swear to that on a stack of bibles.'

Myrtle was smiling, but her gaze was locked with Casey's with a defiant intensity, as if daring Casey to disagree.

Casey smiled slightly, and said again: 'Thanks for your cooperation.'

Myrtle rose from her chair. 'I'll see you out.'

Casey could feel the big woman's presence behind her as she traversed the hall and the cluttered living room. At the door, Myrtle spoke again. 'I hope we were some help; I'd surely like to see Buck's killer caught. No man deserves to die like Buck did.'

Her tone sounded sincere, and as Casey turned to look up into the handsome, bold-featured face, she saw concern there.

'We're doing our best, Myrtle,' she said. 'The Prescott Police and the Sheriff's Department are working on it, and I'll do everything I can.'

The big woman nodded, and closed the door, as Casey headed back down the cracked sidewalk. What a pair! Casey thought. It was easy to see, now, why Steve Randall had been so amused when she said that she was going to talk to Myrtle. Obviously, she was one of the town characters, one of those colourful people that small towns seemed to cherish.

And Taggert? Well, it was difficult to see him in the role of murderer; still, killers came in all shapes and sizes, and with all kinds of personalities. No matter how much you learned about people, it was still difficult, if not impossible, for one person *really* to know what went on in another person's mind and heart. A scenario where Myrtle planned the killing, and Taggert carried it out, was certainly plausible. And why had Myrtle been so vehement about confirming Taggert's alibi, when Casey had not asked her about it? No, she couldn't discount Taggert.

It was growing late by the time Casey drove away from Myrtle's house, and clouds piling up in the south further darkened the late afternoon sun. A summer monsoon was definitely on its way.

Casey decided to call it a day, and headed for Chino Valley and the Farrel ranch. As she passed the Prescott Airport the storm hit, with a cannonade of thunder that startled and rattled the senses and a deluge of water that made vision almost impossible.

Quickly, Casey pulled to the side of the road, as other cars did the same. It was not wise to drive in rain like this; it was like being under a waterfall. Usually such storms did not last long; or, if they did, the rain did not continue with this force. She turned on her radio, hoping to get some weather news. One of the side effects of these summer storms was the flash floods, torrents of water that suddenly filled dry stream beds and low-lying roads. Almost every year vehicles were damaged and people were injured or killed, because they underestimated the force and danger of these walls of water that appeared, seemingly, out of nowhere, and disappeared almost as rapidly.

Between musical numbers the radio announcer gave the usual flash-flood warning, but offered no specifics. So, when the rain slacked off, Casey turned her motor on and moved back out on to the highway. All but the most cautious of the other drivers were doing the same.

The rain continued to lessen, and by the time Casey turned on to the gravel road leading to the Farrel Ranch, the sun, low in the sky, was breaking through. The golden light, on the fresh-washed landscape, was very beautiful. She rolled down her window, and inhaled the fresh, plant-scented air.

As the Cherokee approached the turn-off to the Dyce place, Casey made a sudden decision, and turned on to the side road. She had been tired, but the rain had left her

109

feeling refreshed; and she wanted to keep the pressure on the Dyces – so far, her most logical suspects.

She was glad to see the three Dyce vehicles parked in front of the ranch house. The horse trailer was still hitched to the large, red pickup. As she parked and got out of the Cherokee the front door opened, and the Dyces, father and son, emerged, to stand on the porch.

Darrel spat a stream of brown into the flower bed and glowered at Casey. 'What do you want? Didn't I tell you that Farrels ain't welcome on my property?'

Casey stopped at the bottom steps to the porch, staring up. 'I'm not going to say this again. I'm not here as a Farrel, but as an investigator.'

Darrel's angry gaze wavered under her confident stare. His lips tightened. 'All right. But be quick about it. I've got work to do.'

Casey nodded, turning her gaze to Barney. The boy's face was as closed as a locked safe.

She turned back to his father. 'I have a witness who says that about a month ago, down on Whiskey Row, they overheard you and Barney making some threats against Buck Farrel.'

'Who told you that?' Dyce growled.

'I can't tell you that. Did you make such threats?'

Dyce's eyes narrowed thoughtfully. 'About a month ago, you say. Well, I suppose that could be right. Barney and I were on Whiskey Row about then, and we was pretty sloshed, and that's a fact.' He spat a brown stream, this time close to Casey's feet. 'I ain't made any secret of my feelings about the Farrels. I already told you that.'

'There's a lot of difference between disliking someone and making threats against their lives, wouldn't you say?'

Dyce shrugged. 'So what! People are like to say a

lot of things when they're in their cups. It don't prove nothing.'

'Maybe. Where's Melissa? I'd like to talk to her.'

Dyce's glare turned baleful. 'Lissa ain't got nothing to do with any of this. You stay away from her. Besides, she ain't here.'

Casey looked at the cars parked in the drive. 'Her car is here.'

'She went out riding a bit ago. She does that quite a lot.'

Taking a step forward, Barney Dyce spoke for the first time: 'You leave my sister alone! You got no cause to go hounding her!'

'I'm not hounding her, Barney,' Casey said steadily. 'I'm just doing my job.'

'That's not the way I see it!' Barney said angrily. He took another step, and his father put a restraining hand on his shoulder. 'Gentle down, Barn.' Darrel Dyce gave his ugly caw of laughter. 'Barn gets kind of riled when he sees or hears something that he thinks might harm his little sister. I think you'd better be on your way, little lady.' Darrel's expression grew sanctimonious. 'I might not be able to hold him back. He's younger and stronger than I am.'

Casey stood her ground. 'I told you before, Mr Dyce, it's not a good idea to threaten a law officer. Someone might begin to wonder what you have to hide, and a *real* investigation might be begun to look into why you're so reluctant to answer a few questions.'

Dyce smiled, showing tobacco-stained teeth. 'Why, that wasn't no threat, little lady, just a piece of advice.'

Casey held his stare for a moment, then turned on her heel. She rarely let a suspect anger her, but there was a quality about these two that galled her.

Her anger had cooled by the time the Cherokee topped the rise, and the Dyce ranch house dropped from view.

111

She slowed the Cherokee, hoping to see Melissa riding towards her as she had before; but there was no sign of Melissa Dyce, and she drove on.

TEN

Dan Farrel was pontificating. During dinner, Casey had asked her uncle about rodeoing. She wanted to know how one became a rodeo performer; what desire, what skills were required, and how were they learned?

Dan was happy to oblige. He, Casey, and Donnie were now in Dan's study as he held forth. Alice Farrel was in the kitchen, cleaning up after dinner. She had shooed Casey out, refusing help, saying that she had heard all Dan's stories so many times that she could recite them word for word.

Dan began, 'You know that Prescott lays claim to having the oldest rodeo in the country. Of course a couple of other states and cities make the same claim; but that's neither here nor there. Ask any real old-time cowboy, and he'd probably tell you that the first rodeo began on a ranch somewhere: there was a bronc whose owner claimed that nobody could ride it; and some young cowpoke came along and made a bet that he could, and won the bet. That was the first rodeo.' He smiled at Donnie. 'You know, there's an old saying: "There was never a horse that couldn't be rode, and never a cowboy that couldn't be throwed"!'

Donnie, eyes wide, leaned forward. 'When did you become a rodeo rider, Uncle Dan?'

Dan squirmed a little in his chair, and shot an embarrassed glance at Casey. Then he squared his shoulders. 'What the hey! No reason that you shouldn't know the

113

truth, Donnie. I rode my first bucking bronc in prison. The inmates held a rodeo every summer. I found out that I had a knack for it, and I got pretty good. So, when I got out, I hit the circuit for a few years. I did pretty well; even had one big win, in Pendleton. But by that time I knew that I would never be a real champion, so I took my prize money and made a down payment on this ranch. Land was cheap around here in those days . . .'

'Did you ever ride the bulls?' Donnie asked.

Dan shook his head. 'Nope! Never was quite that foolish, or that brave. I knew my limitations.'

Donnie leaned forward. His eyes were bright. 'I think bull riding would be the most exciting.'

'Exciting, maybe,' Casey said, 'but also the most dangerous; not to mention what it can do to your insides.'

Dan nodded. 'Your mother's right, boy. It takes a special type of man to ride a bull. Like Buck.' He gazed away for a moment, face shadowed by melancholy.

Donnie looked from Dan to Casey, and she gave him a reassuring smile. He leaned forward. 'How did Buck get started riding bulls?'

Dan turned his attention back to Donnie, seemingly grateful for the boy's interest. 'The usual way, I guess you'd say: got up on a horse, got thrown, got up again, until either he or the horse was worn out. From the time Buck was little, he went around the ranch roping chickens or dogs, riding goats and calves. Buck was a natural.

'When he got a little older, and I saw he was serious about it, I sent him to a rodeo school over in California. There are quite a few such schools around, but I knew the old boy who ran this one, Jethro Renfrow. His way was a little different from most. He had all the students select one particular event and a particular rodeo hero to model themselves after. From the start Buck wanted to be a bull rider; and he chose Donnie Gay – who I consider the best bull rider in the world – to model himself after.'

114

'That's my name,' Donnie said excitedly. 'Hey, Casey, maybe I'll be a famous bull rider!'

'Over my dead body,' Casey muttered.

'Anyway,' Dan continued, 'Donnie Gay was Buck's hero.'

He laughed. 'At any rate, Jethro taught those boys to think of themselves as their heroes, and act accordingly. Of course Buck didn't start right out on live bulls. They used mechanical bulls made of rubber and steel, with sprockets and chain drives and an electric motor – the same kind that got to be so popular in Western bars.

'I remember a little lecture Jethro gave all of his student bull riders. He told them that when they were home, they should practise on a barrel. Practise every chance they got. He told them to do just what they would on a real bull, and to keep practising until they got to where they didn't even have to think about it. On a real bull, there isn't any time to think; and if you take that time, well, the bull takes you!

'And I guess he was right. When Buck got home from the school, he must have ridden that barrel six or eight hours a day. Within two years, when he was seventeen, he rode his first bull. Six months later, right here in Prescott, he won his first competition. After that, there was no stopping him. The only thing is . . .' He gave a deep sigh. 'Buck never did have the burning desire to be a world champion. It was the challenge he loved, the competition. That seemed to be enough for him.'

He shook his head. 'But maybe he was smart. It's a rough life, rodeoing. You're always on the road, competing in one city, sleeping in your car, then on to the next. And it's expensive. Unless you're one of the top winners, it's hard to get by. You've got to pay entry fees, buy gas for your car; and if you compete in the calf-roping and bull-dogging events, you've got your horse to feed and a trailer to haul. Buck didn't much like living that way; so

115

he didn't compete all the time, and usually stuck to rodeos more or less close at hand. I can't say that I blame him; still, he had it in him to be a champion if he'd wanted it bad enough. Yes, he might have become more famous than his hero, Donnie Gay.'

Dan shook his head, his mixed feelings clear upon his face. Casey felt a wave of compassion for him. She glanced at Donnie, who, despite his interest, was yawning hugely. But Casey had one more question. 'Did Buck continue rodeoing after he married Pam? Or did he stop for a few years?'

Dan looked surprised. 'Oh, no, he never stopped. In fact, I remember that he went off to a rodeo not two weeks after he married Pamela.'

'Did she go with him?'

Dan shook his head. 'No. She stayed behind. She didn't much care for that kind of thing. Maybe that's one reason their marriage fell apart.'

Beside Casey, Donnie yawned again. Casey said, 'I think it's bedtime for you, sport.'

'Ah, Casey, it's not that late,' he protested. 'I want to hear more about rodeoing.'

'Some other time,' Casey said, ruffling his hair. 'I'm sure Uncle Dan will be willing.'

'Sure, any time, Donnie. Love to talk about rodeoing.' Dan's glance went to Casey. 'Anything I said help you in any way?'

'Not so far as the case is concerned; but it did give me some insight into where Buck was coming from.'

She stretched. Dan was studying her face. 'You look tired, Casey.'

She nodded. 'I am, a little. I think I need to get away from the case for a few hours, maybe a day. Try to get a fresh slant on things.'

Dan leaned forward. 'Why don't you take the boy for a little trip, see some of the countryside, maybe show him

116

Sedona and Jerome? Donnie might enjoy it, especially Jerome.'

Casey brightened. 'That's a good idea. I haven't been to either place in . . . well, it must be several years.'

Dan grinned. 'Well, then you should enjoy it too; though I should warn you that Sedona has changed some; there are even more tourists now, and lots more development. Jerome's busier too. More houses have been restored, but it still looks about the same.'

He turned to Donnie. 'Jerome was once a thriving mining town, the real West. Then, for years, it was a ghost town, almost deserted, the buildings falling apart. Now, people are living there, artists and such, mostly. They have a mining museum, and it's real interesting.'

Donnie grabbed Casey's hand, looking up into her face with eager eyes. 'That sounds neat! And you said when we left Phoenix that we might go to Jerome.'

'Did I say that?' she grinned. 'You think you can stand to be away from the horses for a whole day?'

'Yeah, for one day.' He grinned, and she gave him a narrow-eyed look, thinking that he was a sharp little customer who knew when he was being teased.

'Okay, kiddo. We'll do it. We'll leave right after breakfast, in the morning.'

It was a beautiful morning, sunny and warm, the bright blue of the sky softened by clouds like fat, white cushions. Casey, admiring the view from her bedroom window, felt fit, rested, and determined not to think about the case. Today was for Donnie, and for her, too. They both needed it.

It was about nine a.m, when, full of waffles and fresh strawberries, they got on the road. Casey had decided to go first to Sedona and Oak Creek Canyon, so she headed east to catch I-17.

As they headed in the direction of Flagstaff, Casey

noticed that Donnie was uncharacteristically quiet. 'What's up, kiddo?' she asked him.

He turned to her, his small face serious. 'We were on this road once before, weren't we, when that Dumpster Killer was after us?'

Casey reached over and took his hand. 'Yes, that's right. That was a pretty scary time, wasn't it?'

Donnie nodded sombrely, then his face brightened. 'But you handled that guy real good, didn't you? He won't be able to hurt anyone else ever again, will he?'

Casey squeezed his hand, warm and rough in hers. 'That's right, kiddo. But I didn't do it alone. I couldn't have done it without you. And today is a different day. Today we're just going to have fun.'

They were now dropping down the grade leading into the Verde Valley, which spread below them green and peaceful along the winding Verde River. In the distance loomed the Mogollon Rim, dark blue against the lighter colour of the sky. Just before the highway began the long climb to Flagstaff, Casey took the turnoff towards Sedona.

As the colourful red rock formations came into sight, Donnie sat forward. 'Wow! That's really great. It looks like the movies!'

Casey laughed. 'Yeah, it does, doesn't it? They film a lot of Westerns here, that's why it looks familiar. But it's more beautiful than the pictures, isn't it?'

'Yeah. It sure is. Wow! Look at that one. It looks like a big church or something. How come they're so bright – the colours, I mean?'

'Minerals. There are minerals in the rocks and soil. See, even the dirt by the side of the road is red.'

'Yeah. This is neat, Casey. Can we get out and walk around pretty soon?'

Casey nodded. As she noticed the numbers of cars on the road, she was thinking that Dan was right, Sedona

118

had changed. When she had first visited here, as a child, Sedona and Oak Creek Canyon had been relatively uncrowded. Since then, it had grown into a full-blown resort town, with all the attendant problems that such popularity brings. Recent articles in Phoenix papers had spoken of the damage to the ecology of Oak Creek caused by thousands of feet trampling through the area; and houses had sprung up everywhere in, around and on the edges of Sedona and Oak Creek. New-Agers moved rocks to form medicine wheels and other symbols on sites they considered to have 'power'. The rangers moved them back. The New-Agers moved them again. It might be funny, if all this activity wasn't causing damage to the fragile desert ecosystem.

She shook her head. Well, today was supposed to be for pleasure. She smiled at Donnie. 'You're going to be able to stretch your legs in just a minute. I want to stop at the Chapel first.'

'The Chapel?'

'Yes. The Chapel of the Holy Cross. There it is!' She pointed towards the beautiful building set into a hillside, which was framed by two pinnacles of uniquely coloured, red sandstone.

She drove into the parking lot and parked the Cherokee. Donnie scrambled out of the vehicle and stretched mightily. Casey, exiting more slowly, did the same. From where she stood, she could see a good distance back the way they had come. Out of the corner of her eye, she saw a red pickup pulling up by the side of the road. A vague memory nudged at her mind; but she dismissed it with a shrug as Donnie came around to her side of the Jeep. Despite the gaggle of tourists arriving and leaving the chapel, it was quiet here. Something about this place caused them to keep their voices down respectfully. The sky seemed to go on forever, and two hawks drifted lazily on an updraft, against the spectacular backdrop of red rock.

As if echoing her thoughts, Donnie said in a hushed voice. 'It's quiet here, ain't it, Casey?'

'Isn't, not ain't,' she corrected absently. 'And yes, it's peaceful here. Isn't the chapel beautiful?'

Donnie nodded. 'It looks like part of the hill, almost, only even prettier.'

'You've got good taste, kiddo. Come on, let's go on up. There's a nice view from up higher.'

After inspecting the chapel and its grounds, Casey headed back towards Sedona proper. Here the traffic was almost impossible, and Casey began to wonder if this had been such a good idea after all. It took her a while, but she finally found a place to park, and then she and Donnie set out on a tour of the shops. She realized that shopping, as such, wasn't big with young boys; but the stores were full of Western gear and Indian artifacts, and she thought he would find these interesting. He did, all right. By the time they were ready to eat lunch, Donnie was wearing – proudly – a new tooled leather belt with a silver buckle, a leather vest, and packing a new red-jacketed pocket knife, complete with corkscrew, scissors, screw-driver and spoon, as well as the requisite blades. He had discovered these items while waiting for her to try on, and purchase, a pair of soft, brown leather moccasin-boots, which were on sale. She had seen a beautiful concho belt that she coveted; but, unfortunately, the fifteen-hundred dollar price did not fit into her current budget. Maybe someday. Probably not.

They ate lunch in a pleasant, airy restaurant – despite the large breakfast, Donnie was 'starving' – and then returned to the Cherokee and headed up the old highway, which led to Flagstaff.

Here Oak Creek ran parallel to the road, on their right, the water clear and fresh, as it coursed down from the high country.

A few miles down the road, past the dwindling commercial buildings, Casey crossed over a bridge, and pulled into a small parking area to the left of the road. The area was already packed with cars, but someone pulled out just as Casey pulled in, and Donnie chortled. 'That's good luck, isn't it Casey?'

Casey grinned as she slid the Cherokee into the newly vacated slot. 'You're darned right, it is.'

'Why are we stopping here, Casey?'

Casey pulled on the brake. 'To see the stream, kiddo. This is a famous look-out spot; and, you can get down to the water from here, if you want to.'

Donnie began to bounce. 'I want to go down. Can we go down, Casey?'

Casey laughed. 'Sure thing, kiddo.'

Taking his hand, Casey let him lead her to the well-travelled trail that zigzagged down the steep slope of the canyon to the water below.

As they started down, Casey happened to glance at the bridge, to her left. A red pickup was just crossing. She frowned, but was jostled from her train of thought by Donnie's tug on her hand. 'Come on, Casey! Let's go.'

At the bottom of the trail they found people fishing the stream, some casting from the boulders along the shore, others standing in the swift, but shallow water.

Donnie began to bounce again. 'Can I go wading, Casey? Can I?'

'People are fishing here, Donnie, let's go down-stream so we won't bother them.'

They went under the bridge. Cars crossing overhead made a rumbling sound, like distant thunder. About a hundred yards downstream the stream bed widened, creating a quiet eddy. There were only a few people, and no fishermen. Casey said, 'This should be okay.'

'Yeah!' Donnie quickly removed his shoes and socks,

and rolled his trouser legs up above his knees. 'You coming in, Casey?'

'I think not. I'll watch. Stay close to the bank.'

Donnie squealed as he stepped into the cold water, but soon he was splashing back and forth, retrieving rocks from the stream bed and splashing up to Casey to show her his finds.

It was restful there on the bank in the sun, and Casey had to fight to keep from dozing off. The case, and all its attendant problems and complexities, seemed very far away just now. Feeling the sun on her face, watching Donnie, she wondered, as she sometimes did, if law enforcement was really what she wanted? She could marry Josh – he'd asked her often enough – make a home for him and Donnie. If she found she needed to work, surely there were jobs to be found that didn't entail putting your life, and your mental state, on the line.

She shaded her eyes and tried to see where the sun was. They probably should get on their way if they wanted to see Jerome. She sat up and called to Donnie. He splashed up, like a puppy, dripping water. His face and arms were pink, and she realized, guiltily, that she had not put sun-screen on him. She reached for her bag, and made him sit down while she rubbed the lotion into his arms and face.

'Time to get moving if we want to see Jerome,' she said.

To her surprise, he didn't object. All that jumping and splashing had calmed him down a bit. She shook her head, wishing that there was some way to siphon off some of that energy for her own use. If you could only harness the energy that kids waste, you could power the world.

It was mid-afternoon by the time they hit Clarkdale and Jerome. At the edge of Clarkdale the two-lane highway curved towards the mountain on their left, and a scatter of precariously perched houses could be seen scattered along the slopes.

Casey pointed. 'That's it, kiddo. That's Jerome!'

Donnie stretched to see. 'It don't look like much.'

'Doesn't,' said Casey. 'That's not all of it. You'll see.'

They were already climbing the steep, looping road. Donnie had his face pressed to the window. 'Wow, Casey. How come they built a town way up here?'

Casey, eyes on the road, smiled. 'Money,' she said. 'In this case, in the form of copper. Wherever there is gold, silver or copper, no matter how hard that place is to get to, people will come; and once they're there, before you know it, they've started to build a town. You might not think so now, but in the early 1900s, at the height of the copper boom, Jerome was the fourth largest town in Arizona.'

At the entrance to the town proper, Casey had to slow to a crawl, crowding against the wall on the left. The narrow road – as was often the case – was in the process of being shored up. Donnie shook his head. 'Wow! Do those houses ever fall down, Casey? They're right on the edge. And they're real *rickety*.'

Casey, safely past the construction, smiled. 'Sometimes,' she said. 'They say that a lot of the town is built over the tunnels that the miners made, looking for ore.'

'Gee, neat!' he said, with a small boy's interest in destruction.

Donnie wanted to see everything; and after they found a parking place, they tramped over almost every inch of the town, and the mining museum, below.

By the time they finished the mine tour, Casey had had it. She had wanted to get over Mingus Mountain before dark, and it was now growing late. But Donnie was complaining of hunger, and she realized that her own stomach felt empty. Jerome had only a few restaurants, and all had waiting lines. By the time they had found a

123

restaurant, waited for a table, and had their meal, the sun was beginning to set.

As the Cherokee headed home, there was still enough light for Donnie to see the abandoned mines along the highway, and the twilight view back down into the valley was spectacular; but darkness caught them as they began the switchback climb up the mountain.

Casey, not used to mountain driving, took it easy. For some time she had noticed bright headlights in her rear-view mirror. Now the lights inched closer, the glare in the mirror almost blinding her. There was no passing lane, and no place for her to pull off the two-lane road. The driver would just have to be patient until there was an opportunity to pass.

At that moment, the car behind her surged forward. Casey, her annoyance turning to disbelief, felt the Cherokee jump as the tailgating vehicle hit the back bumper. Anger fuelled a rush of adrenalin.

Donnie, who had been dozing, now yelped. 'Casey! What is it?'

Casey's hands were tense on the wheel. 'I don't know! That idiot behind us . . .'

Her words were cut off, as the following vehicle rammed them again, throwing Casey hard against her seat belt. The Cherokee whipped to the left where the road fell away into a deep canyon. Casey got control of her vehicle only inches from the guard rail, thankful that no cars were approaching from the other direction.

A quick glance at her rear-view mirror told her that the other vehicle had pulled back a few feet. In the headlight's glare, she could not see much, but she thought that the vehicle behind her was a pickup. With the Cherokee under control again, she whipped back over to the right lane, and accelerated.

Behind her, the pickup roared, its lights coming closer. A sharp curve was ahead, and she had to slow or risk losing control of her car. Hugging the mountain wall, she made the curve, and saw that the section ahead was relatively straight.

Before she could regain speed, the pickup was on her again, slamming viciously into the rear bumper. Casey felt the steering wheel twisting in her hands, as the Cherokee began to weave. A desperate glance at the roadside told Casey that the mountain receded here, leaving a bush-covered stretch about the width of two cars for a hundred yards or so. Casey twisted the wheel, and the Cherokee leapt off the macadam and across the shallow depression that ran alongside the road. For a moment, she feared a tyre might blow, but none did. She managed to straighten the Jeep, and carefully brake it to a stop, nose slanted toward the road. Bushes lashed at the right side of the vehicle. To her left, the pickup roared past, and for a moment was illuminated by the Cherokee's headlights, a brief flash of red; then it vanished around the curve ahead.

Casey glanced over at Donnie; his small face was pale in the light from the dash, and his eyes looked to be all pupil. 'Wow!' he said. 'They almost killed us, Casey!'

Casey, struggling to get her breath, touched his hand with hers. Her body was sheathed in sweat, and her heart was pounding. In a moment, she managed to speak. 'Yeah. But it's okay. We're okay.'

'Why did they do that, Casey? We didn't do anything to them.'

'I know. Maybe they were drunk. Are you all right?'

He nodded. 'But my seat belt squeezed my middle.'

'Yeah, I know.' Casey gently massaged her own chest, grateful for the pain, considering the alternative.

'Anyway, they're gone now.' Not wanting to frighten the boy, she didn't want to say what she was thinking: what if the pickup was waiting up ahead at one of the viewpoints?

The Cherokee was still running. Tentatively she stepped on the gas and straightened out the car. Everything seemed to be all right. Engine idling, she hesitated for a moment; then turning the car sharply to the left, she headed back down they way they had come. They would go home by way of I-17; it seemed less chancy.

ELEVEN

When Sergeant Randall strode into the Prescott Police Station early the next morning, he found Casey waiting for him.

He smiled when he saw her. 'Well, you're up bright and early.'

Then his expression grew serious. 'Is anything wrong?'

Casey looked up at him from her chair. 'Depends on how you look at it. Can we talk?'

'Sure. In there.' He gestured to a small room off to the side. Through the open door, Casey could see a table and a few chairs. 'Go on in. I'll be with you in a minute.'

He walked over to the reception desk and spoke to one of the women behind it, then joined Casey, closing the door behind him. He was carrying two cups of steaming coffee, one of which he set down in front of Casey. He sat down across from her. 'Now, what's up?'

Casey took a sip of the fragrant coffee, then told him about the incident on Mingus Mountain.

When she was finished, he frowned. 'And you say you had seen that same red pickup before, in Sedona?'

Casey shrugged. 'Well, I can't *swear* that it was the same truck; but it looked the same; and it *did* seem to show up wherever we were. Under the circumstances, I can't believe that it was simply coincidence!' She hit the arm of her chair with her fist. 'If only I had known what was going to happen later, I would have taken a good look at it. As it is, it was just a peripheral thing, one of those things you notice, but don't really take note of. You know what I mean?'

He nodded. 'Did you notify the local police?'

She shook her head. 'What would have been the point? By the time I got back to where there was a phone, the truck was long gone. Besides, I had no licence number or even the make of the truck. There must be hundreds of red pickups in the area.'

Randall steepled his fingers and looked at them thoughtfully, then peered at her over them. 'Don't the Dyces have a red pickup?'

She nodded.

'And Barney Dyce has threatened you.'

She nodded again. 'I've thought of that, of course; in fact it was the first thing that crossed my mind.'

Randall sighed. 'I warned you, Casey. Those two are dangerous. Have you examined your vehicle? Any traces of paint from the other truck?'

She shook her head. 'I looked the Cherokee over carefully as soon as I got home. Some dents on my back bumper, but no paint.'

'Still, whoever hit you should have some dents and scratches of their own.'

Randall got to his feet, abruptly. 'Come on, let's pay the Dyces a visit.'

In Steve's unmarked car, heading out to Chino Valley, Casey said, 'Anything new turn up yesterday while I was away?'

'Nothing startling,' he said with a shrug. 'We're still trying to turn up a witness at the fairgrounds, someone who might have seen something pertinent. Nothing. I don't think we ever will. Too many people. Too much going on.'

He laughed wryly. 'I spent part of yesterday interviewing some of Buck's old girl friends: the list is long and varied.'

'How did you get their names?'

'Talked to bartenders on Whiskey Row. They all knew Buck, and knew who he came in with, and one person knew another and . . . You know how it goes?'

Casey nodded. 'Anything interesting there?'

'Nope. Most of them claimed to harbour no animosity towards Buck. The ones who do have some bitterness swear it wasn't enough to make them want Buck dead.'

'How about the married ones? I understand there were a few. Any of the husbands angry enough to kill Buck?'

'Most of them swore their husbands never knew, and gave their husbands alibis for the day and time of Buck's murder.'

'Do you have a list of the women you've interviewed so far?'

'Sure, back at the office. You want to see it?'

She nodded. 'Sometimes women will talk more freely with another woman. Besides, then we can compare notes, maybe tell if any of them are lying.'

'Sounds like a plan. Have at it, and good luck.'

'I also think it's time that I scope out Whiskey Row.'

He gave her a quick glance. 'Not alone, you shouldn't.'

'You mean it's dangerous?'

'Oh, I don't think you'll come to any real harm, but it's a whole different territory down there. I think you should let me come with you.'

Casey laughed. 'Are you asking me out, Sergeant?'

'In a way, I suppose. Look, Casey, I know that you have a "significant other" or whatever the hell the latest terminology is; but I like you and enjoy your company.'

'Then it's not just a macho thing, protecting the little woman?'

'Well, maybe partly; but I certainly don't think of you as a defenceless woman, Casey. Far from it.'

She nodded and smiled. 'Well, okay then. How about tonight?'

'Well, okay. Friday night is the night when Whiskey Row really roars, but maybe we shouldn't wait that long. Why don't you meet me at the station about six? We'll have a leisurely dinner, then go honky-tonking!'

She laughed. 'You're on.'

When they topped the rise before the Dyce ranch house, Casey was relieved to see that all three vehicles were parked before the house. Then, she noticed that the red pickup was sitting at a right angle to the black pickup, its nose jammed firmly into the black pickup's side.

Steve hit the steering wheel with his hand. 'Shit!'

Casey knew that he was thinking the same thing she was.

'For someone so stupid and wrong-headed, those old boys manage considerable shrewdness. No use looking at that pickup now.'

He wheeled his car in behind the angled red pickup. They both got out and hurried over to the trucks. It was clear that the red pickup had hit the black with considerable force. Any dents or scratches acquired prior to the ramming would be impossible to isolate.

Casey heard a door slam, and glanced towards the house. Darrel and Barney Dyce stood together on the porch. In a moment, Melissa crept out behind them, placing herself off to one side, as if to separate herself from the two men.

Casey touched Steve's shoulder and, as he turned to her, she nodded towards the house. Steve gave a grunt and began walking, stopping at the foot of the porch.

Darrel Dyce spat out his dark stream into the flower bed. He grinned slyly. 'To what do we owe this pleasure?'

Steve jerked a thumb over his shoulder. 'Appears you had a little accident, Darrel. Kind of unusual to run into one of your own trucks with the other, isn't it? Seems a mite careless.'

Darrel shrugged. 'Well, you know how it is. Barney here got tanked last night and forgot where the brake pedal was. Wonder that he didn't crash right into the house.'

Steve turned his gaze to Barney, who was studiously examining the toes of his boots. 'And just where were you when you were doing this drinking, Barney?'

'He bought a bottle of bourbon and a six-pack and drove around boozing it up,' Darrel said. 'I've warned him about doing that, but you know how these kids are.' His words aside, his tone expressed his pride, and the fact that he was putting one over on the law. Casey felt a strong urge to hit him, the miserable little bastard!

Steve gave the elder Dyce a cold stare. 'I was talking to Barney, Darrel. Surely the boy is capable of answering for himself.'

Barney flushed, and looked up sullenly. 'It's like he says. I was just having a little fun.'

Darrel gave his nasty smile. 'That's right, Sergeant; and besides, it ain't against the law to run into your own truck on your own property, at least as far as I know. Now, if you'd come across him out on the road . . . But you didn't, did you?'

He glanced slyly at Casey, and back to Randall.

Randall looked at him coolly. 'Well, we aren't too sure about that. Barney, do you have a witness to any of this?'

Barney looked back at his boots. 'The guy where I bought the booze is all. But come over here,' he came down the steps and moved over to the red pickup, 'you can see right here I'm telling the truth.'

Pulling on the right door of the pickup, he finally got it open; evidently the collision had sprung the door. Inside,

131

on the seat, there was a near-empty bottle of Jack Daniel, cap off. Empty beer cans littered the floorboards. One can was even wedged underneath the brake and the pedal. An artistic touch, Casey thought.

'You see,' Darrel Dyce said. 'Barn did his boozing in the pickup.'

Casey shrugged. 'That doesn't prove anything. He could have planted the cans and the bottle as a cover-up.'

'Now why in the world would he want to do that?' Dyce's tone was filled with righteous anger. 'Cover up what?'

Steve, ignoring Darrel, spoke to the boy. 'Barney, did you do any of your drinking and driving up in Oak Creek, Sedona, or Jerome?'

Barney opened his mouth to speak, but his father beat him to it. 'Like I told you, Officer, Barn just drove around Prescott and Chino Valley. Don't anybody believe what I say any more? Why in the hell would he be all the way up there? He had no business up that way!'

Steve fixed the older man with a level stare. 'You *do* seem to have a problem with answering for other people, Darrel. Are you afraid of what Barney might tell us, or are you just plain rude?'

Barney flushed, and shot his father a dark look. 'I ain't got nothin' to hide,' he mumbled. 'It was like Pa says: I just drove around Chino and Prescott. I don't know what all the fuss is about.'

'Well, let's just say that someone in a red pickup tried to run Miss Farrel and her boy off the road yesterday up on Mingus Mountain. Since Barney here has been heard threatening Miss Farrel . . . well, you can see that I had to check it out.'

Barney, his face dark, took a threatening step forward, his fists doubled. His father put a restraining hand on his shoulder.

132

'Now, just gentle down boy. Don't pay no never-mind to these two. They're just trying to stir things up.'

Dyce's malevolent stare was fixed on Casey. 'You should be almighty careful, young lady, churning up lies about my boy. Did you actually see who was driving that truck?'

Casey stared back. 'No, Mr Dyce, I did not. If I had, that person would be in jail right now. As it is, Barney is being questioned because of his threats towards me; under the circumstances, a reasonable procedure.'

Dyce spat, this time not bothering to turn his head. The brown stream landed near Casey's shoes. 'You two going to charge my Barn? Go ahead. Then we'll fight her out in court, and I'll file suit for false arrest. Now, get off my property!'

Steve shook his head. 'Oh, we'll be going, in our own good time. I just want to say one more thing to both you and Barn. I'm putting you both on notice. If Miss Farrel is harmed in any way, or threatened again, you two are the first ones I'm going to come looking for. Is that quite clear?'

Darrel Dyce emitted his caw of laughter. 'Mighty protective of the little lady, ain't you, Sergeant? Soft on her, are you? Mighty convenient, you two working together and all.'

Steve's face darkened, and he took a step forward. Casey caught his arm. In a moment she felt the muscles relax. His voice when he spoke was calm. 'Just remember what I said, Dyce. And you better keep a tighter leash on Barney. If one of our boys catches him riding around drunk, like he says he was last night, we'll throw the book at him.

'And as far as charging Barney on this, there will be no charges at this time. However, a witness has come forward who saw the truck and, he says, the driver. After we talk

133

to him, we should have a better idea of the man we're looking for. Thank you for your time.'

He turned away, and Casey quickly followed.

As they walked away she said: 'You're lying about the witness, right?'

He gave a grim smile. 'Yeah, but if they're guilty, it should put the fear of God into them. If not, well, nothing lost.'

He opened the door of the car. 'Boy, that old man has a mouth on him. I haven't been so near to losing it for years.'

Casey settled herself in her seat, and fastened her seat belt. 'I know what you mean. He can really get under your skin. Every time I see that smirk of his I want to kick him someplace vital.'

Steve laughed. 'I'll bet you'd do it, too.'

The car pulled away from the ranch house. As they topped the rise, Casey looked back. The porch was now empty. She sighed. 'I still have no idea whether or not they were involved. But, maybe your warning will keep them away from me from now on. I hope so, anyway.'

Steve shook his head. 'I wouldn't be too sure of that, Casey. Barney doesn't pay much attention to warnings. He gets that from his father. Darrel Dyce has been here since God planted the apple tree. He's a throwback to the frontier mentality: take what you can, and keep it at all costs; and every man outside your own clan is a probable enemy. He's the kind of man who is used to getting his own way, and is mean as a rattlesnake when he's crossed. I hate to sound like your mother, but be careful, Casey. Keep looking over your shoulder, and don't get careless.'

Casey felt a small cold knot settling into her stomach, but she managed a wry smile. 'My mother never talked to me like that, Steve, but thanks. I'll be careful.'

134

TWELVE

Casey spent the rest of the day interviewing the first of the women whose names Steve had given her.

The first name on the list was that of Eileen Brewster. Eileen's husband was an attorney, and their home was in a section of expensive hillside homes. Casey had no difficulty in finding the place. Built into the side of a hill, it had a spectacular view. The beautifully hand-carved sign in front proclaimed that this was the residence of 'The Brewsters', and Casey had a story ready to use in case the husband was home. He wasn't, and she explained to the pretty woman who answered the door, why she was here.

Eileen Brewster was apparently in her early thirties, a tall, full-figured woman with long, ash-blonde hair and a girlish face. When Casey first explained her mission, the other woman seemed a bit startled. 'But I've already talked . . .'

'To the Sergeant, I know,' Casey finished for her. 'But I'd like you to tell me again. I'm mainly looking for background on Buck. I want to know what he was like, what he did with his time, that sort of thing.' Quickly, to forestall the inevitable question, she told the woman of her connection to Buck.

Eileen nodded. 'All right. Come on in.'

Inside the house, Eileen took Casey to the attractively efficient kitchen long enough to put two glasses; two bottles of iced, low-calorie fruit drink; and a plate of

135

low-calorie cookies on a plate; then led her out to the long, wide, covered deck, where a fresh breeze blew.

Casey, seating herself in one of the lounge chairs, sighed. The view, as she had seen from outside, was spectacular, ranging from Thumb Butte on the left, to Granite Mountain on the right. There was no getting around it, money did have its good points.

Eileen gestured to the tray. 'Please, have some. It's all low fat and no sugar.' She smiled and gestured at her pleasantly rounded body.

Casey smiled back, and poured the contents of one of the bottles into the glass. 'Thanks. This is thirsty weather.'

The other woman nodded. 'You say you want to know about Buck. I was wondering,' she blushed, 'how did you get my name?'

Casey took a long swallow of the icy liquid and set down her glass. 'From the sergeant in charge of the case. But it's not common knowledge. It won't be let out to anyone not involved in the investigation.'

The woman sighed. 'Well, I'm glad of that. I'm married, you know. We have two children. They're in school right now. I wouldn't want anything to . . .'

Casey raised a hand. 'I understand.'

'So what do you want to know?'

Casey leaned forward. 'Just what I said. What kind of man was Buck?'

Eileen closed her eyes. When she opened them, her expression was sad. She shook her head. 'I don't know. I mean, I can tell you how he was to me, how I saw him.'

She sighed. 'I guess to me, Buck was excitement. My husband . . . well, Carl is a wonderful man; he's kind, and he takes good care of me and the kids, but . . . you know how it is? We've been married thirteen years, and Carl has never been what you might call a great romantic.

'Buck just happened to come along at the right – or

maybe the wrong – time. I hadn't been around much when
Carl and I married; I was only nineteen, and Carl was the
only man I had ever had sex with. A little while ago, I
started thinking about that, how I had only known one
man in my life, and what I was maybe missing, a delayed
seven-year itch, I guess you might say.'

'And then you met Buck,' Casey prompted.

Eileen smiled wistfully. 'Yes, and then I met Buck.'

She leaned back in her chair. 'I suppose you think it's
odd, a man like Buck and a woman like me. He had
known his way around since he was a boy, and I'd never
been around. But you have to understand something about
Buck. He came across as being a little bit dangerous. He
was like the bad boys in high school that your mother
told you not to go out with – which of course made
them irresistible. But there was more than that; he had
the way of making a woman feel that he wanted to be
saved. He could convince you that all he needed to get
his life straight was the right woman, and that you were
that woman. It was pretty heady stuff.

'And he was very sexy. He had a lot of charisma, and
loads of macho charm. I often thought that he could have
made it big in movies if he'd had the chance. He was a
real heart-breaker.'

Casey leaned forward. 'Speaking of that, were you still
seeing him when he died, or had you broken up?'

Eileen gave her a searching look. 'Oh, we broke up
some time ago. Early in the year.' She looked down at
her hands, and then up again. 'This is a small town, and
it's hard to keep secrets. Someone I know almost saw us
together, and I got frightened. Carl may not be the most
exciting man in the world, but he's my husband, and I do
love him. I really couldn't bear it if I hurt him, or the kids,
so I called it off.'

'So you broke it off, not Buck?'

Eileen frowned. 'That's right. If you're implying that I

had some kind of grudge against Buck because he dumped me, you're way off base.'

Casey raised a placating hand. 'I'm sorry. I didn't mean to imply that at all. I just wanted to know if you parted on good terms.'

Eileen hesitated a bit before replying. 'Well, Buck was a little miffed at first. I gather he was used to calling the shots, and he was surprised when I wanted to end the affair before he did. He called a few times; but when I told him how I felt, he left me alone.'

She shrugged. 'As you can guess, it didn't take long for him to find someone else.' Her tone was somewhat wistful.

'Do you know anything about any of the other women he dated? Were there any who held a grudge against him?'

Eileen shook her head. 'I don't really know. I didn't really run with his usual crowd, you know. In my circumstances I didn't meet many of his other friends.'

'I can understand that,' Casey said. 'Just one more question: Are you certain that Carl doesn't know about any of this?'

Eileen shook her head vigorously. 'I'd stake my life that he doesn't. Carl is not a man who can conceal his feelings. If he knew, I'd know. And I can tell you this. Even if Carl *did* know, he's not the kind of man who could commit murder. Also, he was in San Francisco that weekend, attending a conference.'

Casey nodded, and closed her notebook. 'I want to thank you for your cooperation, and your frankness. I don't think we'll have to bother you again.'

Eileen stood and offered her hand. 'Thanks for being so understanding. This is the first time I've let myself really talk about Buck, and I think I needed to get it out. It's terrible to think of Buck being killed like that.' She shuddered. 'I hope you catch his killer soon. Who would want to do such a thing?'

'That's the question, isn't it? Sooner or later, we'll find out.'

The next name on the list was Sally Foster. It seemed that Sally worked at the City Hall downtown. Casey went inside and asked the supervisor when Miss Foster took her mid-afternoon coffee break.

Over a cup of coffee at a café across from the Courthouse Plaza, Casey told the other woman the reason for her visit.

Sally was a small, young woman, with short, curly brown hair and a pretty face that seemed to be made for to smiling. She looked to be about twenty-eight. At the moment, she was obviously very nervous and anxious. Casey set about trying to ease her apprehension. 'Miss Foster, there is no cause for concern. What I'm trying to do here is to fill in my mental picture of Buck Farrel, get a picture of his background.'

Relief flooded the other woman's face, and she blew out a breath of relief. 'Oh! I thought . . . I mean that other policeman already talked to me and . . . but I'm not a suspect, right?'

'Right.' Casey said, and saw the other woman relax.

'Well,' Sally said, 'I used to date Buck, and I was at the rodeo last Saturday when he was . . .' She swallowed, her eyes suddenly awash with tears. 'When he was murdered.'

'You were still in love with him?' Casey asked sympathetically.

Sally wiped the tears from her eyes with an angry gesture. 'I haven't gotten over him, if that's what you mean.'

'What happened? What brought about the breakup?'

Sally sniffed. 'He got tired of me, and found someone else. That was Buck's way; he never stayed with one woman for long. I knew that, but I believed him when

139

he said that he was through with all that. I thought that I was the one woman who could change him. Stupid, wasn't it?'

Casey put her hand on Sally's arm. 'Not at all. From what I hear, Buck was very good at making women think that.'

Sally sniffed again, and reached into her purse for a tissue.

'One morning, just before daylight, after he'd spent the night in my condo, he told me, as he was putting on his pants, that that was the last time he would see me.'

Again, her eyes filled with tears. 'I loved the bastard! I even begged him not to stop seeing me. He just shrugged it off. He said – I remember his exact words – "Nothing lasts forever, sugar; you're old enough to know that." That was the last thing he said to me.'

'You say you were at the rodeo the day he died. Were you in the stands when it happened?'

Sally nodded. 'Yes.'

'Did you leave the stands during the rodeo?'

'No. I sat through the whole thing, up until Buck was thrown.'

'You didn't go down to check on how he was?'

Sally shook her head. 'No. I thought he was just thrown. I had no reason, at the time, to think he was seriously hurt. And I was still angry with him.'

'Do you know of anyone else who was angry with him, maybe angry enough to want him dead?'

Suspicion filled Sally's eyes. 'No! Why are you asking me these things? You said you only wanted to know about Buck's background. People saw me in the stands. I was with friends!'

Casey tried to soothe her. 'I know it sounds hard, but I have to ask these things. It's routine.'

Sally appeared somewhat mollified. 'Well, Buck hurt me, and I was angry with him for that, but not *that* angry.

140

I mean these things happen all the time, don't they? It hurts, but you get over it. And no, I don't know of anyone who hated Buck enough to kill him. Despite the way he treated women, they all seemed to like him.'

'What about the men?'

Sally shrugged. 'He was popular with the men, too. They thought he was a "good ol' boy", and most of them envied his success with women. What can I tell you?'

Casey nodded. 'By the way, you say he left you for someone else, do you know who it was?'

Sally gave her level look. 'I sure do. About a month after he broke up with me, I saw him downtown in his pickup. He was with Melissa Dyce.'

The third name on Casey's list was that of Myrna Macklin, who owned a small gift shop in Ponderosa Plaza. It was an attractive shop, small, but stocked with many charming items. The general effect was that of a marvellous little box that was just spilling over with goodies.

Casey entered and looked around. It was growing late in the day and there was only one customer in the shop. As Myrna Macklin waited on the customer, Casey studied her. She looked to be older by a few years than the other women Casey had talked to, and not as obviously good looking; yet she was attractive in a quiet, subdued way. Her best feature was her hair, deep black and glossy, which made a shoulder-length frame around her triangular face.

When the customer left, Casey introduced herself and stated her reason for being here. Myrna Macklin studied Casey for a moment with sombre brown eyes. 'Buck? You're the second person in two days.'

'Yes, I know. But it will only take a few minutes.'

The woman hesitated, obviously trying to make up her mind. Then she nodded. 'All right. We can go to the ice cream parlour. It shouldn't be too busy this time of day. Just a minute.'

She turned and went through a narrow door in the back of the shop, then re-appeared with a slender blonde girl in tow.

The girl smiled at Casey, and went around behind the counter. Myrna Macklin nodded at Casey, and walked out into the mall.

The ice cream parlour was just a few doors up from Macklin's shop, and Myrna did not speak as they walked there.

Inside, Myrna chose a small table in a corner. When the waitress came, she ordered a dish of vanilla ice cream. Feeling hungry, Casey did the same.

When the waitress had gone to fill their order, Myrna said. 'All right, what is it that you want to know?'

'What was Buck like? Who were his friends? Where did he hang out? That sort of thing.'

Myrna gave a cynical smile. 'Well, I'll tell you what I know, but it isn't much. Why are you coming to me, anyway? There are many people,' her smile twisted, 'many *women*, who knew him better than I did.'

Casey shrugged. 'I'm talking to everyone and anyone I can find who knew him. Your name was on the list. Do you mind telling me how and when you knew Buck?'

Myrna sighed. 'It was some time ago, about two years back. We went together for almost a year. I thought I was in love. I thought he was, too.' She paused, then added: 'It didn't work out.'

The waitress brought their ice cream, and it looked delicious. Casey took a bite. It was. Swallowing, she said. 'Do you mind telling me why?'

'Well, as I said, I thought he loved me, and I loved him, and that often mentioned device, my biological clock, was beginning to tick rather loudly. I wanted to marry him, settle down, and have some kids before it was too late.

Well, when I talked to him about it, he made it clear that he didn't want to get married, and that he certainly didn't want any kids; in fact he'd had a vasectomy so that he *couldn't* have kids.'

Casey made a quick note in her book. 'He must have trusted you, to tell you that.'

Myrna smiled ruefully. 'When he told me, we had had a few drinks – actually quite a few drinks – and Buck was a bit maudlin. He told me that he'd gotten a girl pregnant once, back when he was very young, and it had ruined her life.'

Casey leaned forward. 'Did he tell you the girl's name?'

Myrna shook her head. 'No. Only that it had happened years ago.'

Casey spooned up the last of her ice cream, and put down her spoon. 'I want to thank you for talking to me, and I have just one more question. This one is none of my business, and you don't have to answer, but what did an obviously intelligent, well-educated woman like you see in a man like Buck?'

Myrna gave her sad smile. 'I often used to wonder about that myself. Maybe it was the lady and the cowboy syndrome; I don't know. But you shouldn't sell Buck short. He was very intelligent, but he didn't like to work at it, as he put it. It was his nature to take the easy way, with everything, even – or perhaps especially – with his women.'

'And you hadn't seen him recently?'

Myrna shook her head. 'No, not in a long time. I don't spend a lot of time on Whiskey Row, and he doesn't seem to shop in the mall.'

'Were you at the rodeo on the day he died?'

Myrna shook her head. 'No. I was in Sedona, with a friend.'

Casey nodded. 'Well, that's all then. Thanks for talking with me.'

Myrna shrugged. 'It's the least I could do. Buck might have been a womanizer, but he was a likable sort of guy; and *nobody*, should have to die like that.'

After Myrna left, Casey sat for a moment, thinking. Finally, with a sigh, she picked up the check, paid the bill, and left. It had been a long day and she felt in the need of a long bath and a short nap before hitting Whiskey Row tonight with Steve Randall.

During the ride home, Casey put on a Carlos Nakai tape, and the combination of the haunting flute music and the golden, late afternoon light leached some of the tension from her.

By the time she reached the turn-off to the Farrel Ranch, she was feeling fairly relaxed and driving on automatic pilot; but when she heard the car horn behind her, she became instantly alert. Her heart began to pound as she glanced in the rear view mirror, expecting to see the red pickup behind her. Instead, she saw the Dyce Cadillac. Her foot started to press on the accelerator; then she noticed the slender arm waving from the vehicle's window, and saw that the driver was Melissa Dyce.

Breathing an audible sigh of relief, she slowed and pulled to the side of the road. The Caddy pulled in behind her, and Melissa got out and hurried towards the Cherokee.

'I'm sorry, Casey,' Melissa said breathlessly. 'I hope I didn't frighten you.'

Casey managed a smile. 'Well, I'll admit I was startled, until I recognized you.'

'I've been parked up there at the turn-off for a least an hour, waiting for you to come along.'

Casey felt a twinge of alarm. 'What is it, Melissa? Has something happened?'

Melissa shook her head. 'No, nothing like that.' She paused to take a deep breath. 'I heard about what

144

happened to you last night on Mingus Mountain, and I just wanted to say that I was sorry.'

Casey looked at her searchingly. 'Then it *was* Barney?'

Slowly, Melissa nodded. In a voice not much louder than a whisper, she said, 'Yes.'

Then she squared her shoulders and looked directly into Casey's eyes. 'Barney came home roaring drunk last night. The noise woke me, and I got up. As I came into the hall, I could hear him and Daddy talking in the study. I heard Barney say that he was only trying to put the fear of God into you, so you'd leave us alone.' Her lower lip trembled. 'I'm sure that's all it was. I'm sure he didn't really want to see you come to any harm. It was Daddy's idea to crash Barney's pickup into our other truck so the police wouldn't be able to find any scratches.'

Casey, remembering the cruel blows the pickup had struck, and how close she and Donnie had come to going off the road into the canyon, was not so certain of Barney's intent, but she nodded. 'That may be true,' she said, 'but we could have been killed.'

Melissa lowered her head. 'I know. That's why I wanted to talk to you, to apologize, and let you know how sorry I am.'

Casey smiled. 'Sorry enough to testify to what you heard?'

Melissa drew back, her face pale. 'Oh, no. I couldn't do that. Daddy would never forgive me. I just couldn't!'

Casey nodded again. 'I understand. Forget it.'

Melissa looked away, down the road, towards the Dyce drive. 'I have to get home now; I've been away too long as it is. I don't want Daddy to start looking for me.'

She turned away from the Cherokee, and Casey stayed her with an outstretched hand. 'Wait, Melissa, there's one more thing. Do you think that your brother, or your father, murdered Buck Farrel?'

Melissa's eyes went wild with panic. She made a choking

sound deep in her throat, then bolted. Casey watched in the side-view mirror as the girl raced back to the Cadillac, almost falling in her haste to be away.

Casey continued watching as the Caddy sped away. She was thinking of one of Josh's favourite maxims: Screw up a suspect's head. Rattle his or her cage; you never knew what might shake loose.

THIRTEEN

'In a way, the history of Whiskey Row is the history of Prescott itself,' Steve Randall said.

He and Casey were having dinner in Murphy's Restaurant, one of town's most colourful and popular eating places. The restaurant was in a building that was, like many of Prescott's buildings, a part of the past. It had once been a mercantile establishment, and still boasted the ornamental tin ceiling that had been part of the original building.

Casey took a sip of her wine. 'I'm sure you're right. Saloons and bordellos were always the first businesses to set up in a new town. After all, first things first, right?'

Steve laughed. 'That doesn't say much for the male sex, does it?'

Casey grinned. 'What can I say? The first people into a new territory were usually men, soon followed by ladies of ill repute. It wasn't until the men were joined by wives and children, that the churches and schools were built.'

Steve smiled ruefully. 'I'm afraid you're right. At any rate, the saloons along Whiskey Row have been on Montezuma about as long as the street has existed. They've been burned out a few times, but they always came back.'

'I've heard the story about the one fire, around the turn of the century. I understand the fire wasn't even out, when the bar owners moved their booze and girls on to the courthouse square and carried on business as usual, until the row was rebuilt. It must have been something to see.'

'Yeah. Well, the row has calmed down some from those days, but on Friday and Saturday nights it can still roar. The tourists love it, real bikers and cowboys on demand – though the tourists don't usually know the difference between the real hands and the cowboy wannabees. Just what do you hope to find there, Casey?'

Casey shrugged. 'Buck hung out there a lot, and since Red Pollock was a boozer, he probably did, too. People let their hair down when they're drinking; I hope that maybe someone will tell me something useful.'

'Sounds reasonable. At any rate, I'm glad you thought of it, because it gives me a chance to know you better.'

Casey gave him a lop-sided smile. 'You may be sorry about that, when you do.'

He shook his head. 'I doubt it. By the way, what about today? What did you learn from Buck's old girl-friends?'

'Not a lot that was new. But, he must have been something, you know. All three of the women I talked to – and they were all very different – seem to have been fascinated by him. They did have one thing in common: they all knew that he was a carouser, and that he played fast and loose with women, but he made each of them feel that they were the one woman who could change him. And, no matter how he treated them, they all still seemed to have some feeling for him. He was amazing. Oh, there was one thing. The last woman mentioned Buck's vasectomy. It evidently came up when she told him she wanted to have kids. He also mentioned a girl he got pregnant, and "ruined her life". Unfortunately, he didn't tell her who the girl was, but it fits in with what we've learned.'

Steve leaned forward. 'Did he say when this hap-pened?'

'Yes, about fifteen years ago.'

148

'Yeah. That fits in.'

He shook his head. 'I wish we knew the girl's name. There's a good chance that the girl had an abortion, or left town to have the child. This is a small town, and fifteen years ago we had a different social climate. But it's too late now. Too much water under the bridge. Also, I can't see how something that happened so long ago could be a factor in Buck's death.'

'Maybe you're right. But it's strange how it keeps popping up in the investigation. Anyway, I've got something else to tell you. Today, as I was going back to the ranch, Melissa Dyce stopped me. It seems that she wanted to apologize for what happened to me on Mingus Mountain!'

She waited for Randall's reaction. He seemed satisfactorily surprised. 'You mean it was her in the truck? I can't believe that.'

'I'm not asking you to. However, it seems that when Buck came home that night, roaring drunk, the noise woke her. When she went to see what was going on, she overheard Barney and his father discussing my near demise. Barney admitted that he had tried to drive me off the road, and his father arranged for the collision in their yard.'

'Well, that should make things easy for us.'

'I'm afraid not. Melissa was willing to apologize – she felt what Barney did was wrong – but she won't testify. She's too afraid of her father.'

'Shit! I should have known. Well, we can write that off, I guess; but the fact that I told them there was a witness may keep them quiet for a while, at least until they find out that I was bluffing.'

He put down his napkin. 'Well, are you ready to hit the row?'

Casey took a last sip of her wine. 'Ready as I'll ever be, I guess.'

149

It was about eight-thirty by the time they found a parking spot, and walked back to the Row. The side of Montezuma Street across from the Courthouse Plaza was a mix of shops and saloons. It was a week night, but since it was the tourist season, the bars were full. Doors opened and closed as people entered and exited the bars, emitting the sounds of country music, raucous laughter, cigarette smoke, and the odour of spilled beer.

About halfway down the block, Steve touched Casey's elbow and pointed to the bar they were passing. 'Might as well start in here,' he said, steering her towards the door.

As they entered the bar, they were hit by a wave of sound that made Casey's ears throb. The long, wooden bar, to the side, was crowded with drinkers; and beyond it, the large dance floor was packed with dancers. Even the over-amplified music could not quite drown out the swell of voices.

Pushing through the standing crowd beside the bar, Steve led the way. Just as they reached the end of the bar near the dance floor, a couple got up from their seats. Casey saw them the same time Steve did, and they quickly grabbed the stools.

From here they had a view of the dance floor and the platform at the rear from which the band performed. Casey turned to study the scene. Most of the dancers were young, but here and there she could spot a few older people, even one or two grey heads. Everyone was dressed to some degree in Western style, lots of stetsons, jeans, cowboy shirts and boots. Everyone seemed to be having a wonderful time.

The band was young, long-haired and good; although Casey would have enjoyed the music more if they had turned the amps down a bit. At this volume it was difficult to hear anything clearly. Next time she came to a place like this, she'd bring her soft ear plugs.

150

She felt Steve touch her arm, and she turned back. Steve leaned forward, placed his mouth almost against her ear, and shouted: 'What will you have?'

Casey thought a moment, then shouted back: 'A tall vodka and tonic, with lime.'

As she spoke, she saw a tall woman coming towards her behind the bar, and recognized Myrtle Carter.

Myrtle leaned towards them, shouting: 'Well, if it isn't my two favourite cops. What brings you two in here? Just having a little break?'

'Yeah. Sort of,' Steve bellowed back.

'Well, what can I get you?'

'A Bud lite and a tall vodka tonic.'

In a few minutes Myrtle was back with the drinks. She set them down just as the musicians finished a number, and for a moment the sound level faded to bearable. Myrtle put her elbows on the bar and gave Casey a stern look. 'You know, Farrel, I should be mad at you.'

Casey took a sip of her drink. 'Why is that?'

'Because Tag took off like a fat-assed bird for parts unknown right after your visit. He took off on that old beat-up dirt bike of his.'

'I'm sorry, Myrtle. I really am. But he shouldn't have done that. It makes people wonder if he has something to hide.'

Myrtle shrugged and grinned. 'Well, no need for tears. I was getting tired of him, anyway. But his leaving doesn't mean that he had anything to do with Buck's death. Tag is just a mite skittish around cops of any kind.'

Steve leaned his elbows on the bar. 'Where did he go, Myrtle?'

'Got no idea.'

'Maybe we should put out an APB on him.'

Myrtle shrugged. 'That's his problem, not mine.'

'Have you thought any more about who may have killed Buck?' Casey asked.

'Yeah, I've thought about it; but no one comes to mind.'

Steve said, 'How well did you know Red Pollock, Myrtle?'

'Not very well.'

'Did he come in here a lot?'

'When he had the money. I guess every bartender on the Row knew old Red. But why are you asking about him? I heard he was shot, but what has that got to do with Buck?'

'We're not sure, Myrtle, but we think the two killings may be connected.'

Myrtle frowned. 'What the hell is the town coming to? Maybe I should follow Tag's example and split. Look, I got to get back to work, can't let Bessie handle it all.'

With a nod, she moved away, muttering.

Steve turned to Casey. 'Excuse me for a sec, Casey. I'm going to call the station and get that APB out on Taggert.'

'Do you think that's justified?'

'Yeah. It'll just be a "wanted for questioning". Be back in a minute.'

As Steve moved away into the crowd, the band started up again, and Casey felt a touch on her elbow. She turned to see Hank Wilder, the rodeo clown, standing beside her, a nearly empty glass in his hand.

'Casey,' he shouted. 'I'm surprised to see you here. Taking a night off, are you?'

Casey looked at him with an experienced eye. His features, beneath the worn stetson he was wearing, looked a bit slack. He appeared to be about half in the bag, but seemed to be in control.

'How are you?' she asked, as he leaned close to hear her answer.

'Fine. In fact, better than fine; I'm well on my way to getting sloshed.'

Casey smiled. 'What's the cause for celebration?'

'No real cause. Do you mind?' He slipped on to Steve's stool.

'It's just that from time to time, when I feel a bit depressed, I feel the need. I know that alcohol is a depressant, but I always feel better after a good drunk. I do this three or four times a year. In between, I'm a model citizen.' He winked.

Casey nodded. 'Well, whatever works; as long as your liver holds out.'

He seemed to find this amusing. 'How are you doing on the case? Any leads yet?'

'Nothing firm. I suppose you'll be leaving town soon?'

He shook his head. 'I thought I'd stay around a while longer. There's nothing at the ranch that needs my attention, and I'd really like to see how this thing comes out.'

He looked into his near empty glass. 'I've been thinking of giving up the circuit. I'm getting a bit old for all of this.'

He smiled, but the expression was sad. 'Listen to me – getting maudlin – well, don't they say that beneath the surface, all clowns are sad?'

He drained the last of his drink. 'Well, better be on my way. When I get to this stage it's time to leave civilized company. Oh, hello, Sergeant: I was just saying hello and goodbye.'

Steve nodded as Wilder slipped from his stool, tipped his stetson, and turned away.

Steve took his place on the stool. 'What was all that about?'

Casey shook her head. 'I'm not quite sure.'

'Well, then, let's do what we came to do, Farrel, let's hit the rest of the bars.'

The next two bars they visited were much like the first, rowdy and noisy, and everyone having a great time.

It was in the third bar – a bit quieter than the previous three – that they hit pay dirt. They were at the bar and Steve had just ordered a beer for him and a designer water for Casey, who felt she had had her quota of alcohol.

After the bartender had served them, Steve asked him, 'Did you know Buck Farrel?'

The man nodded.

'Did he come in here much?'

'Sure, Buck came in,' the bartender said. 'Used to see him in here once a week at least.' He shook his head. 'Sad, what happened to him, isn't it?'

'Yes, it is. I'm Sergeant Randall, Prescott Police, and this is Casey Farrel, from the Governor's Task Force on Crime. We're investigating the murders of Buck and Red Pollock.'

The bartender's eyes widened. 'Are the two connected?' He shook his head. 'Why, Red was in here the night he was killed. I remember because I'd never seen Red so up, and he seemed to have plenty of money! Believe me, that wasn't the usual thing with him.'

Steve glanced at Casey, then back to the bartender. 'He didn't happen to tell you where the money came from, did he?'

The bartender shook his head. 'Nope. I was curious about that, but he wasn't saying, and I had a lot of customers that night.'

'What about Buck? Do you remember the last time he was in here?'

The bartender thought for a moment. 'It must have been about a week before he died.'

'Did you notice anything different about him? Did he seem depressed, or angry, or maybe afraid?'

'Nothing unusual that I remember. He was the usual Buck, drinking up a storm, laughing, having fun.'

'Did anyone come in with him, a woman maybe?'

154

'Not that night. Uh . . . sorry, folks, customer down the bar needs a refill, be back when I can.'

The bartender, wearing a look of relief, hurried down the bar. The moment he was out of hearing, the man two stools down from Casey moved to the stool next to hers.

In a low voice he said to Casey: 'I overheard you asking about Red Pollock.'

Casey turned to face him. The man was of slight stature, balding, probably in his early fifties, with watery blue eyes. His breath was rank with the scent of whisky. Casey turned her head slightly, took a deep breath, then turned back to him. 'That's right, we were. Did you know Red?'

'I knew him well enough to drink with. I saw him in here the night he was killed. He was pretty looped.'

Casey's pulse rate accelerated. Reaching behind her, she pulled on the sleeve of Steve's shirt. He slid from his stool, and moved so that he was standing near both her and the little man.

'Around nine, or thereabouts,' the man said. He flicked a worried glance at Steve, and then looked back at Casey. 'I'm Tim Simmons. I work up at the Chevron station. I know who you two are.'

Casey nodded. 'You say he came in about nine, what time did he leave?'

'At five minutes to ten.'

'How can you be so certain?'

'Cause Red said that someone was picking him up on the Gurley Street side of the square at ten sharp.'

Steve interjected. 'Did he say who he was meeting?'

'I asked, but he wouldn't say. He was real secretive, and that wasn't like Red.'

'He didn't say whether it was a man or a woman?'

Simmons shook his head. 'Nope.' He thought a moment. 'There is one other thing I noticed. At about nine-thirty,

Red went to the pay phone to make a call. It was after he came back that he told me he was being picked up.'

Casey said: 'Did he talk about anything else?'

Simmons nodded. 'He had a lot of money on him, and when I asked him where he got it, he played real cagey, but he did say that there was more where that came from. I got the feeling that the money was a payoff of some kind.'

'Did he happen to mention the murder of Buck Farrel?'

'Yeah, he did. He said that it was too bad about what happened to Buck, but I don't really think he meant it, cause he was grinning when he said it. Of course he was pretty pissed by that time, grinning like a fool at everything.'

'Did he say anything else?'

'Only that he was going to buy a new house trailer.'

Steve said musingly, 'He must have been expecting some big bucks then.'

'That's what I said. Red just rolled his eyes and said that I didn't know the half of it.'

Casey said, 'Do you happen to know how well Pollock knew Buck?'

Simmons shrugged. 'Not real well, would be my guess. They didn't exactly run in the same circles. Buck was in the bars all the time, and Red only came in when he had a few dollars in his jeans, and that wasn't often.'

'Well, thanks for your information, Mr Simmons,' Steve said. 'I'll need a signed statement from you relating to what you've told us.'

'Fine. Any time. Glad to help. I can drop by the station tomorrow during my lunch break. That okay with you?'

'That will be fine, Mr Simmons.' Steve touched Casey on the arm. 'Let's move along, Casey.'

They didn't speak until they were outside the bar, then they both tried to speak at once. Casey broke off, laughing, then said: 'It's beginning to look like

you were right. The two deaths are probably connected.'

'It certainly looks like old Red was mixed up in
something shady; and it may well have had something to
do with Buck's death; but it's not exactly hard evidence.
Still, I know what you mean. It all fits so nicely. In some
way or other Red has knowledge of who killed Buck, and
is blackmailing the killer. Bad move. Killer offs Red.'

Casey sighed. 'It works for me. But I know we need
proof. Do you suppose there's a chance that someone
saw Red take his meeting in the square?'

Steve shrugged. 'Who knows; we might get lucky. It
seems to me we're about due. You know, sometimes
police work reminds me of that legend about the king
who was condemned to roll a huge rock up a hill in
Hades.'

'Sisyphus.'

'Yeah, that was the guy – terrible name, isn't it?
Anyway, that's how I feel about my work sometimes.'

Casey laughed and took his arm. 'Come on, Steve, a
cop's life isn't *that* bad.'

'Maybe not. Maybe I haven't had enough beers, or
maybe too many.' He steered her into the next saloon.
'Speaking of which, you go try to find us a seat at the
bar. I have to make a short pit stop.'

Casey walked the length of the bar and finally found
one stool, which she took. When the bartender came,
she ordered a beer for Steve and a coffee for herself.

She was thinking back over what they had learned from
Simmons, when she felt a rough hand on her shoulder
and heard a harsh voice in her ear: 'I want to know
what the hell you were doing talking to Lissa today! I
saw you!'

Getting a bad feeling, Casey looked around into the
red, angry face of Barney Dyce. Whisky fumes came off
him in waves and he was weaving slightly.

'You'll have to ask Melissa about that,' she said steadily.

'I'm asking you,' he muttered. 'Goddamned government snoop coming around nosing into things that don't concern you. What did she tell you? I want to know.'

'Melissa came to me, Barney; I didn't go to her. What she told me was in confidence, and I can't and won't tell you what it was.'

'Then I'll by God shake it out of you!'

Face contorted with rage, Barney crowded against Casey, pinning her against the bar. Her gun was in her shoulder bag, but she didn't reach for it. She couldn't use it in a crowd like this. Looking around, she saw that no one seemed to consider what was going on anything out of the ordinary.

Suddenly, music blasted on, and Barney's next words were blotted out, as he reached out, grabbed her arms, and shook her so violently that her teeth clicked together.

FOURTEEN

Acting reflexively, Casey clenched her teeth and forcefully raised her right knee. Three things happened simultaneously: Barney gasped in pain; his hands released her arms; and Steve's voice boomed out: 'What the hell's going on here?'

Barney, bent over in pain, only groaned. Casey gave a quick look around; evidently only a few people had witnessed what had happened, and they did not seem inclined to interfere.

Casey turned to Steve. 'Barney here was getting a little physical. I had to stop him.'

Steve frowned. 'Did he hurt you?'

She felt her neck. 'I don't think so.'

'My God, the bitch has crippled me!' Barney moaned, clutching himself.

'Watch your mouth, Barney. We're going to the station. I'm booking you.'

'You can't do that!' Barney grunted, breathing hard. 'Book her. I'm the one who's hurt! I just shook her up a little. That's no reason to book a man.'

'It is in my book. I'm taking you in for drunk and disorderly and for assaulting an officer.'

'She ain't no real officer,' Barney grunted. 'She's just a government snoop, dogging our family for no reason!'

'She has a reason, Barney, and you well know it. You're going to spend the night in jail, my friend. We can't have you banging around town in your pickup in your condition. Where is your pickup anyway?'

'Parked out back.' Barney slumped in Steve's grip, as all the belligerence drained out of him.

'Is it locked?'

'No.'

'Then let me have the keys. We'll lock it, and you can pick it up when you get out.'

'The keys are in the car,' Barney mumbled.

Steve looked at Casey and shook his head. 'Casey, will you lock the truck, while I watch Junior here? I think you know the truck.'

'Yeah,' Casey said drily, 'I believe I do.'

'We'll wait for you in the car.'

Casey opened the door to Buck's pickup on the driver's side. She was immediately struck by a miasma of odours: booze; tobacco; stale food; and something that she didn't even want to speculate about.

Her eyes swept the interior of the cab. It was still littered with empty beer cans, the near-empty whisky bottle and empty fast food cartons.

Wrinkling her nose, she reached for the keys in the ignition, pulled them free, then hesitated, looking around. There was no one in sight.

Quickly, she slid into the driver's seat and reached for the door to the glove compartment. It was unlocked. She opened it and drew in her breath. There, illuminated by the compartment light and nestled in a nest of maps and loose paper was a gun. Closer inspection showed it to be a .22 pistol – the type of gun used to kill Red Pollock.

Leaning forward, but being careful not to touch the weapon, she took a deep breath and inhaled the faint odour of cordite.

Feeling a surge of pure excitement, she drew back and again glanced around. Still no one in sight.

Quickly, she slid out of the cab and locked the door. They would have to have a search warrant. Since Steve had arrested Barney inside the bar, probable cause might not be enough, and she didn't want to take any chances on this.

Pocketing the keys, she hurried back to where Steve had parked his car. Steve was standing beside the vehicle, leaning against the right front fender. She could not see Barney, who was evidently already inside the car.

She strode up to Steve, struggling to keep her excitement under control, and pulled him away from the car. 'What is it?' he said.

'How hard would it be to get a warrant to search Barney's pickup, Steve?'

He gave her a sharp glance. 'Why?'

'I think it should be tossed. Take my word for it.'

'You saw something while you were locking the car?'

'Let's just say I have a feeling we might turn up something.'

'A feeling, nothing more?' He held up a hand. 'Never mind, I don't think I want to know.'

He thought for a moment. 'It shouldn't be too difficult. Are the beer cans and the open bottle still in the cab?'

She nodded. 'Well, with the drunk and disorderly and assault on an officer, I think we have enough to search it without a warrant.'

Casey shook her head. 'I'd like to play this very safe. If we find something, I don't want it declared inadmissible.'

Steve shrugged. 'Another feeling, huh? Well, suit yourself. I'll radio for another unit to watch the truck while we take Barney in, then we'll hop over to the judge's house. He probably won't be thrilled to see us at this hour, but he's usually cooperative. He likes to get the scum off the streets, too.'

*　　*　　*

161

An hour later, they were back in the parking lot with the search warrant. The officer who had been called to watch the pickup was leaning against his patrol car. He came to attention as Steve got out of the car.

'Anybody come nosing around, Denton?'

'Nope. A few people came and went.' He grinned. 'Most of them gave us a wide berth,' he said, pointing at the patrol car.

'Good.' Steve pulled the warrant out of his pocket, and showed it to patrolman. 'I want you and Casey to witness this toss. I want everything nice and legal in case we find anything.'

Casey and the officer stood aside as Steve, using a small flashlight, started the search. He went first to the glove compartment, as if reading Casey's mind.

'Well now, how about this?' he whistled softly. Taking a pen from his pocket, he reached into the glove compartment and backed out of the cab with a pistol dangling from the trigger guard. He looked at Casey. 'A feeling, huh? Yeah, right!' He looked down at the pistol. 'A .22, same calibre that did Red Pollock. Want to bet against it being the same gun?'

He took a plastic bag from his pocket, sealed the gun in it, and handed it to Casey. Then he continued the search of the pickup cab.

While probing under the seat, he emitted a grunt. He pulled back and turned towards Casey, holding out a small object wrapped in a tissue. He shone the light on the object so Casey could see it. The object was a small vial with a few drops of fluid inside. Casey leaned forward. The smell of bitter almonds was unmistakable.

She straightened and shook her head. 'He couldn't be *that* stupid, could he?'

Steve chuckled. 'It's possible. I've known murderers to do dumber things. Sometimes, it's as if they *want* to

162

be caught. Anyway, if this is what it appears to be, I'd say that we have our killer.'

Casey stepped back, her gaze riveted on the vial, as Steve dropped it into another envelope. Could it really be this easy? Was it really all over?

Steve touched her arm. 'Come on, Casey. Denton, you stay here and keep an eye on things. I'll send a tow truck to take the truck to the station so that the lab people can go over it more thoroughly. Who knows what else they may come up with?'

An hour later Steve had Barney Dyce brought into an interrogation room at the station. Barney was reasonably sober now, but he was still belligerent and sullen.

'You have no right to arrest me!' he said immediately.

'We have every right, Barney.' Steve motioned to an empty chair across from where Casey was sitting at a small table.

Barney, eyeing them suspiciously, sidled around the table and sat down. He stared angrily at the tape recorder on top of the table.

Steve seemed relaxed and casual. Casey felt far from relaxed, but she was beginning to believe that they had their killer. The .22 found in the glove compartment hadn't been tested yet, but the vial definitely held cyanide. Both the gun and the vial had been wiped clean of fingerprints.

Steve said, 'You have the right to have a lawyer present while we question you. Do you wish to have a lawyer present, Barney?'

Barney glowered at him. 'Why in hell would I need a lawyer? I ain't done nothing. Sure, I'll admit that I had a little too much to drink, but so what? You start arresting everybody on the Row that's had too much to drink, and you won't have room in the jail!'

'This has gone way beyond your being drunk and disorderly and assaulting Ms Farrel.'

Barney's eyes went wide, and a flicker of fear showed. 'What do you mean?'

Steve picked up the attaché case that had been resting near his feet and put it on the table. Opening it, he took from it the .22 pistol and the vial, still in their envelopes.

Barney gazed at them in fascination. Steve said, 'We performed a search of your vehicle, Barney. In the glove compartment, we found this.' He indicated the pistol. 'The vial, which contains cyanide, we found under the seat.'

Barney's eyes grew wider still, and his face paled. 'I ain't never seen that gun in my life, nor that bottle. What are you trying to pull?'

Casey leaned forward. 'Then how did they get in your pickup, Barney?'

He shook his head wildly. 'I don't know, I swear.'

'When was the last time you had your glove compartment open?'

'I don't know.' He frowned. 'Must've been months ago, best I can remember.'

'And under the seat, when was the last time you looked there?'

He gave her a look of disdain. 'Who the hell looks under their seat unless they've lost something? All I know is that I never saw that gun nor that bottle before. For all I know you put them there!'

Steve shook his head. 'The car was searched in front of witnesses, under a warrant.'

'That don't mean nothing,' Barney said stubbornly. 'It could have been done before. Hell, I never locked the thing. Ask anybody.'

Casey interrupted. 'It was common knowledge that you didn't keep your truck locked?'

'Hell, yes.'

Steve said, 'Still, it's your truck, and that's where these items were found. I'm afraid that's more than enough for us to charge you, Barney. Why don't you make it easy on us all, and admit it?'

'Admit what? Charge me with what?'

Steve leaned forward. 'With murder, Barney. Murder in the first degree of Buck Farrel and Red Pollock. You killed Buck because your families had been feuding, and because he'd been dating your sister, and you couldn't stand that. You killed Red because he either saw what you did to Buck, or because he had some other evidence of what you had done. He tried to blackmail you, and you killed him.'

The colour had completely left Barney's face now. The sudden blow of his fists upon the table caused Casey to jump. 'No!' he shouted; then he slumped in his chair. 'Ain't I allowed a phone call? I'm not saying another word until I get my phone call.'

Steve sat back with a sigh. 'So you've decided you want an attorney after all.'

'No. I want to call my daddy,' Barney said sullenly.

Steve got up from his chair. 'Okay, Barney. I'll arrange it.'

A half hour later Darrel Dyce roared into the station, his face red with anger, his little eyes blazing. Casey and Steve, expecting him, were waiting for him in the small room off the reception area.

Dyce stormed up to the reception counter and hammered on it with his fist. 'Where's my boy? Where's my Barn?'

Steve stepped out of room into Dyce's line of sight. 'In here, Mr Dyce, where we can talk quietly, more or less. No need to rouse the whole station.'

Dyce spun around and stalked over to Steve, getting

165

right in his face. 'I demand to know what you bastards have done with my boy!'

'Your "boy", Darrel, is locked up. Now, unless you want the whole station to know your business, I suggest you step in here.'

Steve turned away and, after a moment, Dyce followed him into the room. Steve closed the door.

Hands on hips, Dyce stood glowering at Casey. 'You! I might have known you'd be behind this! Why are you persecuting my boy?'

Casey looked at him calmly. 'Your son attacked me, Mr Dyce. In a public place, in front of witnesses.'

'He was drunk and disorderly, Darrel,' Steve added. 'And a search of his vehicle led to the discovery of what we think may be the murder weapon used to kill Red Pollock, as well as the type of poison used to kill Buck Farrel.'

For an instant a heavy silence hung in the air, then Darrel Dyce pulled himself together. 'What are you saying?'

'That I believe that Barney killed both Buck Farrel, and Red Pollock.'

Dyce's face turned dark. 'The hell you say! My boy never killed no one.'

'The evidence says otherwise. He had motive, he had the opportunity, and now we've discovered the means.'

Dyce stood as if stunned, and for a moment Casey felt sorry for the man. He was mean as a bobcat, but presumably even bobcats cared about their offspring.

'You people are loco!' Dyce seemed on the verge of a heart attack. 'This is all some kind of conspiracy! I'll sue you! I'll sue the city!'

A knock on the door interrupted him. Steve held up a hand to stay Dyce's invective, and opened the door.

'See you for a minute, Steve?' said a man's voice from outside the room.

Steve went out, closing the door behind him.

Dyce, his jaw clenched, stepped closer to Casey's chair. 'Now you listen to me, young lady. I'd advise you to drop this whole matter and take your nosy self back to Phoenix. Don't, and you're going to regret it, you can be damned sure of that!' He worked his mouth, as if in search of a place to spit. 'Don't think I don't know that you're behind all this. You leave, and the local cops will stop hassling my boy.'

Anger flooded Casey. This man simply would not see what was going on. She stood suddenly, forcing him to move back a step.

'I should think that by now you would know that I do not intimidate easily, Mr Dyce. And you might as well drop the ridiculous idea that if I leave, this will all be forgotten. Your son is in deep trouble, Mr Dyce. The evidence we found tonight makes it look very bad for Barney. The probable murder weapons have been found in his truck; he has assaulted a law officer, twice. I think it's time that you performed a reality check, Mr Dyce. There are some things a father can't fix!'

Dyce glared at Casey murderously, opened his mouth to speak, then closed it again, as Steve reentered the room looking triumphant.

'Talk about timing! The gun found in your son's pickup, Mr Dyce, has just been test-fired. The bullet found in Red Pollock was definitely fired from that .22. I think you should get an attorney for Barney, Dyce. We're charging him with first-degree murder.'

Darrel Dyce paled.

At last, Casey thought, he's beginning to get the picture.

'I'm going to get him out one way or another,' Dyce said in a trembling voice. 'You wait and see. And both

167

of you are going to live to regret framing my boy. You're going to regret ever having heard the name Dyce!'

FIFTEEN

It was nearly two o'clock when Casey finally got away from the station. Darrel Dyce had called his attorney and had him come to the station, to no avail. Barney Dyce had been booked on two charges of first-degree murder and locked in a cell. His bail hearing was set for the next day.

Steve walked Casey out to her Cherokee. As she unlocked the door, he said: 'Look, Casey. I hate to sound like a nag, but I want you to be careful.'

Casey studied his face; it was serious, and so was his tone of voice. 'Well, sure,' she said. 'I always try to be.'

'I know, but I mean extra careful. Old Darrel seems to have calmed down for the moment, but he's erratic and obsessive. He's got this idea that you, personally, are out to do his boy harm, and he's liable to act accordingly. Stay out of his way, and if you do run into him, watch your back.' He hesitated. 'I've grown very fond of you, Casey, and I'd hate to see you hurt. Incidentally, what are your plans now? Will you be going back to Phoenix right away?'

Casey, suddenly aware of how near he was standing, experienced a wave of confusion. Was he, or was he not coming on to her?

She moved slightly away from him. 'I haven't really had time to think about it yet; this all happened so suddenly. I suppose we'll stay on for a few days and finish our

169

•

vacation. I'd like to get better acquainted with my new relatives.'

His smile widened. 'Good! Maybe that'll give *us* time to become better acquainted.'

Casey wasn't certain how she should, or how she wanted to, respond to that, so she said: 'I don't know if my testimony will be required for Barney's trial.' She yawned suddenly. 'Wow, I just realized how beat I am, you'll have to excuse me.'

Steve stepped back as she keyed open the Cherokee. 'Yeah. I shouldn't keep you. Good night, Casey. Have a good night's sleep. You deserve it.'

'Good night, Steve. You, too.'

As she drove away she could see that he was still standing there in the parking lot, gazing after her.

Ordinarily, when Casey had wrapped up a case, she experienced a sense of satisfaction and exhilaration, and then a let-down. This time she felt the let-down, but little exhilaration. Although the evidence seemed clear, it just didn't feel right. She couldn't get rid of the nagging thought that, evidence be damned, Barney Dyce wasn't the killer.

She took three deep breaths to clear her mind, then punched on the tape deck, letting the music flow over her.

When she drove up before the Farrel ranch house, everything was dark. But, as she parked and got out of the Cherokee, a light came on downstairs. As she opened the front door, Dan Farrel stepped into the light spilling out of the study. He was wearing a robe and slippers.

He yawned hugely, stretching. She said amusedly, 'Waiting up for me, Uncle Dan?'

He grinned sheepishly. 'Well, not really. I had trouble sleeping, so I settled down with a bottle of brandy and a good book. I guess I dozed off.'

He stretched again, and Casey watched him, smiling.

170

He caught her eye, and his grin widened. 'All right, so you caught me. With all this stuff going on, I just wanted to be certain you got home safely.'

Casey put her hand on his arm and gave it an affectionate squeeze. 'It's been a long time since anyone has waited up for me. It's kind of nice. And I have some good news for you. It looks like we've got Buck's killer.'

Dan took a deep breath, and his face lit from within. 'Really? Are you sure?'

Casey hesitated, then nodded. 'Pretty sure. Of course, the court will have to decide guilt or innocence, but we have the evidence, and it seems open and shut.'

Dan seemed not to notice her hesitation. 'Come on into my study and tell me all about it. My God, it's such a relief. I don't suppose I'll ever get over Buck's death, and the sorrow will always be there; but knowing who killed him, and why, will let me put it to rest and go on. Do you understand what I mean?'

Casey nodded. 'I do indeed.'

She followed her uncle into the study, but turned when she heard the sound of small feet behind her. She turned to see Donnie in his Ninja Turtle Pyjamas standing behind her. He was rubbing his eyes sleepily.

'What are you doing down here, kiddo? What have we got here, a night watch for the return of Casey Farrel?'

'I heard the car door. It woke me up. And you didn't come upstairs!'

She leaned down and ruffled his already tousled hair. 'Well, you just get back to bed, kiddo.'

Donnie yawned. 'Aw, Casey, I heard what you just said to Uncle Dan. You never let me listen to the good stuff. I want to know who killed Buck, too.'

'Oh, all right,' she said with a sigh. 'I guess you're entitled. You'll hear sooner or later, anyway.'

She seated herself on the couch, and he snuggled against her, looking up at her expectantly.

171

Dan Farrel said impatiently, 'Come on, Casey, what happened?'

Casey smiled. Never had she had a more eager audience.

When she had finished her story, Dan struck his thigh. 'Damn those Dyces! They should all be wiped off the face of the earth, Darrel and both his whelps.'

Casey shook her head, shot him a warning glance, then turned to Donnie. 'He doesn't really mean that the way it sounds, Donnie. He's just very angry, understandably so.'

Dan swung his head angrily. 'I guess I know . . .' He bit his lip. 'Casey's right, boy. When a man gets real angry, he says a lot of things to release the pressure.'

'Besides,' Casey said. 'You shouldn't include Melissa. She's not a bad girl, just under the thumb of her father and brother. She's to be pitied, if anything – another victim.'

Dan was staring off into space, his eyes stricken. 'In a way, it's probably my fault, too. If I hadn't started that ruckus with Darrel over those damned water rights . . .'

Casey shook her head. 'You shouldn't blame yourself, Dan. There was a lot more to it than that.'

But Dan wasn't listening: he was somewhere deep within himself where grief and self-blame warred.

Donnie stirred against Casey's side. 'Now that you've caught the bad guy, Casey, are we going home?'

'I haven't had much time to think about it, kiddo, but I feel that I still have some vacation due, don't you?'

Donnie began to bounce. 'Yeah. We get to stay here?'

Casey put her hand on his shoulder. 'Don't bounce on the furniture. As for staying here, well, I guess that depends on Uncle Dan.'

Dan spoke up. 'Yes, please stay, Casey. Give us all the chance to become better acquainted.'

'Okay, we'll finish out the week,' Casey said. 'Thanks, Dan.'

Dan waved his hand. 'We should thank you. You and the boy have brought some life and excitement back into our lives. It's helped, having you here.'

Donnie began to bounce again, but when Casey put a firm hand on his shoulder, he stopped. 'Can we go riding tomorrow, Casey? You haven't been riding with me yet.'

'Whoa now.' She held up her hands. 'I never promised you I'd get on a horse.'

'Please, Casey. You'll like it.'

'We'll see.' Laughing, she got to her feet. 'And for your information, I *have* been on a horse before, but it's been a long time. It's just that horses and I have never gotten along too well. Now, it's time for you to get back to bed. It's late for a cowboy to be up.'

'Aw, cowboys stay up late. Don't they, Uncle Dan?'

Dan, more at ease with himself now, winked at Casey and said with a straight face. 'Only on weekends, boy. Only on weekends.'

Immediately after breakfast the next morning, Casey called Josh in Phoenix.

He seemed very pleased to hear her voice. 'Casey! How are you, babe?'

'I'm fine. It looks like the case is over.'

'You caught the guy, great!'

Casey had to smile. His voice was so full of pride.

'Well, I did have a little help, you know. Anyway, it looks like we've got him.' She went on to fill him in on what had been happening.

When she was finished, he said: 'Well, it sounds open and shut; so why do I get the feeling that you're not telling me everything?'

173

Casey smiled again. 'Just your naturally suspicious cop nature, I guess.'

She could almost see him shaking his head. 'No, not entirely. Your words say that you think you've caught the perp, but your tone says you're not sure. What gives?'

'You know me too well, Josh. I'm not sure if I like that.'

Josh laughed. 'Girl, as my daddy used to say, you'd kick if you were hanging with a new rope. What's a poor man to do? You women want us to be sensitive, and when we are, you think it's invasion of privacy.'

'Well, I can see that you've got us pegged all right. The thing is, everything is there: motive; opportunity; means; and yet it just doesn't feel right. I can't explain it.'

Josh sighed. 'I hate when that happens.'

Casey chuckled. 'Yeah, you have to go with the evidence, but there's that nagging doubt.'

'Well, it happens. By the way, how do you like working with that homicide dick, Randall?'

'Yeah, Steve Randall.'

'Is he good?'

'One of the best investigators I've worked with.'

'Is he . . . uh?' Josh cleared his throat. 'Is he married?'

'What does that have to do with anything? But no, he's divorced.'

'I see.'

Casey, seeing where this was going, began to feel annoyed. 'You see what?'

'Oh, nothing. I was just curious. Are you coming home now, Casey?'

'Not until the end of the week. I promised Donnie we'd stay till then, and I'd like to spend some time with my uncle and his wife.'

'Okay, I understand. Babe, remember something; remember that I love you.' And, with that flat declaration, he hung up.

Casey sat for a moment with her hand on the receiver, smiling slightly. Josh had a strong jealous streak. She really shouldn't needle him, as she sometimes did; it wasn't fair to him.

Donnie came boiling into the room. 'Who were you talking to? Josh?'

'That's right, kiddo.'

'Why didn't you tell me? I wanted to talk to him.'

'You were busy, doing whatever it is that cowboys do when they're down at the corrals.'

'Aw, Casey.'

'You can call him yourself, later.'

He took her hand, and tugged. 'Come on, Casey. You promised to ride with me this morning.'

'As I recall, I said "we'll see".'

'Come on, Casey. Your case is over, you can take time to have some fun.'

'I'm not all that sure that I'd classify riding a horse as fun.'

She got to her feet. 'But if I don't do it, you'll call me chicken, right?'

He grinned at her. 'Right!'

'Okay. Just let me change into a pair of jeans . . .'

The phone rang, and she picked up the receiver. 'Hello?'

'Casey? This is Steve.'

'Hi. Just a minute.' She cupped a hand over the receiver and waved at Donnie. 'Go on, Donnie. I'll meet you at the corral in a few minutes.'

Into the phone she said, 'Yes, Steve.'

'I'm just leaving to go over to Barney's bail hearing. I thought maybe we could meet for lunch, and I'll bring you up to date.'

Casey thought for a moment. It should work out time-wise. 'That sounds fine, Steve, if you don't make it too early.'

'How does one o'clock sound?'

'Fine.'

'Good, I'll meet you at the Gurley Street Bar and Grill at one then.'

The day was already quite warm, the sky a deep and cloudless blue. As protection against the high-altitude summer sun, Casey slathered sun screen on herself and put on a wide-brimmed hat. She stuck the sun screen in her pocket, so she could put some on Donnie, and grabbed his hat also.

When she got to the corral, she found Donnie saddling his horse. Nearby, stood a taller animal already saddled, a dappled grey with a kindly expression. Casey wondered if she could trust the look, or if it held hidden intent.

Dan smiled down at Casey from the corral fence. 'Donnie's going to make a fine horseman. He's learning fast. But he needs some boots, real riding boots that can stand up to brush and mud and wear.'

Casey nodded. 'All right. Where's a good place to get them?'

'Well, if you wouldn't mind, I'd like to get them for him.'

Casey was about to protest, but then saw the pleading look on his face. She smiled. 'Well, if you insist.'

Dan grinned. 'Good. Buying boots for a boy is a man's job.'

Casey shook her head. Men!

Donnie, finished saddling Brownie, looked up at Casey proudly.

'Did you see? I did it all by myself.'

Casey nodded. 'I'm impressed. That's more than I can do.'

'Well, Uncle Dan saddled Bessie for you.' The words carried a freight of condescension, and Casey had to smile. 'Well, I appreciate that.'

176

'Now, watch me get on.'

Casey watched as he led the bay to a large crate next to the corral fence, and from there mounted the horse with monkey-like agility.

Casey turned to eye the grey, who stared back at her benignly.

'Well, let's see if I remember this: left side, left foot in stirrup,' she followed through with the physical act, 'then raise in stirrup, and swing right leg over . . .'

Donnie started to laugh. Casey had forgotten how much leg strength it took to hoist oneself from ground level up to horse level. Even though the grey was not a tall horse, it took two tries before she managed to hoist herself aboard, and she felt a little embarrassed in front of her uncle.

When she looked at Dan, he was smiling. 'Well, at least you're not laughing, like *some* people I could mention.'

'If you're not used to it, it's more difficult than it looks,' he said, still smiling. 'Now ride carefully. And Donnie, you remember all that I've told you, because Casey's going to give me a report. And Casey, you take it easy; don't go too far this first day or you won't be able to sit down for dinner tonight, if you know what I mean.'

Casey nodded. 'We'll be careful.' She reached over and patted the grey's neck. 'She seems gentle.'

'Well, both horses are past their prime, but they're good for kids or novice riders. Clint's kids ride them.' He frowned. 'That is, when Clint brings them out here. Those stirrups all right for you?'

Casey moved her feet, then nodded.

'Remember, heels down, grip with the knees, but not too hard. Okay then, away you go.'

Donnie gave a gentle cluck, moved his feet in his stirrups, gave his reins a shake, and Brownie moved out at a slow walk.

Casey followed Donnie's example, and Bessie followed Brownie. She risked a glance back over her shoulder. Dan Farrel stood by the open gate, staring after them. He looked, she thought, proud and lonely. Recalling his comment about Clint's children, Casey wondered, not for the first time, if she should tell Dan that Melissa Dyce was carrying his grandchild. Buck's child could go a long way towards easing the pain that Dan felt, but did she have the right? Maybe she should ask Melissa first and see how she reacted to the idea.

Brownie had picked up speed, and Donnie was a good distance ahead of her now. She shouted, 'Hey, kiddo, slow it down, okay? This is the first time I've been on a horse in years.'

Donnie, grinning back over his shoulder, shouted, 'Don't be a weenie, Casey. Make Bessie go faster.'

Grumbling, Casey did as she was bid, noticing, that despite herself, she was enjoying the ride. Bessie had a smooth gait, and Casey was remembering things she had thought she had forgotten. She felt surprisingly comfortable in the big, Western saddle.

In a few moments she had caught up with Brownie, and Bessie automatically slowed so that the two animals were side by side.

'I trust you know where you're taking me,' Casey said.

Donnie looked at her reproachfully. 'Of course. We're going to the pond. It's in a neat little valley with oak trees and all. It's real pretty. You'll like it. When Uncle Dan and I go there he lets me swim in the pond. It's not real deep.'

'It seems that you and Uncle Dan are getting along pretty well.'

'Yeah.' Donnie's grin was shy. 'He's neat. Sort of like a grandpa, you know?'

Casey nodded. Her throat suddenly felt tight. Before

178

she and Josh had taken Donnie in, the boy had known little of conventional family life. Raised by an uncaring aunt and her live-in lovers, he had experienced emotional and physical deprivation. It was amazing, but he had come through the experience relatively unmarked. His native intelligence, good nature and practicality had seen him through. He was a real survivor.

The little valley proved to be all that Donnie had promised. The pond – more like a small lake – was blue with reflected sky, and the big, old oaks stood around it like an enclave of Druids. One of the oaks reached a thick branch over the water, and from the branch hung a knotted rope.

They dismounted under one of the trees and tied up the horses. Immediately, Donnie began to strip off his clothes. 'Hey, pardner, wait a minute. What are you doing?' Casey said.

'Going swimming,' Donnie replied with a grin. 'I put my shorts on under my clothes.'

'Are you sure it's safe?'

He grinned, pulling off a sock. 'Heck, Casey, there's no sharks or anything, just catfish and bass, Uncle Dan says. Come on, you come in, too.'

She gave him a look of mock severity. 'Well, I would, if you'd told me where we were going, so that I could have worn a suit.'

He stopped, sock in hand, his face full of dismay. 'Oh, gee. I'm sorry, Casey, I didn't think. Maybe you could go in your underwear. There's nobody here but us.'

Casey shook her head. 'No thanks, I don't want some cowboy riding up and catching me in my skivvies. You go ahead, but be careful.'

He expression cleared. 'Thanks, Casey. You're the best.'

In a moment he was out of his clothes, all thin brown arms and legs and bright red swimming trunks. She watched him head for the water at a run. He was a thin child, but well muscled and nicely proportioned. He would be a handsome man someday. Casey sighed, thinking of all that he must be taught so that he would become a good man as well.

Settling herself under one of the oaks, she watched him as he swung on the rope, yelling like Tarzan, then dropped with a splash into the water. She yawned, feeling suddenly sleepy. Her sleep had been interrupted last night by a dream, a nightmare really, which had wakened her and left her with a bad feeling.

She frowned now, thinking about it. At first the dream was pleasant; she was standing in a wide meadow inhabited by placid cows and horses. Then, abruptly, it had turned dark, as a black bull appeared. The animal's eyes were red, and it pawed the earth. She had known he was going to charge, but she was powerless to move, even as he came towards her. And still she stood frozen. Then, with the seeming rightness of dream logic, she knew that she would be saved. The clown would save her. And there the clown was, with his red cape, drawing the bull away, and everyone was clapping, Uncle Dan and Aunt Alice, all of Buck's girlfriends, even the Dyces. So she clapped, too, and the clown turned and looked at her, and he had no eyes, just black holes in his painted face, and she had felt such fear!

She shook her head. Dreams were fascinating, and sometimes they even made sense, in an elliptical way; but she could make no sense of this one, except for the connection with the fake rodeo clown.

She glanced at her watch. She would give Donnie a half hour in the water, then they would have to get back, if she was to meet Steve in town at one.

Steve was waiting for her at the grill. After they had been shown to a table and had given their orders,

Casey said, 'Well, tell me what happened at the hearing.'

'The judge denied bail,' Steve said with satisfaction. 'When he heard the charges, including the fact that Barney attacked you twice, he ruled that Barney represents a threat to the community.'

'How did Barney take it?'

'Sullenly, as usual; but his old man sure raised a stink. He went wild. They had to remove him from the courtroom.'

The waitress came with their food. Casey was hungry; the fresh air and the horseback ride had given her an appetite, and she dug into her pasta for a few moments before she spoke again.

'I still find it hard to believe that even Barney is stupid enough to keep two murder weapons in his truck, where – if he is telling the truth about his truck usually being unlocked – anybody might find them.'

Steve shook his head. 'It happens. All murderers aren't Hannibal Lecters, you know. A lot of them don't think logically. How about that woman who tried to kill her husband, but couldn't get it right? They made a movie about it with Kevin Kline and Tracey Ullman. I don't remember all the details, but the wife found out the husband had been unfaithful, and tried to kill him several different ways, none of which worked. Finally, she shot him; but he didn't die, so she just let him lie there. Really weird. As I said, I don't remember all the details, but he lived, and he forgave her!

'Then there was that case in San Diego, where a young Marine wife solicited several other Marines to kill her husband. Not only that, but she talked about it to a lot of people. After a few tries – these guys couldn't get it right either – they finally killed the poor guy. The unbelievable part is that this woman didn't seem to realize that if you're contemplating murder, it's not real smart to tell all your friends about your plans. And

181

then there was that Amy Fisher business, really bizarre. I could go on and on.'

Casey nodded. 'Point taken. But I still don't feel comfortable about this one.' She shrugged. 'And I can't really tell you why.'

They ate for a bit in silence, then Steve glanced at his watch. 'I have to run, Casey. I have a busy day today. I have to finish up the paper work on Barney, as well as a couple of other cases.'

He looked at her intently. 'You going to be around for a few days then?'

'Yes. Until the end of the week.'

'Then, how about dinner and maybe a movie one night before you go?'

She hesitated. 'I don't know, Steve. I'm not sure it's a good idea.'

'Think about it, okay? I'll call you.'

It was about three o'clock when Casey got back to the ranch. Dan's pickup was parked in front of the house. She got out of the Cherokee, and looked toward the corral to see if Dan and Donnie were there.

She saw Dan, throwing a saddle on a high-standing buckskin. Donnie was nowhere in sight. Vaguely disquieted, without knowing why, she started toward the corral.

As she reached the gate, Dan looked up and saw her. He stopped what he was doing, and hurried towards her. 'Casey, am I glad you're here. Donnie is missing! I was just going to look for him.'

'Missing?' she said in alarm. 'What do you mean?'

'Just that. I took him into Chino. I had to pick up some things, and we bought him some boots. When we got back about an hour ago, I felt like a nap, so I left him helping Alice peel apples. She says they finished that and he went outside to play. When I got up from my nap

I went looking for him, and couldn't find him. Alice is frantic.'

The pasta that Casey had eaten for lunch became a cold weight in her stomach. 'But where could he be?' she said. The words sounded foolish in her ears.

'He usually hangs out here at the corral, so that's where I came looking for him. Then I saw Brownie there.' He jerked his head toward the small bay who stood, saddled, head hanging, inside the corral.

'When I spotted Brownie, he was coming from the direction of the pond, and Donnie wasn't on him. I've told the boy never to go riding alone, but . . .' He spread his hands. 'It was those new boots; he kept saying that he wanted to try them out, but I told him to wait until tomorrow. I'm sorry, Casey. I'd cut off my right . . .'

Casey waved his words away. 'It's not your fault, Dan. Let's not waste time, let's just find him. Maybe he was thrown and hurt. Maybe he's lying out there . . .'

Dan shook his head. 'Brownie's never thrown anyone yet, but if something scared him . . . Anyway, if Donnie's out there, I'll find him.'

Casey grabbed his arm. 'Wait, I'm going with you.'

Dan hesitated for only a moment, then: 'All right. Take Brownie, he's already saddled.'

SIXTEEN

A few minutes later Casey and Dan were riding at a canter towards the pond where Casey and Donnie had ridden this morning. Casey fought to hold back her panic and anger. Donnie was going to get a severe scolding as well as restrictions on his freedom for disobeying her and Dan's orders not to ride off alone. But, oh God, if he had been hurt . . .

There was a well-worn trail from the ranch to the pond, and Casey scanned both sides of it as they rode. Dan was doing the same. Casey flinched at the distant sight of every hummock and rock, thinking each time that one of them might be Donnie's small, still body.

But they reached the pond and the grove of oaks without seeing the boy. They reined in at the pond and both Dan and Casey shouted Donnie's name. There was no response. They dismounted, and Dan, head down, began covering the ground around the pond and under the trees. Casey followed his footsteps, but being inexperienced at tracking, could make little sense of what she saw.

Dan stopped abruptly, and Casey almost ran into him. 'The boy was here. Those are the prints of his new boots.' He pointed a finger at the damp earth near the water's edge. 'And those are Brownie's hoofprints!'

Casey clasped her hand to her mouth, as she looked at the water. 'Oh, God, Dan, do you suppose?'

He put his hand on her arm. 'No. No, girl, he's not in the pond. See here? Here are other bootprints, man-sized,

184

and the hoofprints of another horse, right alongside. Someone else was here the same time as Donnie. Look, you can see where he struggled with the boy!'

Casey looked and saw a mishmash of footprints. She scanned the ground around them, slowly, then suddenly froze, feeling the fine hairs along her back rise as if touched by an icy finger. She heard her uncle's voice only vaguely: 'Somebody took the boy, but the ground here is some churned up. I can't make out which way his horse came or went.'

Casey looked up. 'That doesn't matter, Dan. I know who took Donnie! See that?' She pointed to a large, brown stain in one of Donnie's footprints. 'That's tobacco juice, and I'll bet you anything I have that it came from Darrel Dyce. Darrel Dyce took Donnie!'

Dan squinted at her. 'You're right. I know you are. His rotten son killed my boy, and now, because you've caught the little slime ball, he's taken Donnie. I always knew the bastard was crazy, but to kidnap a child! I'll kill the bastard, so help me I will!'

Casey put her hand on his arm. 'No, Dan. Calm down. We have to think this through. We can't just go barging over there; Dyce will have him hidden, and he'll just deny everything.'

'But he could hurt the boy!'

Casey shook her head. 'I don't think he took Donnie to hurt him. Dyce may be crazy, but he's clever in his way. No, I think he took Donnie for a reason, perhaps as a hostage for Barney's release. If that's true, we should hear from him soon. Let's get back to the house.'

As they rode back to the ranch, Casey's thoughts turned to the judge in Phoenix who had finally approved Donnie's adoption. One of the reasons she had been reluctant to do so was because of Casey's profession.

Casey had managed to persuade the judge that her job would not put the boy in jeopardy, that Donnie would be

185

safe in her care. Now it appeared that she had been wrong. Donnie was certainly at risk right now, and it was, just as certainly, because of her job.

As Casey and Dan rode up to the corral in a cloud of dust, Alice Farrel came out of the house, running toward them, calling, 'Casey!'

Dan dismounted first, and met his wife at the gate. 'What is it, hon? Word about the boy?'

She brushed past him. 'It's for you, Casey. A man on the phone, a Sergeant Randall. He called just as I saw you riding up. He's holding.'

Casey ran to the house and into the study. Snatching up the receiver she said, 'Steve? Is it about Donnie?'

'Well, yes,' he said. 'But how did you know?'

'In a minute. First, about Donnie, is he all right?'

'As far as we know, yes. Darrel Dyce has him.'

Casey grunted. 'I thought so. What does he want with him?'

'He wants to exchange him for Barney, all charges dropped.'

'But that's impossible!'

'I know, but I didn't want to tell him that. I tried to buy some time.'

'Dyce has gone around the bend, hasn't he?'

'I'd say so. When he called he was ranting and raving, nearly incoherent.'

'Does he have Donnie at his house?'

'Yes, and he's threatened to shoot him if we come on the premises. I'm sorry, Casey, but I thought you'd want it all laid out.'

'I do.'

'And he wants the media there, in front of his house, and the Governor. He wants the Governor to swear, in front of cameras, that Barney will be released in exchange for Donnie.'

Casey sighed. 'Doesn't want much, does he?'

186

'The whole nine yards.'

'So what did you tell him?'

'That we'd go along. I figured that would stall him while I called the Sheriff's Department and the State Police. I told them that it was a hostage situation. I also called a couple of Phoenix TV stations. Crews are on their way up. I told Dyce that I called the Governor, but that he's out of town, and it will be several hours before he can get here.'

'Is that true?'

'It's true that I called the Governor; but he's not out of town. He could come here, but there's no way he can do what Dyce wants. We figured that it was best to say that he was out of the city, and that it would take time for him to get here. That way we buy some more time.'

'Did Dyce swallow that?'

'I think so. I can be pretty convincing when I have to be.'

'So you've bought us some time. And after that?'

'We'll just have to play it by ear, Casey. A hostage negotiator is being flown in from Phoenix. Maybe after a few hours Dyce will calm down, and see reason.'

'Do you really believe that, Steve?'

'It's possible.'

'But not probable.'

'Maybe not, but we have to go with what we've got. I have to go, I'm heading out there right now. The state boys and the county men should already be there.'

'I'll see you there.'

'You'll probably beat me. Don't do anything foolish, Casey. We'll get him back, okay?'

'Okay.'

Casey hung up the phone, and turned in her chair. Dan was standing behind her, staring at her questioningly.

'I was right,' she said. 'Dyce has Donnie. He called the Prescott Police and told them he wants to exchange him for Barney, and a promise that Barney will not be prosecuted.'

Dan shook his head. His face reddened. 'The damn fool! Doesn't he know they can't promise him anything like that?'

Casey sighed. 'He's past reasoning with, Dan. He wants the Governor to appear on TV and make the promise. Steve told him that he was having trouble reaching the Governor, but that the TV people will be there soon. Steve hopes that will stall Dyce until the hostage negotiator gets here.'

Dan spread his hands helplessly. 'So what do we do now?'

'Head over to Dyce's ranch, and then we wait. As Steve says, we have to play it by ear, and hope for the best.'

They drove to the Dyce farm in Dan's pickup. Near the turn-off, they saw several police cars ahead and behind them. When they topped the rise and could see the ranch house, Casey saw that cars from various law enforcement agencies had circled it. Both uniformed and plainclothes men were sheltered by the cars or standing in groups a safe distance away from the house, talking and gesturing.

As Dan parked, Casey looked around for Steve, but she didn't see him anywhere. A man in a Yavapai County Sheriff's uniform approached the pickup as Dan and Casey got out.

'Do you have business here?' he demanded.

'I'm the boy's mother,' Casey said, 'Casey Farrel, and this is my uncle, Dan Farrel. Have you learned anything more? Is Donnie all right?'

'We assume so,' the officer said. 'We haven't yet tried to communicate with Dyce. We're waiting for the hostage negotiator, and Sergeant Randall . . . Oh, there's Randall now.'

Casey glanced up the road, and saw Steve's vehicle coming fast. He slowed to a stop behind the pickup, and slid out. He came up to them, nodding at the deputy, 'Hello, Gene. Anything happening?'

'Nope. I was just telling the lady, we've been waiting for you and the hostage guy.'

'I have a phone in my car, Casey. Let's go have a chat with Darrel, and see if he's calmed down.'

Casey went with Steve to his car, leaving Dan talking to the deputy. Casey watched impatiently as Steve punched out Dyce's number and waited for him to pick up the line. At last he nodded to Casey and spoke into the phone. 'Hello, Darrel, this is Sergeant Randall. I just called to give you a report on how things are . . .'

He pulled the phone away from his ear, and grimaced. 'Still raving,' he said to Casey, and then back into the phone: 'Yes, Darrel, the TV people are on the way, and the Governor has been notified. But, as I said before, it will take several hours for him to get here. We'll all just have to be patient and . . .'

Casey pulled at Steve's arm. 'Ask him if Donnie is okay.'

'Donnie's mother is with me, Darrel. She wants to know if Donnie's okay.' He listened for a moment, then said to Casey, 'He says the boy is fine.'

She pulled his sleeve again. 'Let me talk to him.'

'Casey wants to talk to you . . . Come on, what would it hurt? She's worried about her son.'

He handed the phone to Casey.

Before Casey could speak, Dyce was snarling in her ear, 'Now you listen here, girl. Your kid is okay, but he won't be for long if you don't do what I want. You want to see him get out of this alive, you convince those bastards to let my boy go. It's all your fault anyway, that he's in jail. He don't belong there!'

'Mr, Dyce, why don't you let Donnie go? This isn't going to gain you anything.'

His caw of laughter rattled her ear. 'That's where you're

189

wrong, girl. I'll get my Barn back. If these cops try to double-cross me, you'll all be sorry. I'll kill your boy. I swear I will! So you'd better just see to it that they do as I ask.'

Casey realized that there was no use trying to reason with him. 'I would like to speak to Donnie, Mr Dyce.'

'That you're not going to do, little lady. You're trying to run something by me here, I can smell it.'

Casey's hand was white on the receiver. 'I'm not trying to trick you. I just want to know that he's all right. If you won't let me talk to him, how can I be sure that you haven't already harmed him?' She had to fight to keep her voice steady.

Dyce was silent.

'What harm can it do? If things were reversed, wouldn't you want to be assured that *your* son was all right?'

At last Dyce spoke: 'Okay. But no tricks, you hear? I'll have my old .45 against the back of the boy's head; and I won't hesitate to use it! Don't think I'm bluffing.'

The line went silent, then Donnie's voice said in her ear: 'Casey!' His voice sounded high, and a little shaky.

'It's me, kiddo.' She strove to keep her own voice light. 'How are you holding up?'

'I'm . . .' His voice broke, and he sounded close to tears. 'I'm okay, but I'm scared, Casey.'

'I know you are, kiddo. But hang in there. We'll have you out safe and sound soon. We're doing everything we can. Has he harmed you in any way?'

'No.' She heard him swallow. 'But he keeps threatening me, telling me what will happen if you don't do what he says.'

'You tell him that we're trying our best to do what he wants.' She hesitated, then said: 'Donnie, I'm going to ask you a question, just answer yes or no, do you understand?'

'Yes.'

190

'Is Dyce's daughter, Melissa, in the house?'

'Yes.'

Casey heard Dyce's grating voice in the background, 'That's enough, boy.'

'No. Wait!' Casey said frantically. A loud crash made her pull the receiver away from her ear. When she returned it, the line was dead. She put down the phone, staring towards the house through a blur of tears.

Steve handed her a tissue. 'Did he seem all right?'

Casey nodded. 'For the moment. But Dyce is so far over the edge I can't even imagine how his mind's working. Oh, Steve, I'm so frightened. I don't know what I would do if anything happened to Donnie!'

Steve moved as if to put an arm around her, then drew back.

'He won't make a move until he's certain that his plan isn't going to work. Hopefully, before that time, we'll be able to defuse the situation. I heard you ask about Melissa?'

'Yes. He said that she was there.'

Steve grunted. 'Great. Another person to worry about.'

Casey tucked away the tissue and looked up. 'Her presence may work to our advantage. Melissa isn't cut of the same stuff Darrel and Barney are, and she's pregnant. I think it's unlikely that she would hurt another child, or allow her father to hurt Donnie.'

'That may be true, but you said yourself that she's scared to death of the old man. Do you really think that if push comes to shove, she'll be able to stand up to him?'

'I can only hope so.'

'What if he turns on her, too?'

'Dyce may be a mean son of a bitch, but he dotes on his children. I can't believe he would hurt her.'

'Well, let's hope that you're . . .'

'Hey!'

Steve turned his head to see a man's head and shoulders in the driver's side window. 'You Randall?' said a deep, mellifluous voice.

'Yes, I'm Steve Randall. Who are you?'

'Jack Clements, the hostage negotiator you sent for.'

Steve opened the car door, and the man stood back. 'Good, let me fill you in on the details.'

The two men began to talk, and Casey slid out the other side. She was surprised to see that it was growing dark. Somehow that fact made the situation seem more pressing.

While she and Steve had been talking, the media had arrived. There were TV vans and equipment all over the area in front of the house, and the technicians for the news teams seemed to be everywhere.

As she stood by the car, her uncle came up. 'Did you talk to Dyce. Is Donnie okay?'

'So far. Dyce let me talk to him. Donnie is keeping a stiff upper lip, but he says that Dyce keeps threatening him. I know he's frightened.'

Dan knotted one large fist. 'If I could get my hands on that sonofabitch, I'd . . .'

'I know, Dan. I feel the same way.'

'But we have to do *something*, Casey! We can't just stand around out here while the boy's in danger in there. You said yourself that Dyce has gone over the edge.'

'Dan, I feel the same way you do,' Casey said. 'But we have to wait, at least for now. Maybe this hostage negotiator can talk Dyce out.'

She turned away to avoid further conversation with him. She knew he was hurting, but so was she; and at the moment, she didn't feel she could deal with both him and Donnie's situation.

Looking again at the house, she saw that lights had been set up, bathing the house and the surrounding area with brilliant, white light. The only area not clearly lit was the

192

barn, some forty yards east of the main house. As Casey watched, a helicopter came whomping in from the east. It slowed, hovering directly over the house, throwing dust and noise in all directions.

To Casey's right, a mobile TV unit had been set up. A woman with short blonde hair and an attractive figure stood before a camera, holding a mike. She wore a serious expression, like a mask that could be removed and instantly replaced with a smile. Now, she half-turned, pointing towards the house, talking animatedly. A blast of air from the hovering copter blew a few strands of hair across her face, and she glanced up in momentary annoyance as she brushed the hair back.

Casey turned back to Steve's vehicle. Clements was talking on the phone, while Steve stood at the open door of the car, listening.

'Any progress, yet?' She said in a low voice.

'Negative!' Steve snapped. And then, as he turned and saw it was Casey: 'Sorry, Casey. Guess I'm wound a little tight.'

Casey shivered and hugged herself. 'We all are. So he isn't getting anywhere?' She nodded towards Clements.

'It takes time. Dyce keeps hanging up on him, but at least he picks up the phone. We have to have patience.'

But Casey's patience was wearing thin. Feeling the need to move, she patted Steve's arm, and turned away, prowling the perimeter of the scene, just beyond the light.

There were lights on in the house now, too, in several rooms.

Looking at them, she wondered if Dyce had given Donnie something to eat and drink; how Donnie was feeling; what was going on in Dyce's mind.

She remembered another hostage situation in Phoenix. She had not been directly involved, but she had been on the scene as an observer at the horrific, climatic moment.

A man had been holed up in an apartment for hours with his wife and four-year-old daughter, with a small arsenal at his disposal. He had called 911 with threats that he would kill his wife and child, and police had surrounded the building and cleared out the other tenants. A hostage negotiator had been called in, and he talked to the man until his voice was hoarse.

All to no avail.

Seven hours after the call to 911, three shots rang out in the apartment. When the police broke into the apartment, they found the man, his wife and the child, dead.

They never did uncover a reason for his act.

She jumped as a hand touched her on the elbow, and a voice said softly, 'Casey?'

Her head snapped around, and her mouth fell open. She was facing Melissa Dyce.

'Shh.' Melissa put a finger to her lips. 'I don't want anyone else to know I'm here.'

Casey said, in a whisper, 'How did you get out here? Not twenty minutes ago I asked Donnie if you were inside, and he said yes.'

'I was.' Melissa said simply.

'But the house is surrounded, and lit up like a stage show.'

'I'll tell you in a minute. Come with me.'

Melissa took Casey's arm and led her further into the darkness. Casey's mind was reeling with the implications of Melissa's presence.

When they were well away from the light, Melissa stopped.

Casey said, 'Does your father know you're out here?'

'God, no! Look, I want you to come back to the house with me. Will you come?'

'You have some secret way in and out?'

'That's right.'

'Listen, Melissa, we must tell Sergeant Randall. If there is a way in, we can . . .'

'No!' Melissa said vehemently. 'No one else must know. I've thought about it, and if you come in alone maybe you can talk some sense into my father; but if he sees the police, I don't know what he'll do.'

Casey hesitated, then said: 'Melissa, why do you think your father would listen to me? He hasn't so far. He hates me!'

'He *is* angry at you,' Melissa said. 'But you're a woman, and the boy's mother. Father's a strong believer in family. If you stop . . . well . . . being so *strong* with him. If you could act like . . . well . . .'

Casey felt both like laughing and crying. 'You mean if I act as he thinks a woman should act, plead with him, be humble?'

Melissa sighed with relief. 'Yes, that's it exactly. Look, I know that it might be hard for you, but . . .'

'But it might be a chance to save Donnie without anyone getting hurt.'

Melissa sighed again. 'Exactly! I know what my father is. But even so, I don't want him killed, and I certainly don't want him to kill Donnie: he's a sweet little boy. This way, there's a chance. I figure that it's worth taking.'

'All right. I'll do anything to get Donnie out of there alive. How do we get in?'

'Not yet. First you have to promise me that you won't tell anyone else what I've told you, or that you're going in.'

Casey thought for only a moment. This was a risky business. Was there a chance that Dyce would listen to her; or would the sight of her inflame him further? She had to take the chance.

'I give you my word,' she said. 'Let's go.'

Melissa took Casey's arm, and led her carefully along

the perimeter of the light, and Casey realized that they were circling their way towards the barn.

When they reached the building, Melissa led her to a side door, eased the door open, and edged inside. Casey followed. If Melissa was leading her into a trap, there was little she could do. She had to trust her.

Inside the barn, it was very warm and the air smelled of hay and horse droppings. Melissa turned on a flashlight and shone it on the floor, sweeping it back and forth.

Casey whispered: 'Why have you brought me in here?'

'Because there's a tunnel under here leading into the main house.'

'A tunnel?'

'Yes. My grandfather dug it when he built the house at the turn of the century. He came from Minnesota, where the winters are terrible, and they often built a tunnel from the house to the barn. Here. Would you hold this please? Shine it right there.'

Taking the light, Casey shone it on the designated spot. Melissa squatted and began feeling along the hay-strewn floor, as if searching for something.

'Also,' Melissa continued, 'Grandpa was afraid of an Indian attack. He'd read all the dime novels about Indians massacring the settlers. He figured he and his family could hide in the tunnel, and escape that way. There!'

In the light of the flash, Melissa's fingers found purchase – in what, Casey could not see – and pulled, lifting. She gave a soft grunt, as a section of the floor, hay and all, swung aside, exposing a dark hole about two and a half feet square. The top rungs of a sturdy wooden ladder could be seen.

Melissa dusted off her hands. 'You go first. I have to shut the trap. I'll hold the light for you, so you can use both hands.'

Casey shook her head. 'I'd rather keep the flash, if you don't mind.'

Melissa shrugged. 'Okay.' Gingerly, Casey began descending the ladder, holding the flash in her right hand, feeling for each rung; wondering what she would do if Melissa were to close the trap and leave her there.

She judged the hole to be about eight feet deep. When she reached the bottom, she saw the tunnel stretching ahead into the darkness. The tunnel was about three feet wide and five feet high; braced and walled with split logs that were grey with age. Cobwebs moved in the current of air set up by the open trap, long and silvery, like witches' hair. Casey shivered and aimed the beam of light upward to where Melissa was just pulling the trap closed. The solid 'thunk' of its closing made Casey shiver again.

Melissa was down the ladder now, and holding out her hand for the flash. 'I'll take the lead now.'

Casey handed over the light, and squeezed against the wall so that Melissa could pass.

'It looks pretty well shored up,' said Casey, wanting reassurance that the tunnel was safe.

Melissa shown the light into the tunnel. 'Oh, it was built to last. Grandpa didn't do things by halves. Come on. It's not really far.'

Maybe not, thought Casey, but after a few feet it began to seem so. It was an uncomfortable way to travel, bent over like an old woman, attempting to keep that bobbing circle of light in sight.

Casey's back was beginning to protest in earnest, when Melissa stopped. Casey did likewise, lifting her head so she could see what Melissa was doing; she heard the friction of wood on wood, and saw a sliver of light grow into a doorway.

Following Melissa, who had extinguished the flashlight, she found herself in a dimly lit basement, immediately behind a large furnace. When Melissa closed the door behind them, Casey saw that it fit tightly into a wooden wall, unnoticeable unless you knew where to look. Looking around, she saw the small night-light that dispelled what otherwise would have been the total darkness of the room.

Melissa put the flash on a work bench across the room, beside a flight of steps leading upwards.

'This leads into the kitchen,' she whispered. 'Be quiet so we don't alert Daddy until you're ready to face him.'

Casey followed the other woman up the steps. Adrenaline fizzed through her blood and made her heart pound. She took a deep breath to calm herself.

At the top of the basement stairs, Melissa eased the door open, and, blinking like a mole, Casey shielded her eyes from the sudden glare. When she could see, she found herself in a rather Spartan kitchen. As Melissa led her through the brightly lit house, she noticed that all the blinds and drapes were drawn. The rooms were all unexpectedly neat. Melissa's doing, she decided.

Before they reached the study, Casey heard Dyce's angry voice on the phone. As they stepped through the open door of the study, Casey saw Dyce and Donnie across the room. Dyce, a .45 revolver in his right hand, had his back to them; but Donnie, on a straight chair by the desk, where Dyce could keep an eye on him, was facing the doorway.

Casey raised a hand to signal to him, but it was too late, his eyes went wide, and he half rose, emitting a strangled cry.

Dyce dropped the telephone and whirled. At the same time, his left arm went around the boy, bringing the child's head against the barrel of the gun. Looking into Dyce's glaring eyes, Casey glimpsed madness.

'Don't come any further,' Dyce said wildly, 'or I'll blow the boy's brains into the next county.'

SEVENTEEN

Casey held up her hands. 'Please, Mr Dyce, I'm not here to cause any trouble; I just came to talk.'

Dyce glared at her, and then at his daughter. 'How did you get here? Lissa? You brought her through that damn tunnel, didn't you?'

Melissa took a step towards him. 'Daddy, I couldn't let this thing go on. Somebody is bound to get hurt.'

'You betrayed me, girl,' he said in an agonized voice. 'How could you betray me to these outsiders. And your brother? What about your brother?'

Melissa began to tremble, but she stood her ground. 'Daddy, what you're doing is not going to help Barney: it will just make things worse, for him, and for you, as well. If you were thinking straight, you'd realize that!'

Dyce's eyes seemed to cloud over. When he spoke his tone was almost apologetic. 'I had to do something, girl! I couldn't just stand by and see them put my boy in jail for something he didn't do!'

Casey was surprised to see tears leaking from the man's reddened eyes; he was near the breaking point. She said gently, 'Melissa is right, Mr Dyce. Holding Donnie hostage only worsens the situation. Kidnapping a child is . . .'

'Well, what about *my* child? Barney didn't kill anyone. I know he's a little wild sometimes. I know that he steps over the line, especially when he's boozed up; but he's not a killer.'

Touched by Dyce's evident pain, Casey's next words came out without any forethought whatsoever. She heard herself saying: 'I believe you, Mr Dyce. I don't believe Barney killed Buck Farrel, or Red Pollock!'

Dyce blinked at her, and the hand holding the gun lowered. 'You telling me the truth, girl? Do you mean what you say?'

Casey took a deep breath, experiencing a great feeling of relief. The nagging doubt she had felt over Barney's arrest came into full focus. 'I meant what I said. More than that, I'll do my best to prove it.'

Dyce's gun hand dropped to his side. He looked from Casey to his daughter. 'Can I trust her, Lissa?'

Lissa was crying and smiling at the same time. 'Yes, Daddy. She'll do what she says.'

'You'd better!' Dyce said to Casey, but his voice did not carry its usual sting. She could see how tired he was.

'I'll do everything I can to find the real killer. You have my word.'

He shook his head. 'I hope it's enough!' he said. He released Donnie and gave him a push toward Casey. 'Go on, boy. Go to your mother. No use in two innocent boys being hurt.'

Donnie stood for a moment as if not knowing what to do, then with a quick look at Dyce he ran towards Casey's outstretched arms, burrowing his face against her. A single sob racked his body.

Casey smoothed his hair, murmuring comfort. He finally looked at her with wet eyes. 'I'm sorry, Casey. I didn't mean to cry, but I got so scared.'

Casey looked up at Dyce, who glanced away. She turned back to Donnie. 'It's all right to cry, kiddo, you have every reason. But it's all over now.'

She heard a faint yammering sound from the direction of the desk, and realized that it came from the dangling telephone receiver. Her glance went back to Dyce. He had seated himself on the couch, his face in his hands. Melissa knelt by his side, murmuring to him softly.

Casey stepped over to scoop up the dangling receiver. 'Hello?'

There was a startled pause, then an unfamiliar voice said, 'Who is this?'

'This is Casey Farrel, investigator for the Governor's Task Force on Crime. I'd like to speak to Sergeant Randall, please.'

'But, what's happening in there?' the voice demanded.

'Put Sergeant Randall on, please. I'll only speak to him.'

She heard the babble of voices, a silence, and then Steve said, 'Casey?'

'That's me.'

'My God, what are you doing in there? How did you . . . ? Has he got you, too?'

Casey felt her temper fraying. 'Settle down, Steve. No. I'm not a hostage, and neither is Donnie. Everything is under control. Just warn everybody; we're all coming out.'

'Is anybody hurt?'

'No, damnit! We're all walking out; just call off the dogs. I don't want any trigger-happy sniper blowing one of us away.'

'Give me a few minutes. Hang on to the phone; I'll be right back.'

Casey kept the receiver to her ear. She reached out and drew Donnie to her. Dyce hadn't moved from the couch. Melissa had just poured him a glass of whisky and was kneeling before him, urging him to drink it.

Steve's voice said in Casey's ear, 'It's all arranged, Casey. You can come out now. How many of you?'

'Four: myself, Donnie, Dyce, and Melissa.'

'There's just one thing. You said that none of you are hostages. If you were forced to say that, it might get

201

hairy outside. Just answer yes or no. Are any of you hostages?'

'No.'

Steve gave a sigh of relief. 'Good. Okay, come out of the front door. Dyce first, alone, hands over his head, then Melissa, then you and the boy.'

All of a sudden relief flooded Casey. She felt giddy and light. 'It shall be as you say, O Great Chief,' she said.

She replaced the receiver, and turned to the others. 'It's all set up. We can leave.' She explained the order of their departure, wondering if Dyce would protest at going first; but all the fight seemed to be drained out of him. Almost docilely, he let Melissa lead him to the door.

It was eerily quiet outside, considering the fact that a crowd of people stood out there beyond the blinding lights. Casey watched from a window as first Darrel, then his daughter, walked out into the glare and into the arms of the police.

Then it was time for her and Donnie. As they stepped into the light, a loud cheer went up, and people came running towards them. She stopped, Donnie pressed against her side; and then Dan was there with his arms around them, and Steve, with a big smile on his face. 'Casey! You're a wonder! I want to hear how you did it, but first, let's get you away from here before . . .'

But it was too late. The reporters were upon them, surrounding them with a wall of avid faces, cameras, and microphones. The air was loud with shouted questions and pleas. Casey closed her eyes and tried to control her temper. She had a particular aversion to the way the media was allowed to overrun the scene of every major crime and disaster. The only thing they cared about was 'the story', and in the process of getting it, they often interfered with the work of whichever agency was attempting to cope with the situation. Casey always thought of them as a rude nuisance, much like the tail that wagged the dog; and she was in no mood just now to put up with them. Turning her back, she faced Steve. He took one look at her expression, grabbed her arm, and followed by Dan and Donnie, pushed their way through the crowd, saying: 'Miss Farrel has no statement at this time,' over and over, until they were in the clear, near the car.

As they reached the vehicle, Casey could see that several police cars were now parked nearby. Standing by one of them, Casey could see Darrel Dyce and Melissa. Dyce's hands were cuffed and an officer was holding each arm. As she watched, he turned his head and spat a brown stream that barely missed the feet of one of the men holding him. Melissa cried out, 'Don't hurt him!'

Steve turned and walked over to the other car. 'We're not going to hurt him, Melissa.'

Dan put Donnie down, and placed a hand on Casey's shoulder. 'You're not hurt?'

She shook her head. 'Only tired as all get out.'

'And the boy?'

She smiled down at Donnie. 'A little frightened, but otherwise in good shape.'

Donnie held out his foot. 'Look, Casey. My new boots. I can ride real good with them.'

A wave of anger washed aside Casey's fatigue. She clenched her fists as she thought about what she had just been through, how she had felt when she thought Donnie might be hurt or dead. Unable to control herself, she hit at the boot with one hand. It hurt her hand, but it startled Donnie, who looked at her with wide eyes.

'Do you know what you've done?' she said angrily. 'Do you have any idea how worried Uncle Dan and I were when we found you gone? Do you realize that you might have been hurt or killed?'

Donnie's small face was pale. 'Gee, Casey. I'm sorry

203

. . .' he gulped back a sob. 'I just wanted to try out the new boots, and neither of you was around to ride with me. I didn't think . . .'

'That's just it,' Casey snapped. 'You didn't think; and look what happened! I want you to promise me that from now on you *will* think before you do something so foolish. When I tell you not to do something I'm not just being arbitrary. I have a good reason. I want you to remember that!'

'Stepped into it again, I see,' a deep, familiar voice said behind her.

She wheeled around. 'Josh! How on earth . . .'

Donnie jumped down from Dan's arms and ran past Casey, yelling, 'Josh, Josh!'

'Hi, sport.' Josh scooped the boy up in his arms and swung him high.

A big man, Josh Whitney, big in every way. Well over six feet with the shoulders of a linebacker, a big head and a craggy face. His grey eyes were warm as he looked at Casey. He grinned crookedly. 'Well, babe, what do you have to say for yourself?'

'How did you know what was happening? And how did you get here so fast?' Casey said.

'It's all over the TV news in Phoenix: "Adopted son of task force investigator held hostage". I headed for the airport right away.'

Casey, her anger gone, smiled at him. 'Always coming to my rescue, aren't you, Detective? And always arriving a few minutes too late.' She began to laugh, and had difficulty stopping.

Josh put a big arm around her, pulling her close. 'Well, at least I arrive. You have to give me points for that.'

She hugged him back. 'I do. I really do.'

'Here.' She took his arm. 'I want you to meet my Uncle, Dan Farrel. Dan, this is Sergeant Josh Whitney, I think I've mentioned him.'

Dan nodded and held out a big hand. 'Pleased to meet you. Any friend of Casey's has to be good people.'

Josh shook the proffered hand. 'I can see that she has you fooled, too.'

Suddenly, they were plunged into darkness as the lights were cut off, except for one mobile TV unit, where a reporter was still interviewing. At that moment the police car carrying Dyce moved away, and Steve came towards them through the gloom. Casey was surprised at how ill at ease she felt over introducing Steve to Josh. Josh was going to be difficult, she just knew it.

After her introduction, the two men shook hands warily, taking one another's measure. Casey thought you could almost see the hair bristle. Men!

'Sergeant Randall,' Josh said coolly, 'Casey has told me about you. She says that you're a more than competent investigator.'

Steve shot Casey an unfathomable look. 'That's very flattering,' Steve said, equally cool. 'But I'm afraid that you have me at a disadvantage; she hasn't told me much about you. What brings you to Prescott?'

'Oh, I'm not here on business.' He put his arm around Casey's shoulders possessively. 'Casey and I are close friends.'

Casey's face was growing hot. Josh hadn't said a thing that wasn't true, but it was the *way* he said it: he might as well have pounded on his chest and bellowed: 'This woman mine! Keep away!' It was embarrassing, and not a little demeaning!

She stood stiffly under the weight of his arm. 'Josh and I have known one another for a long time', Casey said to Steve, trying not to sound apologetic.

'He's the one you mentioned,' Steve said noncommittally.

'Yes,' said Casey.

'Mentioned?' said Josh.

They all jumped at a sudden flood of light blinded them.

Casey, shading her eyes with her hand, saw the blonde TV reporter that she had seen earlier at the mobile unit. She was accompanied by a cameraman and another man carrying the light.

The woman thrust a microphone at Casey. 'Miss Farrel, could you spare me a few minutes, just a short interview with you and your son, telling the viewers how you felt when you learned your son had been kidnapped, and . . .'

Case instinctively drew back, 'No. Not now!'

The woman shoved the mike closer. 'But surely . . .'

Steve stepped in between Casey and the interviewer. 'This woman and her son have just gone through a terrible ordeal. Give her a break, okay? I'm sure she will talk to you later, when she has had time to . . .'

'But that will be too late. This is going out on the ten o'clock news.'

Josh stepped up beside Steve. Together they made a formidable wall. 'The lady said not now. That should be clear enough. Now, turn off that damn light.'

The reporter glared at Josh for a few minutes, then turned on her heel, muttering to the men with her, 'Come on, guys. Let's fold our tents and get the hell out of here. This kind of treatment is about what you'd expect from these rednecks!'

'Thanks, men,' Casey said to Steve and Josh. 'But I could have handled it myself.'

Josh replaced his arm around Casey's shoulder. 'You shouldn't have to put up with that crap, after what you've been through.'

'Well, I am beat. That's for sure.'

'I should think so. Let's get out of here.'

'Just one thing, Casey,' Steve said. 'I've got to know. How did you get in there, and what did you say to Dyce that got him to let you go?'

Casey smiled. 'I could say that it was my womanly

206

wiles, but the truth is that Melissa took me in through a hidden tunnel. By the time we got in there, Dyce was about ready to break. He kept saying that Barney wasn't guilty, that he hadn't committed the murders; and I told him that I agreed; that I didn't think Barney was guilty either, and that I would try my best to prove it!'

'And that's all it took?'

She nodded. 'That's all it took.'

He shook his head. 'Well, like I've said before, a lie can be forgiven in a good cause.'

Casey took a deep breath. It was now or never. 'But I wasn't lying. I've never felt right about arresting Barney. I think you know that.'

He stared at her, his expression puzzled.

'Aw, come on, Casey! We've got Barney nailed, good and proper. Don't mess around and open up a whole new can of peas.'

'I had you figured for a good cop, Steve,' she said steadily. 'I never thought that you'd settle for the easy solution, closing your mind to anything else.'

Even in the darkness she could see him flush; and Josh's arm tightened around her shoulders.

'I'm not closing my mind to anything,' Steve snapped, 'but we have all the evidence we need to convict. What more do you want?'

'I want the truth, and I don't think we've found it.'

Josh laughed. 'You don't know Casey very well, Sergeant, or you'd know that she is one stubborn female. When she gets her mind set on something, it takes a bomb to derail her. Sometimes, even that won't do it.'

Steve ignored him, still staring at Casey. 'Well, it looks like maybe I've misjudged you, too, Casey. I thought that you were a reasonable and logical person. I know the value of hunches, and feelings, but in the end, you have to go on the evidence, and we have that. If you go on with this, you're doing it on your own!'

'If that's the way you want it.'

'It's not the way I want it, but that's the way it is!'

Turning on his heel, he got into the car, slammed the door, and started the engine.

Josh chuckled. 'Well, it looks like you've ticked off your "excellent investigator", Casey.'

Casey slumped, all the cumulative fatigue of the day hitting her. 'You don't have to be so damn smug. Let's get out of here.'

Donnie, who, with Dan Farrel, had been standing somewhat aside, chimed in: 'Yeah, Casey, I'm starving. Can we stop someplace for something to eat?'

Casey, realizing that her own stomach felt hollow, nodded. 'Okay, kiddo. I could manage to eat something myself.'

She looked around, noticing that almost everyone else was gone.

She turned to Dan. 'Dan, did you see where Melissa went?'

Dan nodded. 'I saw her hotfoot it for the house when those TV people got after her.'

Casey slipped out from under Josh's arm, and went to her uncle. He cleared his throat. 'Do you really think that Barney is innocent?'

She put her hand on his arm. 'I doubt that you could call him innocent; but I don't think he killed Buck or Red. Look, I know how you feel about the Dyces; but there wouldn't be much satisfaction in putting Barney away if he isn't the one who committed the crime.'

Dan sighed heavily. 'I'm a reasonable man, Casey. I think you know that. I want Buck's killer caught; and if you say Barney didn't do it, well, despite what Randall said, I believe you know what you're doing. I'll go along with you, at least for a while.'

Casey nodded, and gave his arm a pat. 'Good. There's

one more thing, something I think it's time you knew. Melissa Dyce is carry Barney's child, your grandchild.'

Dan's expression was something to behold. 'A grandchild? Buck's son?'

Casey held up a hand. 'Whoa! I didn't say it was a boy. I don't know *that* much.'

'But how? When?'

'That's a long story, which I'll tell you later; but you should know that despite the fact that Darrel is Melissa's father, she's a nice kid, and she loved Buck very much. She told me that she and Buck were going to get married. I think she's telling the truth. And I think Buck must have been serious about her, or why would he have had his vasectomy reversed? I think you two should talk.'

Dan was staring at the house. Despite the day's ordeal, he looked more vital than Casey had seen him so far.

'Not tonight, Dan. Give her a day or so, okay?'

He nodded.

'Food!' said Donnie. 'I'm starving.'

'Yeah,' said Josh. 'I second that. My treat, okay, Mr Farrel? Casey?'

Casey nodded. 'By all means, but it's going to cost you. I'm hungry as a bear, and so is Donnie, right, kiddo? Where do you want to go?'

'The Dry Gulch! They've got the biggest pieces of Mud Pie!'

'And great steaks,' said Casey to Josh.

The Dry Gulch was located in a country-residential section just off Iron Springs Road. The parking lot beside the rustic building was full, but some of the dining crowd had come and gone, so they didn't have to wait for seating in the no-smoking section. Josh, who had never been to the restaurant before, shook his head. Pointing at the full-size carving of a goofy looking cowboy near the bar, he said: 'I wasn't sure from the name of this place, but it's Western, right? It must be, because it's rustic as all . . .'

'Josh!' Casey warned, giving him a poke with her elbow. 'Now behave yourself. You don't have to let them know you're a city boy.'

He grinned. 'I'll try to fit in, but with my natural sophistication, it might be difficult.'

Casey gave him a wide grin. God, it was great to see the big lug again. She gave his arm a squeeze as the waitress came to lead them to their table.

When Donnie saw where they were headed, he gave a low whoop. 'Hey, we're gonna get the table by the Indian.'

'Why, sure enough. We are,' Josh said, raising an eyebrow. In the corner of the small room they had entered, sat the figure of an Indian, very close to the table where they were being seated.

'If you sit in that chair,' said Donnie, pointing, 'and the Indian's behind you, if you turn around real sudden, you think he's alive.'

'A treat, I'm sure,' said Josh, picking up the menu. 'You say the food is good?'

'If you like steak,' Dan said, 'and they cook it like you want it.'

When they had all ordered, Josh beamed at them all. 'Well, considering what you three have been through today, you look in pretty good shape.'

Casey said, 'Then looks must be deceiving. I feel like the last rose of summer.'

'You'll feel better with some food in you,' Dan said.

Casey looked over at Donnie. He had pulled his chair as close to Josh as was possible at a square table, and he had his hand on Josh's arm.

Casey felt what a friend of hers referred to as 'the warm fuzzies' as she watched the pair. Donnie had never

210

really known his father, and Josh filled a real need in his life.

'How's Spot II?' Donnie was demanding. 'Are you giving him enough to eat? Does he miss me?'

Josh looked thoughtful. 'I think he's gained at least five pounds since he's been staying with me. Probably have to put him on a diet when you get back. He'll probably be so fat that he won't be able to get around.'

'Aw, Josh,' Donnie grinned happily. 'You're kidding me!'

'Now, would I do a thing like that?' Josh said. 'And as for missing you,' Josh winked at Casey over Donnie's head, 'to be honest, I don't think so. He sleeps at the foot of my bed, and in the afternoons I take him rabbit hunting. He really likes chasing those rabbits. He just may want to stay with me even after you come back. Too bad.'

Donnie narrowed his eyes, unsure of whether he was being teased. 'I can take him rabbit hunting, too!' he said firmly.

Casey, engrossed in watching the two males she cared so much about, jumped when she heard her name spoken.

'Casey!'

She looked up into the face of Hank Wilder. She was glad to see that this time he was sober. 'Well, hello, Hank.'

He smiled. 'I was just leaving, and I saw you in here. Thought I'd come over and say hello. I'm mighty glad to see that you seem to be all right.'

Casey nodded. 'Yeah, it was pretty hairy there for a while. Hank, you know my uncle, Dan Farrel. This is my friend, Josh Whitney, from Phoenix homicide; and this is my son, Donnie.'

Hank held his hand out to Josh, and then to Donnie. 'Glad to meet you.'

211

He studied Josh. 'So you're from Phoenix Homicide. Are you working on the case, too?'

'If you mean Buck Farrel's murder, no. I came up to see Casey and Donnie. I had planned to come soon anyway, but when I saw the news tonight, I made it a bit sooner.'

Wilder shook his head. 'Yes, I saw it, too, but when I left the hotel, the situation hadn't been resolved. Like I said, I'm real glad that you got out safely. What about Dyce?'

'He's in custody.'

Wilder nodded. 'Well, he can keep his boy company now, can't he? At any rate, I'm very glad it's all over. They have charged Barney Dyce with both murders, haven't they?'

Casey hesitated, then nodded.

'Guess I'll be going home then. It was a terrible thing, but I'm glad I stayed till it was over. I'll sleep better for knowing.'

'Barney hasn't been convicted yet, Hank.'

He shrugged. 'I know, but I understand that the evidence is very strong. I'm sure the jury will do the right thing.'

Casey bit back her rejoinder. Let the man be on his way.

'When will you be leaving?' asked Dan.

'No later than the end of the week. Glad to have seen you again, Casey, and you, Dan; and pleased to have met you two.' He nodded at Josh and Donnie, and turned away.

'Who is he?' Josh asked.

'A rodeo clown,' said Dan. 'He was the one tied up in the barn while the killer took his place.'

Josh looked at Casey. 'Why didn't you tell him that you weren't sure that Barney Dyce was the killer?'

Casey shrugged. 'Since my view is not the official one,

I didn't feel I should. Besides, I'd rather that everyone, particularly the killer, thinks that it's all over.'

'Catch the killer with his guard down,' Josh said.

She nodded. 'Exactly. When do you have to leave, Josh?'

'In the morning, I'm afraid. I'm on my own case, and I really shouldn't have left, but . . .' He shrugged. 'Maybe I should take Donnie back with me?'

Donnie groaned. 'I want to stay, Josh. I want to see what happens. I miss you and Spot, but I've invested a lot of time in this case.'

The corners of Josh's lips turned up as he heard his own words come out of the boy's mouth. 'Well, I'm sure you have,' he said.

Casey hesitated. The offer was tempting, particularly in light of the day's events; yet the pleading look in Donnie's eyes could not be denied.

'Do you promise to behave? Do you promise to stay close to your Uncle Dan and myself, and to do everything we tell you?'

Earnestly, Donnie nodded, and crossed his heart.

Casey and Josh exchanged looks, and Casey said: 'Okay, kiddo, but if you don't keep your promise, off you go.'

She turned to Josh. 'Josh, where are you staying?'

'You can stay with us,' Dan said. 'I'm sure we can make . . .'

Josh shook his head. 'No, I don't want to impose. I'll get a motel room out by the airport. I've got to catch the first plane back in the morning.'

He leaned close to Casey and spoke in low voice. 'The only thing is, a motel room is awfully big just for one man. I don't suppose . . .'

Casey shot an embarrassed look at Dan and Donnie. 'Josh!' she said warningly, glancing again at Donnie. The child had the hearing of a bat.

213

Donnie leaned forward. 'You won't have to stay alone, Josh. I can stay with you!'

Casey and Josh exchanged looks and exploded into laughter at the same moment. Donnie looked from one to the other in puzzlement, then shrugged at the strange ways of grown-ups and turned his attention back to his hamburger.

EIGHTEEN

Casey sat alone in the breakfast nook of the Farrel home, having a final cup of coffee, mulling her options. Dan and Donnie were already out for a morning ride, and Alice had gone grocery shopping.

The problem, Casey was thinking, was how to proceed. She had promised Darrel Dyce that she would do all that she could, but where to start? Before the evidence had turned up in Barney's truck, she had been exactly nowhere. If Barney wasn't guilty, then she was back in that same spot.

It was too bad that she wouldn't be able to work with Steve. She felt bad about what had happened last night, but done was done, and there was no use in worrying over it. She was on her own now; but she had been on her own before, and she could handle that.

But where to begin? That was the question. All leads, such as they were, had been investigated, and the only one which had led anywhere had led to Barney Dyce.

She smiled, thinking of one of Josh's bits of advice. 'If you're at a dead end, start over: look for new leads, go over old ground. In any homicide there are always things left undiscovered the first time around, so go over it again, and again, if necessary. It's dull work, but that's the way most cases are solved.'

Well, it was good advice, and she would follow it.

There was nothing else she could do. Draining her coffee cup, she gathered up her things and went out to the Cherokee.

The first thing she did was to revisit the scene of the crime, the Yavapai County Fairgrounds. Although it was only mid-morning, there was some activity. Horse racing, interrupted by the rodeo, had resumed, and a number of owners were working their horses on the track.

Casey parked the Jeep, and walked over to the chutes, where Buck had met his death. Standing by the chute, Casey closed her eyes, reliving the scene as it must have played out back here: Buck mounting the bull; taking a few seconds to toss back the fatal drink of whisky handed him by the clown; the release of the bull – Buck already dying and losing his grip on the bull rope. Something stirred in the back of her mind, wispy and indefinite, and was gone. She hated it when that happened, but maybe it would come to her later.

Next she went to the barn where they had found Wilder, bound and gagged. Horses now occupied most of the stalls, and the odour of horse droppings was strong. Down at the far end of the building a man was forking hay into the stalls.

She closed her eyes again, hoping that the tickle in the back of her mind would return. Nothing.

'Hey, lady, you're not supposed to be in here, unless you own one of the nags.'

Her eyes flew open. Confronting her was the man with the pitchfork. He was staring at her sternly. 'Do you?'

'Own one of the horses? No. I'm investigating the death of Buck Farrel.'

His muddy brown eyes regarded her with suspicion. 'And so?'

'The rodeo clown, Hank Wilder, was found about here, bound and gagged.' She gestured. 'Were you working this building that day?'

He shook his head. 'Nope. I don't work the rodeo, just the races.'

'What's your name?'

'Benton. Pete Benton.'

'Did you know Red Pollock?'

'I thought you said you were investigating the death of Buck Farrel?'

'I did. I am; but I'm also investigating the death of Red Pollock. Did you know him?'

He nodded. 'Yeah. I knew old Red. Fact is, we went to school together here in Prescott.'

'Do you know of anyone who would benefit from his death?'

He snorted. 'Hell, no. Old Red wasn't much, and I don't suppose he did anyone much good, but, on the other hand, I can't think of anyone who would benefit if he was dead. He was a harmless sort of guy. I can't think of anyone who would have a hard-on for Red, enough to waste him.' His expression was sly, as if he hoped the vulgarity would offend her.

Casey found this annoying, but wasn't going to let him know it. She said calmly, 'You've known Red a long time then. Did he usually work the rodeos and fairground events?'

'Sure. Never did anything much else that I know about, at least not in the last few years. Before that, he used to work the rodeo circuit as a bronc rider. He was never much good at it, barely got by. Then he got stove up some, the boozing got to him, so he ended up working stables and the like.'

'What rodeos did he work?'

'Oh, in the state here, and up in Montana and Wyoming, Nevada, sometimes out in California. It was mostly the small rodeos, Old Red was never good enough for the big time.'

'I know he was a drinker. Did he ever get belligerent when he drank?'

'Naw. He was a happy drunk; used to get plumb foolish. Besides, he couldn't fight his way out of a paper bag even when he was sober.'

'When was the last time you saw him?'

Benson tilted his head to the side in thought. 'The day before the rodeo started. I was helping move some horses out so they could move in the rodeo stock, and I ran across Red.'

'Did you have a conversation with him?'

'Yeah, we talked.'

'How did he seem? What did he say?'

Benton shrugged. 'He was real upbeat, and half in the bag, and he said something real unusual, for him: he said that he had gotten his hands on a few bucks, and that things were looking up for him.'

Casey frowned. 'And that was the day *before* the rodeo started?'

'That's right.'

'Did he mention where the money came from?'

'Nope, and I didn't ask.'

'Do you happen to know if Pollock and Buck Farrel were acquainted?'

'Not at first hand, no. But they must have been. Both guys worked the rodeo here, and other places as well. Usually, everybody on the circuit knows everybody else.'

'When was the last time you talked to Buck Farrel?'

He thought for a moment. 'Can't rightly recall. Never knew him all that well. Look, lady, I've got to get back to work here before my boss catches me screwing off.'

Casey nodded. 'Thanks for your help.'

'Yeah, any time.' He gave her a long look, top to bottom, finishing with a self-satisfied leer.

Casey, in no mood to take any crap, gave him the same once-over, but finished with a shake of her head and a frown. Pete flushed and stomped back to his work.

Casey, feeling guilty at sinking to the man's level, but nevertheless pleased with herself, went back to the Cherokee. One thing Benton had told her was intriguing. How had Red Pollock come into a windfall *before* Buck's death? Her assumption, and Steve Randall's as well, had been that Pollock had seen and recognized the killer and had tried a little blackmail. The fact that he had come into the money before the killing invoked a different scenario. Was it possible that Red had been working with Buck's killer?

She drove downtown to the courthouse square and pulled into the Chevron station on the corner, to the full-service pump. Tim Simmons, the man she and Steve had talked to on Whiskey Row the night Barney Dyce was arrested, ambled over as she got out.

Wiping his hands on a rag, he said, 'What can I do for you?'

'Fill it up, please.'

As the man poked the hose into the gas tank, she said, 'Mr Simmons, do you remember me? Casey Farrel. We talked the other night in the bar, about Red Pollock.'

He squinted at her, then nodded. 'Sure, I remember.'

'Good. That night you mentioned that Red had been flashing a lot of money around.'

'Right.'

'And he said that he had come into some money, and was set to meet someone that night and get more.'

'Yep.' Simmons turned off the hose and hung it up. 'Check under the hood?'

'No, don't bother, Mr Simmons, about this money Pollock had that night. Did he say *when* he got it?'

219

Simmons rolled his eyes skyward and tapped a finger-nail against his teeth. 'I seem to recall him saying he picked it up the night before.'

'That would be the Friday night before the rodeo performance during which Buck Farrel was killed.'

'Yeah, I guess so.'

'And he never mentioned who he got the money from?'

'Not a word. That'll be sixteen dollars and twenty-two cents, for the gas.'

Sighing in frustration, Casey gave him her credit card. He filled out the slip and gave it back to her to sign.

As she was signing, he snapped his fingers. 'I just remembered something.'

Casey's head snapped up. 'What?'

'When old Red was leaving the bar, he did something that struck me as a little off the wall. He went out singing. Red never could carry a tune in a bucket, and loaded as he was, he was even worse.'

Disappointed, Casey said, 'What was so strange about that?'

'Well, it was the song. I mean it wasn't New Year's Eve or anything like that, and he was bellering "Auld Lang Syne"; you know, "should old acquaintance be forgot".'

Casey opened the door to Farrel & Associates and went inside. This time the receptionist was not at her desk, and Casey went right on past without stopping. The door to Clint Farrel's office was open. Clint was leaning back in his swivel chair, his feet on the desk, talking into the phone. He sat up, his feet hitting the floor, as he said into the phone, 'I'll call you back in a few minutes, Roger.' He slammed down the receiver, and glared at her. 'What are you doing here?'

'I have a few more questions.'

220

'More questions? I thought the case was over, and I thought that you'd be on your way back to Phoenix by now.'

Casey, determined not to let him get to her, smiled. 'Thought, or hoped?'

Her pleasant answer seemed to leave him nonplussed. 'Look, I just talked to Sergeant Randall, and he told me that Barney Dyce had been arrested and charged with Buck's murder.'

Casey nodded. 'I know. But I believe that we arrested the wrong man. I don't believe that Barney is the killer.'

He slumped back into his chair. 'Then who the hell is?'

'That's what I'm trying to find out, but I need a little help. Look, you want them to get the right person, don't you? Barney Dyce is no prize, and certainly no saint; but he shouldn't be put away or executed for a crime he did not commit! Your father, by the way, is going along with me on this.'

Clint's expression showed obvious surprise. He sighed. 'Well, if the old man is going along, he must think you're on to something: he wants Buck's killer mighty bad. And no, I wouldn't want the wrong man executed, even if it's a Dyce; and I sure don't want the real killer to go free. So ask away, cousin.'

Now it was Casey's turn to be surprised. 'Cousin? You accept that then?'

He nodded. 'I guess I'll have to. But don't let it go to your head. Fire away.'

Casey pulled up the chair opposite the desk and seated herself. 'When I talked to you before, I mentioned that Buck had had a vasectomy.'

He nodded. 'And I didn't believe you.'

She leaned forward. 'I have proof, Clint. I talked to the doctor who performed the operation.'

221

'Okay. So he had the operation. But as I recall you said that it was done before he married the bubble-head. That would have to have been more than fifteen years ago.'

Casey nodded. 'Around that. Now, you've admitted that you and Buck didn't get along very well. Was it always that way, even when you were young?'

Clint clasped his hands behind his head. 'Pretty much. We were just different, something I realized early on. Hell, Buck was rodeoing even when he was in high school. During his last two years of high school, every summer he'd go off to one rodeo or another, all across the country. I never did understand why Dad let him. He was just a kid, and a wild kid at that. The year he graduated, he was gone most of the year, up in Montana, Nevada, God knows where. He only came home once, for the Fourth of July rodeo.'

'But I thought he and Pamela got married right after they graduated.'

'Not right away. Let's see . . .' He paused, considering. 'If I remember correctly, they were married the second summer after graduation. In August, I think it was.'

Casey nodded. 'Yes, that fits. One of Buck's old girlfriends told me that he got a girl pregnant just after he got out of high school. He told her that was the reason he had the operation. She didn't know who the girl was. Do you know anything about that?'

'No, but I can't say that I'm surprised.' He gave a bark of laughter. 'I am surprised that he didn't get more women pregnant in those days.'

Casey got up from the chair. 'Well, thanks for talking to me. 'I won't bother you again.' She started for the door.

'Casey . . .'

She turned.

'Dad called this morning to invite me and my family out for dinner tonight. I said I'd think about it. Now I've decided to go. Will you be there?'

'So far as I know.'

'Good! That will give you a chance to meet my wife, Ruth, and our kids.' He smiled: it appeared to Casey that it was an effort, but at least it was a smile.

'That will be nice, Clint. I'll look forward to it.'

She stopped at the first pay phone she came to, and called Pamela Morgan in Prescott Valley. 'Pamela, this is Casey Farrel.'

'Oh, Miss Farrel! I read in the paper that they caught the man who murdered Buck!'

'I know. But I think they may have the wrong man.'

'You mean it's not over yet?' Pamela's voice expressed her dismay.

'I'm afraid not. I have a few more questions. Do you have a few minutes?'

'I guess so.'

'When I talked to you the other day, you said that you married Buck right after you both got out of high school. Is that accurate?'

'Well, I didn't mean to say it was *right* after we graduated; in fact, it was the next summer. Buck felt that he just *had* to have one last fling at the rodeo thing, so I said I'd wait. Why?'

'It may be important. Did Buck ever mention to you that he had gotten another girl pregnant, just before he married you?'

There was a moment of silence, then: 'No. He never told me anything like that! Where did you get such an idea?'

'From an ex-girlfriend of Buck's.'

'Do you think she was telling the truth?'

'She has no reason to lie. She said that he told her the story to explain why he didn't want to have children. When did you learn about the vasectomy?'

'About two years after we were married. I had been

223

pestering him to visit the doctor for a check-up. I wanted to have kids, and nothing was happening. I had been checked out, and my doctor told me that there was no reason why I couldn't conceive. He suggested that Buck be checked. When I talked to him about it, that's when he told me. But he never told me he got someone else pregnant. The bastard! Did he say who it was?'

'No. My informant said she had no idea. That's why I'm asking you. Can you think of anyone . . .?'

Pamela said, 'No.'

Casey sighed. Each fact she uncovered was never complete, never enough. 'I thought that maybe he might have said something, when he was drunk maybe; it might not even have made much sense to you at the time . . .'

'You know something. When Buck got really drunk, he never came home. He said once that he didn't want me to see him like that. Of course, probably what he did was go home with some woman. But at least he wasn't like some men who get drunk and go home and beat up their wives. He had his faults, God knows, but he could be sweet, too, when he wanted to be.'

A sob caught in her throat, and she was silent for a moment. 'I'm sorry that I can't be of more help, and I'm sorry to be such a baby. I swore that I was never going to cry over Buck Farrel again.'

'Old loves die hard, Pamela, and old wounds often take a long time to heal,' Casey said, and felt like an unctuous ass for saying it. But it seemed to help, and when Pamela spoke again her voice sounded brighter. 'Well, I wish you luck in whatever it is you're doing. Goodbye.'

Casey hung up the phone. Yeah. Whatever it was she was doing; she only wished she knew what that was.

It was a little early for lunch, but Casey was hungry, having eaten a quick, sparse breakfast. She drove out to the edge of town to the Sheraton. Hank Wilder was staying there, and she wanted to talk to him again, too.

224

Using the house phone, she asked to be connected to the room of Henry Wilder. The desk clerk let the phone ring for a long time before she said, 'I'm sorry, Mr Wilder doesn't answer.'

'He hasn't checked out, has he?'

There was a pause, while the clerk checked. 'No, he's still registered. It appears that he's checking out tomorrow.'

'Thank you.'

Casey hung up the phone, and turned towards the dining room. Wilder would probably have nothing to add, anyway. I'm grasping at straws here, she thought ruefully. Maybe Steve was right. Maybe she should just chuck the whole thing, enjoy the weekend with Donnie, then head back to Phoenix, her ego bruised. But she couldn't do that, either. She had promised Darrel Dyce that she would try to free his son, and it was very important to her that she keep her word.

So after indulging in a leisurely and modestly sinful lunch, she doggedly returned to her investigation. Driving to the park, she parked the Jeep in the shade, opened the windows, and took out her notebook. Carefully she re-read all of her notes, looking for something she had missed, anything that would give her a new lead. After reading through this mass of material, she was struck again by the thought that the answer to the mystery lay in the past. There was something there, but she couldn't put her finger on it.

By mid afternoon she was tired, sweaty and cranky. She was strongly tempted to head for Chino Valley and a long soak in the tub, but she decided on one final stop.

Parking before Myrtle Carter's old house, Casey noticed that Taggert's motorcycle was missing. Apparently, he had not returned.

She rapped on the red door, waited a few moments, and

rapped again. She heard footsteps inside, and Myrtle's deep voice rumbled: 'Yeah, yeah, I'm coming!'

The door swung open, and Myrtle's blue eyes widened in surprise. 'Well now, the lady cop! Didn't expect to be seeing you again, sweetie. Thought the case was all wrapped up.'

'Not quite.'

'And here I was thinking that old Barn was going down for the count.'

'He may yet, I'm just tying up some loose ends.'

Myrtle grinned. 'And, as usual, you have some questions.'

Casey laughed; there was no way you could dislike this big, brassy woman. 'Don't I always?'

'Then come in.' Myrtle stepped back. 'I've only been up a half hour or so, trying to jump-start myself with some black coffee. Would you like a cup?'

'No coffee right now, but I could sure go for a cold soft drink.'

'I can handle that. Follow me.'

Casey followed the big woman towards the back of the house, and the Arizona room. Myrtle was dressed pretty much as she had been on Casey's previous visit, in tight, faded jeans, sleeveless shirt, and low-heeled boots.

As they drew near the room, Casey felt a rubbing across her ankles, and she paused to bend down and rub Buck, the cat. The animal purred up a storm, long bushy tail a waving question mark.

'That tail expresses about the way I feel, Buck,' she muttered. 'Questions, questions!'

Myrtle stamped her foot. 'Go, Buck! Leave the lady alone.'

Buck looked at her disdainfully, and made no move to leave. Casey gave the cat another scrubbing of the ears, then started on. Buck trotted right along with her, looking up, talking plaintively.

226

Myrtle laughed. 'I don't know why I ever bother to tell him to do anything. He always does just the opposite. I think he likes you, Casey.'

She motioned to Casey to precede her, blocked the cat with a booted foot, then closed the door in its face. Buck immediately set up a howl, scratching at the door. 'Bitch all you want, catface, you're not getting in here.'

She turned to Casey. 'I have to show him who's boss once in a while. It's a matter of pride.'

She crossed to a small refrigerator in one corner of the room. When she opened the door, Casey could see cans of beer stacked high. Myrtle rummaged around inside, finally extracting a can of soda. She popped the tab, and handed it to Casey, then sat down on the end of the couch and picked up a full coffee mug. Casey joined her on the couch.

Myrtle said, 'I have to go to work in a couple of hours, and I usually need a gallon of coffee to get me going.'

'Working nights and sleeping days must be tough.'

'Naw, I'm used to it,' Myrtle said. 'Been doing it for years. Now, what can I do for you, Casey?'

'First, have you heard anything new that would have any bearing on the deaths of Buck and Red Pollock?'

'Heard plenty, but it's all bar talk; you know, everybody talking about it, but nobody really knowing anything. Most of the talk lately has been about you and the Dyces. How's your boy, by the way? Is he doing all right?'

'He's fine. He may have nightmares about it for a while, but he's taking it pretty well. He's a tough kid, and he had a rough life before I adopted him.'

'So what about Barney, did he kill Buck or not?'

'Well, everyone except me seems to think so.'

'You don't think he did it?'

Casey shook her head. 'No, I don't: that's why I'm still asking questions, thereby not making any friends.'

Myrtle shrugged, causing her large breasts to jiggle.

'Ask away, I don't mind. Never been in any way involved in a murder investigation before. It's kind of interesting.'

'From one of the women I interviewed, I learned that Buck got a girl pregnant just before he married Pamela Morgan. I thought that you might have heard some gossip about it, know who it was.'

Myrtle shook her head. 'Nope, not a word; but that was a long time ago.'

'Well, I guess it was too much to hope for. I'm not sure why, but I've got a feeling that it's important.'

'Do you think Buck wronged some local gal, and that she killed him, after all these years? That's a long time to hold a grudge.'

'People have held them longer; take the Montagues and Capulets, or the Martins and the Coys.'

'Yeah, whatever.' Myrtle looked thoughtful. 'You know, the girl he got pregnant, she might not even be from Prescott.'

Casey sat forward. 'What do you mean?'

'Just what I said. She could have been a rodeo groupie, someone he met on the circuit.'

'I never thought of that. Someone told me that a lot of women hang around the riders.'

Myrtle smiled. 'They sure do. These girls fix on some old rodeo boy with a cute butt, and they follow him from rodeo to rodeo. And old Buck had a real cute butt, he really did!'

Casey slumped back. 'If that's the case, I probably won't ever find her. She could be anywhere.'

She got up wearily. 'Thanks for your time, Myrtle. I hope I won't have to bother you again.'

Myrtle stood up and stretched – an awesome sight – and laughed. 'Hell, I'm getting kind of used to it, and like I said, I like you, honey.' Her laughter exploded. 'Never thought I'd hear myself saying that about any cop!'

* * *

228

Leaving Myrtle's place, Casey headed for Chino Valley. As she neared the turn-off to Granite Dells, she slowed and turned right. When she reached the Dells she drove to the spot where Red Pollock's body had been found. She parked and walked down to the edge of the stream where the body had lain. She could see no one else in the vicinity. Looking at the peaceful scene, Casey could see no trace of the violence that had ended there. The wind blew, and the trees rustled. Birds sang. But then nature was used to violence, she thought. Beneath this lovely exterior there was waged a fierce war for survival, as, out of necessity, animal stalked animal. She shook her head, thinking of Red Pollock, and then of the young girl whose body the medical examiner said had been found here, in almost the same spot – an eerie coincidence. Or was it coincidence?

When she got back to the Farrel Ranch, Dan Farrel opened the front door for her. The savoury odour of roast meat came from the kitchen. Dan said, 'I invited Clint and his family out for supper, Casey. I hope you don't mind.'

'I know. I talked to Clint today. And why should I mind, they're your family,' she said, then added, 'and this *is* your house.'

Dan smiled apologetically. 'I know, but Clint can be pretty obnoxious when he puts his mind to it, and you two didn't seem to . . .'

'Hit it off,' said Casey, smiling back. 'But today he was very pleasant.' She thought it wouldn't hurt to exaggerate a little. 'I'm looking forward to meeting his family.'

Dan sighed. 'They're good people. Ruth's a wonderful woman, and the girls are great kids. I should make more of an effort to get along with Clint for their sake. We should see more of each other.'

Casey nodded. 'Sounds like a good idea. Where's Donnie?'

'He's in the kitchen, helping Alice.'

She laughed. 'You and Aunt Alice must be a good influence on him. I've never known him to be so helpful.' She looked at her watch. 'Do I have time for a shower before dinner?'

He nodded. 'Certainly. It will be another hour before we eat.'

Casey gave him a grateful smile.

By the time Casey had finished her shower and donned a colourful skirt and cool blouse, Clint and his family had arrived. As Casey came down the hall, she heard the sound of girlish voices. Turning into the kitchen she saw Alice and a pretty blonde woman of around thirty working at the butcher-block table. Two girls, one blonde and fair, one dark and olive- skinned, were trying to help. The girls looked to be about two years apart in age: Casey estimated them to be about seven and nine years old. Donnie was just starting into the dining room with an armload of plates.

Casey intercepted him. 'Hi, kiddo. Looks like they put you to work, but I see you have a couple of buddies.'

Donnie screwed his face into an expression of disgust. 'Girls!' he said in a stage whisper.

Casey patted his cheek. 'Get used to them, kiddo. Girls are here to stay. And, believe it or not, within a few short years, you will be crazy about them.'

Donnie looked at her as if she had grown two heads. 'Aw, Casey. How come you say things like that!'

She turned away, toward Alice Farrel. 'May I help?'

Alice smiled. 'I have enough help now, maybe too much.' It was clear that she was pleased to have her family together. 'Casey, this is my daughter-in-law, Ruth, and my two granddaughters, Marcie and Jessica. Ruth, this is Casey Farrel.'

After introductions had been exchanged, Alice said, 'Casey, why don't you go into the study and join Dan and Clint for a drink? Supper will be done in a few minutes.'

In the study, Casey accepted a drink from Dan and sat down. Clint was surprisingly cordial. The conversation was also surprising: not one word was said about the murders. Talk was general, ranging from sports to political topics, both local and state. Casey was included from time to time; Clint seemed particularly interested in Casey's work; and although she gathered that the current governor wasn't popular with Clint, he expressed approval of the fact that the man had established the task force.

Listening to the two men, she found that both of them were volatile and somewhat arrogant in their beliefs, and obviously enjoyed a good and rousing discussion. It was interesting to watch them debate.

She wondered if Dan had taken her advice, and had gone to see Melissa Dyce this morning; but she didn't think it was her place to quiz him about it. She had done what she could. Now it was up to him.

After they all sat down to the delicious meal that Alice had prepared, the conversation turned to family matters. The conversation was restful, and a little dull, and after partaking generously of the good food, Casey found herself struggling to stay awake.

When they had finished desert, Clint performed a few simple magic tricks for the children. He was, Casey decided, not bad. She watched him make a quarter disappear, and then retrieve it from Donnie's ear.

Donnie was amazed. 'How'd you do that?' he asked. 'Could I learn to do it?'

Clint laughed. 'I'm sure you could. It's all misdirection; the hand is quicker than the eye.'

Casey muffled a yawn, and Dan looked a question at her. She said apologetically, 'I've really had a day, and I hope that you will all excuse me, but I need to go to bed.'

Donnie looked at her accusingly. 'Aw, Casey, it's early yet.'

She gave him a weary grin. 'That doesn't mean you have to turn in, kiddo; that is, if Uncle Dan and Aunt Alice will keep an eye on you.'

Alice said, 'Of course, Casey. You go along. We all know how hard the past few days have been on you.'

The bed looked wonderful, and Casey barely got out of her clothes and into her long, Mickey Mouse tee, before falling on to it. She lay for a moment in that drowsy state between sleep and waking, details of the case floating through her mind: Red Pollock, coming into money *before* Buck was killed, there was more where that came from. The girl Buck had impregnated fifteen years before; was she here, in town, or had she been a rodeo groupie, wandering from rodeo to rodeo? Had she had the child? Another girl, a girl with no face, dead beside a trickling stream. Who did she belong to, did anybody care? A person, man or woman, in a clown suit, offering Buck that last, fatal drink. Why? And then, just before the soft waves of sleep enveloped her, she thought of a word, misdirection, and of Red Pollock, drunk out of his mind, singing Auld Lang Syne, and it all fitted. She was certain that she knew who had murdered Buck Farrel.

NINETEEN

Casey awakened the next morning as if coming up from a very deep dive; feeling herself rise from sleep reluctantly. There was something that she should remember, that she *must* remember, something important.

Pulling the sheet over her head, she tried to pull her thoughts together.

Slowly, she sat up and stretched. Was the memory really important, or just 'dream scam'? Then, as she came fully awake, it came flooding back, and she shivered with excitement.

Within the hour, Casey was at the offices of the *Prescott Courier*.

She was greeted cordially, and her request was granted without delay. Soon, she was going through the back issues of the paper, starting about a year before Buck and Pamela were married. It took some time, but finally she found what she was looking for. The story was headlined on the front page: BODY OF YOUNG WOMAN FOUND IN GRANITE DELLS.

The article stated that the young woman had been in her late teens or early twenties, and that she had died of a gunshot wound to the head. A .22 revolver had been found near her right hand. It had been fired once. Identification of the body had not yet been made.

Eagerly, Casey looked through the following day's issues, until she found the follow-up. The young woman

233

had been identified as Sue Anne Taylor, last address Las Vegas, Nevada. Her body had been found by a jogger, lying beside Granite Creek. The coroner had placed the time of death at approximately midnight, on 5 July. Miss Taylor had been two months pregnant.

Slowly, Casey lay down the paper. The similarity to the manner in which Red Pollock had been killed could not be coincidental. There had to be a connection. She read on, and learned that the police had been unable to find any ties between the young woman and anyone in Prescott. It was surmised that she had come to town for the rodeo. Investigation in Las Vegas had proved almost as futile. Miss Taylor had only lived there a few months, and had checked out of her rooming house just three days before she was found dead in Granite Dells.

Future issues of the paper disclosed little more. The death had been declared a suicide. Casey made copies of all the articles.

When Casey arrived at the police station, she found Steve Randall in his office. He glanced at her warily. 'I wasn't sure I'd see you again, Casey, after I let fly at you the other night out at the Dyce place. I'm sorry about . . .'

She waved him off. 'No apologies are necessary, Steve. Under the circumstances, you had a perfect right to your opinion.'

He frowned. 'Why do I have a feeling you're leading up to something I won't like? You look awfully self-satisfied.'

Casey couldn't help but smile. 'You know, you're right. Steve, I think I know who murdered Buck and Red, and it wasn't Barney Dyce.'

He groaned. 'Please, Casey, not again!'

'I have new evidence,' she said softly. 'And I'm pretty sure I can prove what I'm saying.'

He leaned back in his chair. 'All right then, let me hear it. Convince me! Who is the killer?'

234

She sat down opposite him. 'I need your help first to check out a few things.' She held up a hand to forestall further questions. 'Look, Steve, I think you know by now that I'm reasonably dependable, and that I know my business. Granted?'

He nodded slowly. 'Okay, I'll give you that. What do you need?'

'Just a little information.' She opened her notebook. 'Do you remember when we found Pollock's body in Granite Dells? The Medical Examiner told me that the body of a young woman had been found there some years before.'

'And?'

'What if I was to tell you that she was found in the same spot, the exact same spot that Red was found!'

He frowned. 'I'd say that it was a pretty wild coincidence.'

She nodded. 'I don't think it was, a coincidence, that is. Do you still have a file on the case?'

He scratched his head. 'It happened about a year before I came here. That was fifteen years ago, Casey!'

'I know, but will you check? Please?'

He rubbed his chin thoughtfully, staring at her intently. Then he gave an abrupt nod, got up without a word, and left the room. He was gone for almost a half hour. Casey used the time to go over her notes again, thinking through her theory and finding that it played.

When Steve returned he was carrying a file. Seating himself, he said, 'It's pretty slim. What is it that you want to know?'

'Were they certain that her death was a suicide?'

Steve opened the file, read for a moment, then looked up. 'It appears so. All the evidence pointed that way: the wound, her fingerprints, and hers only, on the gun, powder residue on her hand. It was pretty obvious.'

'Is there anything in the file about who picked up the body?'

He leafed through the file. 'Here it is. It was held in the city morgue for two weeks, then released to the Rutkowski Funeral Home. That's the usual procedure when a body isn't claimed. She was probably buried here, at city expense.'

'Would it be possible to call the funeral home and find out?'

Steve looked at her, obviously puzzled. 'Casey, do you really think any of this has a bearing on Buck's murder?'

'I'm convinced of it. I think the motive for Buck's death lies in the past, and that Red's death came about because he was involved in some way with Buck's killer. And I think the death of this young woman, this Sue Anne Taylor, may be the genesis of the whole thing.'

Steve shrugged. 'Well, I said I'd go along with this; and I have to admit that I'm curious.'

He thumbed through his card file, then punched out a number. When the phone was answered, he talked for a few moments, then cradled the receiver on his shoulder. 'They have to check old records. They wanted to call back, but I told them it was important, and that I'd wait. You'd better be right, Casey.'

Casey hoped she was, too. Several minutes passed in silence, then Steve sat up. 'Yes?' He listened for a few minutes more, interjecting a question now and then. Finally, he hung up.

'They don't have much. It seems that the very day Sue Anne's body was turned over to them, they received a special delivery letter. Inside was a money order for five thousand dollars, made out to the funeral home. There was also a typed, unsigned letter stating that the money was for the casket and burial of one Sue Anne Taylor.'

Casey sighed. 'That's not much, is it?' she said. 'Where was the letter mailed from? I don't suppose they saved it?'

236

'No to both questions. I asked.'

Casey pounded on the arm of her chair in frustration. 'Damn! I was hoping . . .' She leaned forward. 'Will you make another call for me? This one's long distance. I could do it, but I think we'll get more cooperation if it came from a Prescott officer.'

He eyed her warily, then threw up his hands in resignation. 'All right! I might as well go the whole nine yards. Who do you want me to call?'

She leaned forward and told him.

Casey feared that they might be too late; but when they reached the room they could hear the television playing inside.

Steve tried the door, and finding it unlocked, he entered, Casey close behind him.

Hank Wilder stood in front of the bed upon which his suitcases lay open, surrounded by piles of clothing.

Casey made a small sound of relief, evidently audible to Wilder. He spoke without looking around. 'I told the desk to send someone up in half an hour. I'm not finished packing yet.'

She said, 'It's not the bellman, Mr Wilder.'

He stiffened, and turned slowly. His melancholy eyes widened. 'Casey! And Sergeant Randall. I didn't expect to see either of you again.'

'I'm sure you didn't,' Casey said.

Wilder looked from one to the other. 'Is this an official visit? Has there been a new development in the case?'

'Yes, and yes,' Casey said, her gaze never leaving his face. 'We've discovered some new facts.'

Wilder returned to his packing. Steve stepped forward. 'I think you can forget that for a minute, Mr Wilder.' His eyes were on Wilder's hands.

'But, as you see, I'm checking out. I have to finish my . . .'

Steve put a hand on his arm. 'I said, leave it, Mr Wilder. This won't take long.'

Wilder's face assumed an expression of annoyance, but he left his packing, and seated himself in the room's one comfortable chair. He seemed perfectly at ease, but Casey, watching his face, saw his eyes were uncharacteristically bright, and that his hands moved nervously. 'All right,' he said, 'but I don't see . . .'

Without preamble Casey said: 'Fifteen years ago, the body of a young woman was found in Granite Dells.'

Wilder grimaced. 'That's all very interesting, but what has that got to do with me?'

'She was identified as Sue Anne Taylor,' Casey said. 'And the interesting thing is that she was found in the same spot where they found the body of Red Pollock.'

'An odd coincidence, I'll admit. But I still . . .'

Casey raised her hand. 'The autopsy showed that the young woman, Sue Anne Taylor, was pregnant. The verdict was suicide.'

Wilder's lips thinned. 'That's a very sad story, but I still don't see what it has to do with me?'

'I believe that Sue Anne Taylor was your daughter, Sue Anne Wilder.'

'You can't be serious! That's about as crazy an assumption as I've ever heard.'

'Not so crazy,' said Casey firmly. 'When I was going over the notes of my conversation with you, I remembered that you had mentioned a child you had lost, and it aroused my curiosity. I asked Sergeant Randall to make a couple of calls to your home town, Elko, Nevada. He learned some interesting things. Thirty-five years ago, Mr Wilder, you had a daughter. When the girl was fifteen, your wife ran off with another man, taking your daughter with her. Eventually, your wife divorced you and married again, a man by the name of Taylor. It seems that by that time your daughter's mind had been poisoned against you, and

238

she took her step-father's name, Sue Anne Taylor. Shall I go on?'

Wilder looked away from her. He took a toothpick from his pocket, put it in his mouth, and began to roll it from one corner to the other. In a low voice he said, 'No need to root through all that old dirt. Yes, I had a daughter, the only child I ever had. She was the sweetest little thing when she was little. My wife, Nettie Fay, was a dirt tramp. But Sue Anne could never see that. When Nettie took her away, she taught the girl to hate me.' His voice was no longer dispassionate. 'When Nettie Fay died, Sue Anne was eighteen. I tried to get her to come and live with me, but she would have none of it. Said she despised me. By that time she was just like her mother. She started following the rodeos around, sleeping with any performer who'd have her. Sometimes I wondered if she didn't do it just to spite me; she always seemed to choose the rodeos where I was performing.'

'And one of the men she slept with was Buck Farrel, wasn't it?'

He looked up, his eyes filled with pain. 'Yes, one of the men was Buck, the last one, in fact.'

'And she became pregnant?'

'You've got that right, too. I was here, working the rodeo that Fourth, and Sue Anne came to me, in tears. Finally come to her old daddy, after all that time. Came to me for help, but what could I do, go after the boy with a shotgun? Two days later, she was dead. I felt terrible, felt that I should have done *something!*'

'Didn't you talk to Buck about it, before she died?'

Wilder turned to look at Steve. 'Yeah, I went to Buck, but the bastard laughed in my face. Sue Anne was of age, he said, and he hadn't forced himself on her, she had come to him. He said that if she was pregnant, it was her own fault, and that considering all the men she . . . all the men she had been with, the child probably wasn't even his.'

239

'Why did you wait fifteen years to kill him?' Casey asked.

Wilder gave a bark of laughter. 'Now you're getting into the realm of fantasy, Casey. I couldn't have killed him, now could I? I was tied up and unconscious at the time he was killed. Whoever hit me and tied me up is the killer.'

Casey shook her head. 'No, Hank,' she said softly. 'The second clown was only misdirection, because there was no second clown, just one, you! You gave Buck the cyanide in the whisky bottle, then hurried to the horse barn where your accomplice, Red Pollock, was waiting. He tied you, gave you a rap on the head so that you'd have something to show the police, then went about his business. Later, when he attempted to blackmail you for more money, you eliminated him, putting his body in the same place where your daughter had died, as a bit of poetic justice perhaps. I don't suppose you thought that anyone would remember her case, after all this time, or if they did, they wouldn't tie her to you. Then, to finish things off neatly, you put the murder weapons in Barney Dyce's truck, knowing that he was already a suspect.'

Wilder looked over at the shirts stacked beside the suitcase, than back at Casey. When he spoke, his voice was again calm. 'Is that how you conduct your cases, Casey, by making wild guesses, with no proof to back them up?'

'I'll admit that what I have is circumstantial, but it's all there, and cases have been won on less. You must have gotten the cyanide somewhere, and the gun. It may take some legwork, but we'll work on connecting them to you.'

Steve stepped forward. 'I'm going to have to place you under arrest, Mr Wilder . . .'

Wilder's hands came up from the depths of the cushioned chair, holding an automatic fitted with a silencer. He stood, and said in a mild voice, 'I'm afraid I can't let you do that, Sergeant. I've never taken well to the idea of a jail cell.'

Steve stopped short. 'You should have thought of that before you started killing people.'

Casey said, 'What are you going to do, Hank, kill both of us? If you do, you won't get far. This is your room, they know who you are.'

Wilder looked at her sadly. 'I don't want to, Casey. It seems that I've grown to like you. If my daughter had been more like you, she might be alive today; but I don't know what else to do. I've already killed two people, do you think they'll do any more to me if I kill two more?'

Steve said harshly, 'Yes, they will. Special treatment is given killers who kill law enforcement officers. Every cop in the state, in the whole country, will be on your ass!'

Casey saw a shadow of indecision flicker across Wilder's face. Maybe if she could keep him talking? She said. 'Reprehensible as these crimes are, you had a reason for killing Buck and Pollock. Tell me, do you think that your daughter's death wasn't suicide? Do you think Buck killed her?'

Wilder blinked, but his gun hand did not waver. 'He might as well have. She came here to see him, to tell him about the baby. She got herself liquored up, for courage, went to him, and asked him to marry her. I guess she made a scene, threatened suicide if he didn't. To calm her down, he took her for a ride to Granite Dells. They talked, and he told her that there was no chance that he was going to marry her, particularly since he couldn't be certain that the baby was even his. She had a gun in her shoulder bag, and when he said this, she pulled it out. Before he could stop her, she shot herself in the head. Coward that he was, he got into a panic, and just drove away.'

'How do you know all this?'

'The next morning it was on the news; they had found her body. I knew that Buck had to be involved, so I went to him and beat the shit out of him. He told me what had happened.'

'There's one thing I still don't understand. Why did you wait fifteen years to kill him?'

Wilder sighed. 'Because normally I'm not a violent man. I would have happily seen him dead, but I didn't want to be the one who did it. And he made a promise to me.'

'A promise?'

'Yes, he promised that he would get himself fixed so that he would never get some poor girl pregnant again.'

'And when you came to Prescott this year, you found out that he had had the operation reversed.'

Wilder blinked. 'How did you find out? But yes, you're right. He came up to me, bold as brass, and announced that he figured that he'd paid enough for whatever wrong he had done Sue Anne. He was in love, and he wanted a child.' His mouth took on a bitter twist. 'His words brought it all back, all the pain and the hurt. Why should he have a child, when I didn't? There was only one way to stop him, and I took it.' He smiled bitterly, 'And you know what? Don't let anyone ever tell you that revenge isn't sweet. It is! I killed him, like I should have done fifteen years ago, when he left my little girl no way out but to end her life. I was too soft-hearted then, but fifteen years of grieving fixed that.'

Casey looked at his eyes, his sad eyes that still held that eerie glitter. Still, he seemed calmer now that he had voiced his feelings. The man was not a killer by nature. Would he really take out Steve and her in cold blood? She decided to take a risk in the hope that he would not. She began to move slowly towards him.

He pointed the gun at her chest. 'Stop right there, or I'll shoot. I swear I will!'

She kept moving, very slowly. 'I don't think so, Hank. You said it yourself, usually you are a peaceful man. I don't think you'll shoot me in cold blood. I don't think you want that on your conscience.'

His eyes flickered, and she sensed that he was losing it. Her heart began to pound. What if she was wrong? The mouth of the silencer looked small but deadly as a rattler, and all of her senses seemed to quicken.

Wilder backed away, towards the bed, keeping the gun pointed at her chest. She kept moving towards him. If he was capable of killing her, he would either do it now, or later, so she did not see that she had any choice.

'Casey!' Steve called warningly.

She risked a glance at him out of the corner of her eyes. He seemed about to throw himself at Wilder.

'No, Steve,' she said, 'it's all right.'

Her glance went back to Wilder. She was only a few steps from him now. 'You don't want to do this, Hank,' she said gently. 'You know you don't.'

A deep groan game from Wilder, and the hand holding the gun wavered, then dropped. He squeezed his eyes closed. Trembling, Casey reached out and took the gun from his hand. He offered no resistance.

He slumped down on the bed, tears flowing down his cheeks. Steve hurried to him, handcuffs ready.

On shaking legs, Casey walked over to the bureau, and lay down the pistol. She turned, her back against the sturdy wood. Through the window she could see the panorama of Prescott spread out before her, as Steve read Wilder his rights. This was the second time in as many days that she had faced a man with a gun, and she hoped that it wasn't setting a trend.

'Casey?' Steve said.

She looked up. Wilder, hands cuffed behind him, was standing quietly, head down.

'Jesus, lady, you've got some guts!' Steve said. 'How did you know he wouldn't shoot?'

She shrugged. 'I took a chance.'

243

He shook his head. 'I'll say you did. I have to say this, it was running through my mind as you faced him down: Casey, you were right, and I was wrong. You're one hell of an investigator. I'll never doubt you again.'

She gave him a wan smile. 'Do you know what I was thinking? I was thinking that if Wilder killed me, Donnie would lose his mother, and he's already lost one!'

TWENTY

By the time all the paperwork was completed on Henry Wilder, it was well past noon. Steve walked Casey out to the Cherokee.

'What about Barney Dyce?' she asked. 'When will he be released?'

Steve said, 'He'll be on the street before the day's over. He still faces the charge of assaulting an officer, but that probably won't get him more than a suspended sentence, under the circumstances.'

He arched an eyebrow at her. 'Do you want to press charges against him for trying to run you off of Mingus Mountain?'

She shook her head. 'Not enough evidence. Besides, I guess he's suffered enough. Maybe the experience will make a better man of him.'

Steve grinned. 'Well, any improvement would be a godsend.'

'What about Darrel?'

'Oh, he'll have to stand trial on kidnapping charges. He'll be going away for a while.' His grin widened. 'Maybe it'll make him a better man, too; at least it will keep him out of Melissa's hair. Maybe now the poor kid can have a life of her own. She's had a rough time of it.'

He touched her arm lightly. 'You know, you really showed me up, Casey.'

She looked up at him, searching his face. He waved his hand. 'Oh, I didn't mean it that way. I mean that I really learned something. I was too complacent, too sure that we had the right perp in Barney. Yes, I've learned an important lesson from you; I'll be more careful next time.' He held out his hand. 'Goodbye, Casey. I hope that I see you again.'

She took his hand, ignoring the question in his voice. 'I'm sure we'll meet again, Steve, sometime. It was good, working with you. Goodbye.'

Getting into the Cherokee, she put it into gear, and drove out of the lot, purposefully not looking back. She liked Steve Randall very much, and felt a tug of regret at having to say good-bye. Under other circumstances . . . But there was Josh waiting for her in Phoenix.

When she drove up before the Farrel ranch house, both Dan and Alice came out on to the porch. Casey got out and went towards them, realizing, after a moment, that Donnie was not with them.

Mounting the steps, she said, 'Where's Donnie?'

'Out riding,' Dan replied with a grin.

She said in alarm, 'Alone?'

'Oh, no, Casey, you don't think I'd let him do that again? He's with . . .' He glanced towards the corral. 'There they come now.'

Casey followed his glance, and saw Donnie and Melissa Dyce, riding up to the corral.

Dan said, 'I took your advice, and had a long talk with Melissa.'

'That's good,' said Casey in relief. 'Barney is being released this afternoon, and hopefully he's learned his lesson, but when he learns that Melissa is pregnant, I don't know . . .'

Alice smiled, and put her hand on Casey's arm. 'Melissa is going to stay with us, Casey, at least until the baby comes, and I hope afterwards.'

Casey glanced at Dan and saw that he was frowning.

'You say that they're releasing Barney Dyce? Why? What's been going on, Casey?'

Casey laughed. 'I can't believe I haven't told you. So much has gone on today . . . Dan, Alice, we found the real killer. He's behind bars right now.'

Dan shook his head. 'Then it *wasn't* Barney? Then who was it? Who killed my boy?'

Casey took his arm. 'Let's go into the house, and I'll explain everything.'

When Casey had finished her story, Dan and Alice sat quite still for a long moment: then, tenderly, Dan took Alice's hand in his, and sighed deeply. 'So it's all over then. This time you're certain?'

Casey nodded. 'Yes, this time we've got the right man.'

Dan shook his head. 'It's a sad story all around; but at least now Alice and I can begin to heal, and go on. Thank you, Casey. I can't tell you how much we appreciate what you've done.'

'Having Melissa here, and the baby, will help,' Alice said softly. 'Nothing will ever completely take away the hurt, and no one can ever completely fill the void; but a baby can go a long way towards easing a person's heart.'

Casey, feeling tears threatening, sniffed, and got hold of herself. 'I understand,' she said, as calmly as she could. 'Look, I need to call Phoenix, is that okay?'

Dan shook his head. 'You don't need to ask, Casey. We've told you that our house is yours.'

'You go right ahead, dear,' said Alice. 'I'm just going to fix us all a bite of lunch. Donnie is always starving after a good ride.'

In the library, Casey picked up the telephone. It took her a while to track down Josh, but finally he was on the line. His deep voice sounded wonderful.

247

'Hi, Josh.'

'Casey! Are you all right? Is Donnie all right?'

'We're both fine. He's been out riding again, with Melissa Dyce. They just got back. I called to tell you that we'll be driving back in the morning.'

'Case finished? Were you right? Was the killer someone other than Barney Dyce? Come on, give. I'm going crazy here.'

Casey laughed. 'You mean you had doubts? Of course I was right. We have the real killer locked up, and good ol' Barney is being released this afternoon.'

'So who was it?'

'The rodeo clown, Hank Wilder.' Quickly she filled him in on the details, adding, 'But I owe some of it to you, Detective. I followed your advice about going back over the data, re-checking your original leads, remember?'

Josh chuckled. 'Good girl. You always give credit where credit is due. Hurry home, and I'll show you how much I appreciate you, and how much I've missed you.'

'Is that a threat or a promise, Detective?'

'Both.'

'You sound eager, Detective.'

'I am, I am. You guys are my family, and I've missed you like hell.'

'I'll be happy to be back, too, Josh. We'll see you tomorrow.'

As she hung up the receiver and turned around, Donnie came charging into the room, all smiles. 'Me and Melissa had a good ride. She's nice people, Casey.'

Casey reached out and ruffled his hair. 'Yeah, she is, kiddo.'

'Uncle Dan says that you caught the bad guy, Casey. I'm real glad.'

'That's right, kiddo. Surprised?'

'Nope.' He pressed close to her knees. 'You always

catch the bad guy, Casey. Josh says that you're like the Mounties, you always get your man.'

She hugged him fiercely. 'Ah, the faith of the young.' She smiled over his head at Dan Farrel, who was just coming into the room.

Donnie pulled back, staring at her. 'Who were you talking to, Casey. Was it Josh?'

She nodded. 'We'll be going home tomorrow.'

She had expected a protest, but Donnie just smiled. 'Good.'

She looked at him in surprise. 'Good? I thought you'd be complaining.'

He smiled slyly. 'Oh, I like it here, Casey. I like Uncle Dan and Aunt Alice, and Brownie and all; but I kinda miss Josh, and Spot II must be getting real lonesome for me. Besides, Uncle Dan says that I can come back anytime I want to, didn't you, Uncle Dan?'

Dan smiled. 'That I did, young man; and you can even bring Casey, in fact you can bring your whole family, Casey, Josh, and Spot II. We're all one big family now. Ain't that right, Casey?' He stared into her eyes.

Casey nodded and swallowed the lump that was forming in her throat. 'That's right, Uncle Dan. We're all family now.'